The Angels
of Sinkhole County

Praise for

"I just finished reading *Remedios* and it blew my mind completely! It's pure narrative adrenaline. Deborah Clearman once again shows her keen understanding and delicate power of observation of life in rural Guatemala. I am still processing the multiple emotions evoked by this masterfully crafted novel."

—EDUARDO JUAREZ,
Guatemalan author of *Marioposas del vertigo* and *Serenatas al hastío*

"Deborah Clearman has written a tense, tragic, deeply authentic book that shares DNA with such cartel-tinged masterpieces as *Power of the Dog* and *Breaking Bad.*"

—BEN DOLNICK, author of *The Ghost Notebooks*

"A riveting journey through the savage and explosive world of the Latin American drug trade, where innocence and evil are intertwined and the flip sides of friendship, family, love and redemption lead to an ultimate betrayal. This compelling page-turner was hard to put down and, even at the finish line, I was reluctant to leave *Remedios* behind."

—JUDY CHICUREL, author of *If I Knew You Were Going to be This Beautiful, I Never Would Have Let You Go*

"This isn't normally a genre I tend to read, but I'm so glad I branched out. It provided enough of an adrenaline jolt for me to skip my morning coffee!"

—*Literary Quicksand*

"It's an intense page-turning novel but at the center is a likable innocent family who has lost their way."

—SUSAN ROBERTS, *Girl Who Reads*

CONCEPCIÓN AND THE BABY BROKERS

"A collection of stories about hard choices borne of desperation and the stark delineations between classes in both Guatemala and the United States.... The author offers the same photographic eye and acute vision of Guatemalan culture throughout ... stories of strength and ethical quandary."

—*Kirkus*

"In these vivid and often heart-wrenching stories, Deborah Clearman illuminates Guatemalan culture at ground level, through characters whose struggles are palpable and moving. The collection couldn't be more timely, or necessary."

—JULIE SALAMON, author of *An Innocent Bystander* and *The Devil's Candy*

Deborah Clearman

The Angels of Sinkhole County

LIBRARY OF CONGRESS CATALOGING-IN-PUBLICATION DATA

The Angels of Sinkhole County
Authored by Deborah Clearman

ISBN: 9798988023418
LCCN: 2023949572

Contents

1. FROM THE HIGH PLACE TO THE HOLLOW   1

2. DEAD RINGER   15

3. MISS BEATRICE SHUFFLES OFF THE MORTAL COIL   27

4. HOW TO SHOOT YOURSELF IN THE FOOT   39

5. WHAT LIES BENEATH THE SURFACE   53

6. WHAT CAN BLOOD TELL?   63

7. A MORAL DILEMMA   69

8. MORE CATS OUT OF THE BAG   77

9. A MAN OF THE CLOTH IS ALARMED   91

10. REVELATIONS   97

11. ENCOUNTERS AT THE END OF THE WORLD   109

12. AN UNEXPECTED VISIT ENDS ABRUPTLY   119

13. INSOMNIA   131

14. WHAT THE HEART KNOWS   139

15. WORDS COMING BACK   155

16. UP MUD LICK HOLLOW   165

17. HELL HATH NO FURY   181

18. CRESCENDO   193

19. MORE REVELATIONS   203

20. A WOMAN'S WORK IS NEVER DONE   219

21. AND THEY ALL DIED HAPPILY EVER AFTER ...   233

For the caregivers
and
In memory of D.B.C.

Listen! you hear the grating roar
Of pebbles which the waves draw back, and fling,
At their return, up the high strand,
Begin, and cease, and then again begin,
With tremulous cadence slow, and bring
The eternal note of sadness in.

—MATTHEW ARNOLD, *from "Dover Beach"*

From the High Place to the Hollow

A SUNDAY IN AUGUST

The night the Major passed, Loretta Hardwick smoked too many cigarettes, perched on the edge of the glider on the front porch. Anybody would of. The smoke curled up into the night sky and gave Loretta uneasy thoughts about the awful beyond.

Headlights blazing through the dark, Cass drove in, parked by the front gate, and hurried up the walk to the house. "What're you doing out here, girl?" she demanded as she swept past.

Loretta dropped her butt into the pickle jar stationed by the glider for that purpose and went in after her boss, like there was something she could do about the Major's plummeting vitals. Major lay on his hospital bed in the front room, illumined by an inadequate antique lamp. His head, propped up by pillows, was thrown back. He gazed at the ceiling with wide eyes. His mouth gaped open and he sucked in rattling breaths. Tammy sat next to the bed, holding and patting his hand and looking stoic. She was a large and placid woman compared to scrawny little Loretta ("I'm little but I'm strong," Loretta liked to protest). Cass swooped in with her stethoscope and cuff, like they were going to pull Major back from wherever it was he was going. Loretta didn't know whether to cry or scream.

"What happened here?" Cass looked accusingly at Tammy and wrapped the cuff around Major's arm. Cass was Major's care manager and took herself seriously.

"I come in at three, Major was fine, joking with me as usual," Tammy said. "He had some potato soup at five. A couple hours later, he started vomiting and looking real bad. That's when I called you."

Major drew in one long shuddering breath. The three women held theirs and waited for another. Waited interminably. The stethoscope dangled uselessly. Loretta felt ghosts gathering in the room. Photographs of Miss Beatrice lined the marble mantelpiece—Miss Beatrice as a debutante in the early '40s, Miss Beatrice selling cattle in the '80s, Miss Beatrice riding horseback through the mountains just two years ago, still thin and ramrod straight, shortly before she died. Loretta could almost feel her barging into the front room to intimidate the caregivers, as she had when Loretta started out, cursing at Major to get his damn ass out of bed. Finally Tammy felt Major for a pulse. "I reckon he's gone," she said. Tammy had sat at the side of the dying before, first her husband, and then within the last year her daddy and mama, leaving her to raise her daughter alone.

Cass dropped the inflation bulb she was still holding and burst into tears. "This wasn't supposed to happen!" She said it like an accusation, like it was Tammy and Loretta's fault. For losing him on their shift. Loretta felt culpable, as if she deserved the blame. Even *if* Major had been going downhill the whole time Loretta had worked there, the victim of myriad maladies including strokes and mini-strokes and several slow-acting cancers, as well as the normal bouts with UTI and pneumonia. Even *if* in the last three months Major had hardly been out of bed and had been hallucinating people in the room who weren't there and travels to his boyhood home in Massachusetts. Loretta had told the other girls she could not be present when he went. She couldn't bear it. He still had his good days, when he told them stories out of his past and flirted with them and asked them to be his girlfriends. He'd been so lonely since Miss Beatrice died. Cass bawled into a tissue. Loretta felt her own tears welling. "What's going to happen to us?" she asked. A question that could have multiple meanings, she knew, all of them terrifying.

"You know," Tammy said. She was a pragmatist, and they'd talked about it, of course, as Major had wasted. "We won't have no jobs. I heard not even Walmart is hiring." Jobs were sparse in Sinkhole County, West Virginia, and Major had kept a double staff and paid one-and-a-half times the going rate. For these last two years he'd been the only thing preventing Loretta from losing her house.

"Don't talk about that now," Cass snapped. Her husband had become a worthless drunk since he retired and she'd had to throw him out. Major was more than a paycheck to her. She was still fighting sobs while removing the cuff. "Loretta, get me the phone. We've got to call the kids." Hume Thorndike lived fifty miles north, in Powhatan County, and could be at his father's side in an hour and a half, pushing his bright yellow Mazda Miata to its max on the twisting country roads. Ruth, the daughter they referred to as Ruthless behind her back, lived in New York City.

"Just hold on half a minute," Loretta said. "There's something you should know."

THREE MONTHS EARLIER

Loretta came in through the kitchen door, stashed her evening snack in the refrigerator, and said hey to Kristy Mae and Dellisha, the seven-to-three shift. "Anything new?" she asked.

"Same old same old," Kristy Mae said. "I gotta run pick up my kids."

Dellisha was out the door behind her and Loretta headed for the front room. There she found Major in his hospital bed weeping, tears streaming down his pale cheeks.

"Lorda mercy, Major honey, what's wrong?"

Between sobs he gasped, "I've had an altercation with my daughter, the artiste."

The telephone lay on the tray table where Kristy Mae must have left it so he could converse in private. He had a tendency to set the phone on speaker and shout at it, on account of his deafness.

"She refuses to come and visit her poor old father. She claims she's too busy. I reminded her that her mother and I moved in with her grandparents for two years before they died. Two years I was wiping my mother-in-law's ass! The old battle-ax hated me! But Ruth ..." here he broke to sob and hiccup, "... Ruth won't come for a weekend when she promised."

"She promised?" Loretta asked.

"Yes, this weekend, though she denies it."

"Well now, I didn't hear about Ruth visiting." In fact, Major often imagined conversations that hadn't taken place and forgot those that had from one moment to the next. In addition, Loretta was pretty sure he had never wiped anyone's behind except his own. Nevertheless, she ached to comfort him. "Did she say when she *would* be coming?"

"I told her not to come! I never want to see her again! I'm sorry I didn't cut her out of my will last year. You know, she tried to put me in a nursing home."

"No she didn't. That was a misunderstanding." Loretta had been present for that crisis, one of a series of storms that had whirled through the household, keeping the caregivers busy with gossip and Ruth shuttling between New York and West Virginia, trying to put out fires. It was when Loretta had gotten to know Ruth, when Loretta started calling them the hillbilly and the Yankee. "She wants you to stay right here at home and let us take care of you. Don't fret, she loves you." She dabbed at his cheeks with a Kleenex and patted his back to calm the hiccups.

"She doesn't deserve this farm. Doesn't want it either. Nor does her brother. What would they do with 360 acres?"

"Now, Major, you know Hume is coming tomorrow, like he does every Friday. You're lucky to have kids who love you and look after you, lucky you ain't all alone in the world like that old man up on the mountain."

"What old man?"

"Your spitting image. Remember? That collapsed in the aisle of Dixon's IGA last fall with a stroke. I told you the whole story."

"I don't remember." Major scowled. He hated to be reminded of his failing mind. He'd been so proud of his memory when Loretta first met him and he'd recited Caesar to her in Latin to show off.

"I take care of him when I'm not with you. He could be your double. He could be *you,* except he lives alone in a miserable cabin at the head of a holler, without a neighbor or family member to care if he's alive or dead. What he would give to live in a nice house with all us girls around!"

"Well then," Major said, a devilish gleam lighting up his water-soaked eyes, "bring him on down when I'm gone. Ruth and Hume don't need to know. He really looks just like me?"

"It's spooky! I get the creeps every time I go up there and think I'm seeing you in that tumbledown shack."

"Bring him down when I'm dead. Don't tell a soul. Just bury me up in the High Place next to Beatrice. It won't be long now till I'm out of the way."

"Don't say that!" Loretta said. She didn't wail, she didn't cry, but she wanted to.

The conversation came rushing back at her as she recounted it to the others without exactly spelling out its implications. All the while vague thoughts were forming in the depths of her imagination—dangerous, bold, tantalizing thoughts flitting in and out of murky shadows in her mind, calling on her to notice them. She ended her tale, ruminating, "He's a widower, no kids, no family, no one cares about him. It's pitiful."

"You felt sorry enough for him to do his shopping and cleaning without hardly getting paid, is what I remember," Tammy said.

"He pays me what he can, which ain't much. But that's not the point. Nobody should be so lonesome. It's sad." Loretta followed her idea through mental thickets like a hunter stalking prey, through darkness toward light, her own pulse quickening, not knowing if what she was pursuing was salvation or perdition or how she would know the difference. "When there's this nice big house with all of us."

Tammy placed Major's hand on his chest, on top of the blanket, and smoothed it wistfully. It was a fine hand. "What do you mean?"

"It's what Major asked us to do. We should do it for him." It was a raw moment, with Major staring up at who knows what, and all their nerve endings pinging with sorrow and anxiety. "He don't have to die. We can keep him alive in our hearts."

Cass stopped sniffling and looked at Loretta like she was the devil. "Are you crazy, Loretta? Screw loose?"

"No I ain't." By now she was getting close enough to the idea to see it more clearly. It didn't appear overly diabolical, but she approached it cautiously, testing out its moral threat, on her guard against any whiff of foul intentions. "Major dies, it's pure heartache for Hume and Ruth. Ruth has to drag her fancy ass down here and get everything in order. They got this big farm neither one of them wants, and all their parents' stuff to sort through and disturb their lives." A good person would surely want to spare the kids from such affliction. It would be only righteous. "If he don't die, we still have our jobs. His kids don't have to stress, we just carry on like we've been doing. Everybody's happy."

"So how exactly are you planning to pull this off?" Tammy asked.

With a touch of bravado Loretta revealed the outlines of her idea, now beginning to glow in something like holy luminescence, its details still coming into shape. "There's no one to go looking for that old man up in the holler if he disappears."

Silence greeted this suggestion. Loretta waited nervously for the vision it conjured to insinuate itself from her imagination into theirs, so that they could share in its magical awakening. Loretta listened for a sign, something to guide them. Sometimes the old farmhouse creaked, but there was no wind tonight. They were deep in the country, not a car engine or a nearby house to break the solitude. All the girls were afraid of the dark, and kept the curtains drawn at night to keep it out. Coyotes had killed Major's favorite cat, and now bears were coming down from the hills.

"You *are* crazy, Loretta," Cass said. "I've got my professional reputation to think about."

"Think about this. You still get to come to work, nothing changes. We get our Major back."

"Suppose your old man gives us away?"

"He don't talk. He can't. Stroke took him. No one will ever know. Just us three."

"Suppose he don't want to come here?" Tammy asked. "Old folks can be stubborn."

"He's real fond of me. He'll do what I tell him," Loretta assured them. She could see into Tammy's and Cass's thoughts; she knew them that well from all the months of gossip and drama they'd spent together. She saw their fears, and argued against them with her confidence, saw their resistance, and its softening, moment by moment. She saw the wheels turning, spinning fast, then slowing, little by little. Tick. Tick. . Tick. . . They would click into a safe and comforting place. All three of them would realize that an alive Major could ease the threat of destitution as well as salve the pain they were feeling in their hearts. Loretta saw the release of panic on the other faces, replaced by the soft light of acquiescence.

"Well, it would be a blessing to have the Major back," Cass said in a dreamy voice at last. "He was a sweet man."

Tammy harrumphed, and Loretta almost laughed. A sweet man was one thing the Major was not, but they let it pass because Cass was only putting into words the love they all felt. Cass packed away the stethoscope and stood up. "I'm leaving now. I don't want to know how you do it. If I come back in the morning and Major's looking better, I'll consider it a miracle."

After she had hustled herself out, Tammy said to Loretta, "I guess that makes you a miracle worker."

That would remain to be seen, but strengthened Loretta's resolve. "I'm going into the other room. I can't do this in front of Major." He was still staring up at them with his beady eyes, as if he could see into her mind and discern the plan that had now attained its perfect form, like a chainsaw carving emerging from a tree stump. His plan, his last joke against the world.

"You go on. I'll sit with him," Tammy said. She touched Major's forehead with her comforting hand and pulled his eyelids shut. "Time to rest, Major."

From the bay window alcove in the dining room where the girls always sat to gossip and pass the time while Major slept, Loretta called her husband. "Beaver, you got to get Bo and Nate and come on out here right away."

"What's up, Loretta? It's the middle of the night."

"I'll explain when you get here. Bring a pick and shovels. We got a burial to attend to." She made her voice sharp and brooked no nonsense. She'd kept Beaver on a short leash ever since she had busted him for an affair with the girl in the office at Hard Rock Construction and made him quit his truck-driving job. The call made, the wheels of the plan put into action, she returned to Major's side.

"My husband and his brothers will be here soon," she told Tammy.

"I thought only us three were to know about this," Tammy objected.

"You aiming to dig a grave by yourself? You can trust the Hardwick brothers, Major always said so. Said he would trust them with the keys to his kingdom."

"Hmph." There wasn't much more Tammy could say. Loretta would like to have told her to go on home, but didn't want to keep watch alone with the presence of death so near. So they waited quietly by the Major until headlights shone again in the drive and the three Hardwick brothers clomped up to the porch of the Thorndike house and the women met them at the door.

"Major's passed," Loretta told the men. They looked startled and a little uncomprehending. "He's done gone to his Maker." The Major was an atheist, Loretta knew, but she didn't take that seriously, considering it a pose on his part to rile people up. Despite Major's faults, she counted on Jesus to take him in. "We got to take him up to the High Place and bury him next to Miss Beatrice."

"Now?" Bo Hardwick looked aghast. The Hardwick brothers had been looking after the Thorndikes for years, fixing the house and outbuildings, clearing out downed trees on the property, shoving dead cattle into the bottom of the big sink— as if Major were their own daddy. Bo had been particularly close to Major, kidding around with him while he worked inside the house on the plumbing, wiring, and whatnot. Nate, the wild, rangy-looking one, had taken care of Miss Beatrice's horses when she got sick and after she died, until Hume and Ruth gave them away to the therapeutic riding place in Sweetwater County. "That's pretty damn irregular, Loretta," Bo said, furrowing up his forehead like a field of red clay.

Loretta attempted to soften her demand. "Look, I know you're upset. None of us was ready for Major to go. But this ain't no time for tears. It's what he asked me to do, right before he died. He didn't want no priest or minister, just wanted to go straight to the High Place with no fuss. Ain't that so, Tammy?"

"Dear Lord, Loretta!" she said.

"Maybe you'd gone out of the room to get him a glass of water, when he reminded me of his plan to help us all through this hard time." Loretta remembered this conversation as clearly as if it had actually taken place.

"Dear Lord, Loretta," Tammy repeated. "I better get on home."

"You do that, Tammy. The boys and I will take care of Major. Boys, you better pull the truck around to the kitchen door."

Tammy slid on out. Bo Hardwick looked uncomfortable. "Look, Loretta. Don't we have to get a death certificate first? Don't we have to call someone?"

"Bo Hardwick, are you going to forget how Major stood by your daddy when the hanging judge sent him to prison? You want to get the law in here? Are you going to deny Major his last request?"

"I ain't arguing what Major done for our dad. Major told everyone it was prison that killed an innocent man."

"Are you denying Major's right to be buried on his own property, like a good American?"

Bo didn't know anything about burial laws; his legal expertise was limited to electrical and plumbing codes, and he was willing to cut corners on those. He did believe that private property was an inalienable right, and that government had no business butting in. Mountain people had a proud history of standing up to the law.

"I think we should do what Loretta says," Beaver said. "She's the one Major confided in, and he knew what he was talking about."

"Lately he was getting pretty confused," Bo said.

"He was real clear when he told me this three months ago." By this time Loretta was firm in her belief that the Major had worked out all the details with her, that their earlier conversation had not been the ravings of dementia or momentary pique but a true bequest that it was her responsibility to carry out.

Beaver backed her up. "Are we going to stand here in the doorway all night or should I pull the truck around?"

"No," Loretta said. "Bo, you get the truck. Beaver and Nate will help me bundle Major."

"Then what?" Bo still stalling.

"I'll explain the plan to you up at the High Place." She didn't give Bo any more time to object, but hastened the other brothers into the front room and directed them as she wrapped the Major's mortal remains in a clean sheet, kissing him tenderly on the forehead before she covered his face. "This is how he wanted to be buried, so that his body will go back to nature and feed the buttercups." She well remembered Miss Beatrice insisting on her deathbed that she be buried in a woven willow casket. Biodegradable, Miss Beatrice called it.

While the boys carried Major outside, Loretta gathered pillows and Miss Beatrice's favorite quilt that had been put away after she died. Thus prepared, they drove up the farm roads that traversed the pastures to the highest point on the Thorndikes' 360 acres, a grassy hilltop that overlooked the rolling valley in the moonlight, under the ramparts of Ragtop Mountain. It took several hours for the brothers to dig a hole in the rocky soil. When the grave was three feet deep Loretta lined it with pillows. They laid the Major in the quilt and lowered him into the grave with all the respect they could muster. Loretta said the Lord's Prayer, since she didn't have the burial service committed to memory, and added in her own words a plea to Jesus to forgive the Major's sins.

They were all pretty worn out by the time the hole was filled and smoothed out and tamped down to prevent any incursions by wild animals. They stood by the pickup smoking, and Loretta finally explained the Major's plan. If its logic didn't quite add up, she wasn't about to admit to any doubts now.

"Damn! That's some scheme, Loretta." There was admiration in Beaver's voice.

"It'll never work," Bo said, his outrage plain. "How you going to fool all those people—the Major's kids, the nurses, the doctors?"

"Wait till you see that old man. He could fool the Major's mother," Loretta said. "As for Dr. Nightingale, she's so spacey she couldn't pick Major out of a lineup."

"Seems risky to me." Nate was a man of few words.

"Y'all have come too far to back out now." This was an understatement. Not that Loretta had exactly intended to snare them into the plan before revealing it, but rather she had followed her instincts, taking one step at a time. The first step being to lay the Major to rest. Now she tried to make her apparent subterfuge up to them. "We'll leave Nate and Bo out of it. Go on home. Me and Beaver'll do the rest." And so Loretta prevailed, as she so often did. They dropped the brothers off, Bo slamming the truck door and exclaiming, "A fine thing you've gotten us into!" before stalking off.

Beaver drove the pickup with Loretta riding shotgun, up an almost impassable dirt track into the mountains. It was near dawn of an August morning when they arrived at the old man's ramshackle cabin at the head of a hollow rarely visited by outsiders.

"You wait in the truck, Beaver. I'll bring him out."

"Whatever you say." Loretta was a small, sinewy woman, but Beaver knew she was strong, and as hard as the rock from which the mountain people were hewn. She went in through the unlocked door, through the front room with its rack of antlers and its wood stove visible in the early light, and into the messy back room where the old man slept. He sat bolt upright when she shook him.

"It's only me, dear," she said in a reassuring tone. "Family Services sent me up here. They don't want you living up here on your own no more. It's dangerous, DHHR says. They found you a nice house with some ladies to take care of you. All paid for by the county. Aren't you glad?" She took his arm to help him out of bed.

"Unh?" He tried to wrench his arm away.

"Now don't you fuss, Major. That's your name now. Long as you answer to it the county will send your checks. Hurry up. We got to get you down off this mountain."

The old man being addled, either from his stroke or from being awakened at such an early hour, and being used to Loretta and her authoritative ways, allowed her to help him put on his pants and shirt and shoes and lead him outside to the waiting truck. He was actually quite physically capable for his age and didn't really need her assistance, but who among us will turn down care when it is freely offered, when we are old and alone and confused by all the changes in the world? At any rate, the old man couldn't speak, so his opinions will remain a mystery.

Loretta got him into the front seat of the pickup and the three of them drove down the mountain as morning broke.

2

Dead Ringer

MONDAY

Kristy Mae and Dellisha, the morning team, met Loretta at the door of the Thorndike house. They had only just arrived and found the house ominously empty. No Major. No night crew. Kristy Mae was about to call Cass and ask what disaster had befallen—a sudden ambulance ride to the emergency room?—when Loretta's pickup appeared, then Loretta herself, leading the Major by the hand.

"He's walking!" Kristy Mae exclaimed. "Where you been?" And what was Loretta doing here?

"Getting him checked out. He had a stroke. But he's OK. Tired is all. We had quite the night," Loretta said.

Kristy Mae studied Loretta. Something was not right. "They discharge you, or did you just walk out, Major?" she asked. She knew he hated the hospital, but it was odd they hadn't kept him in for at least a few days. He glared at her but didn't answer.

"He can't talk, because of the stroke. Let's get him to bed." Loretta pushed past Kristy Mae and led the old man into the front room, the morning crew following. "Here you are, Major dear. Kristy Mae'll take off your shoes and tuck you into bed. You can keep your shirt and pants on, but don't give the girls no backtalk." He sat on the edge of the bed and looked around, his eyes a little wild.

"Where'd he get them clothes?" Dellisha asked. "Major don't have blue jeans."

"Borrowed them. There was a accident."

"Loretta, what's going on?" Kristy Mae asked. "What have you done to him?"

"Nothing! I ain't done nothing! Beaver's waiting for me in the pickup. I'm wore out. I gotta go home and sleep. I'll be back at three." She pecked the old man on the cheek. "Remember what I told you. Be good." She rushed out of the room, not letting Kristy Mae get in another word.

"That was weird," Kristy Mae said to Dellisha. "What got into her?"

"I've always thought Loretta was crazier than the hind leg of a mule," Dellisha said.

"Never mind that. Let's get Major settled." She knelt down to unlace his boots.

"Where'd he get them shoes?" Dellisha asked. "Major don't wear work boots. He mail orders those special Earth shoes for his flat feet. I put in the order myself for him, on the Internet."

"Beats me." The old man peered down at Kristy Mae as she pulled off the boots but left his socks on. Then she lifted his legs up into the bed, as she'd been doing for Major for months, ever since he lost the ability to do it himself. The bed was raised to the sitting position, and she pushed him back into it, fluffing the pillows around him. "Comfortable?"

He made some noises in his throat and blinked his eyes rapidly.

"You may not be able to talk, but you should at least be able to nod your head yes or no," Kristy Mae reprimanded. Dellisha looked on with pursed lips.

"Looks like he don't know what's going on," Dellisha said. "That stroke must have addled him."

"Maybe he's hungry. I'm going to get his breakfast. You watch over him. Don't slack off." She ignored Dellisha's indignant harumph and went out to fix the Major's cereal and coffee. She made the coffee weak and sweet, the way he liked it. When she came back, Cass was standing by the bedside, holding the Major's hand, tears in her eyes.

"Look at you, Major. Pink cheeks, bright eyes! You're looking better than you have in months. God moves in mysterious ways!"

"You heard he had a stroke?" Kristy Mae said sharply. "Spent the night in the hospital? Loretta just brought him back." Why Loretta? Kristy Mae thought. Where was Cass?

Cass looked defensive. "Course I heard," she retorted, dropping Major's hand. "I was babysitting my grandkids, otherwise I would have gone to the hospital. Loretta offered. Right now I'm going into Buckfield and pick up supplies, like I always do Mondays. Go on and give Major his breakfast."

Cass left and Kristy Mae sat in the chair next to the bed. Dellisha in the corner worked on her nails. "Here you are, Major. Cheerios, your favorite!" Kristy Mae said.

She attempted to spoon some cereal into the Major's mouth. He couldn't hold a spoon because of the trembling from his Parkinson's and the staff had to feed him. Kristy Mae was a pro. She had perfected the art of coaxing another spoonful into him, baby-talking him and congratulating him when the bowl was clean. Suddenly he grabbed the spoon out of her hand, uttering some unintelligible cries.

"What on earth!" she exclaimed. He fixed her with a fierce look, warding off tenderness, and gobbled his food.

"I guess that stroke turned him ornery," Dellisha observed. "But if he can do more for himself, I suppose it's less work for us."

Dellisha was one of the new girls hired on by Cass, and Kristy Mae didn't think much of her tendency to shirk chores. "More time for you to cruise the Internet for a wedding gown you mean," she said.

"Look at you on your high horse while he's makin' a mess." Dellisha snapped her nail kit shut.

It was true; Cheerios had gone everywhere and milk dribbled down the old man's chin. Kristy Mae took the empty bowl, whipped off his bib, and dabbed at his face with a napkin, then announced, "It's Monday morning, Major, bath time!"

She'd noticed a funkiness about him when she got close and would have made it Monday no matter what. Major never knew what day it was. "You want to sit on the potty first?"

"Unh! Nah gitray feer!" The Major's eyebrows went up and down.

"I'll take that as a yes," Kristy Mae said, perturbed. "I'm going to swing your legs around while Dellisha helps you sit up." They settled into their customary teamwork. Kristy Mae pulled the blanket back and Dellisha took hold of his shoulders to heave him around. But Major gave a roar and sat up on his own accord, kicking Kristy Mae away from his feet. "Take it easy! You want to do it on your own, OK. But you got to behave." She positioned the wheelchair next to the bed. "That means riding to the potty in your Mercedes Benz. I don't want you falling."

The Major stood up and allowed the two women to push him into the wheelchair, growling at them. They wheeled him a short distance to the potty standing next to the fireplace, which was stacked with packages of diapers, wipes, disposable gloves, paper towels, and other care supplies. When Major saw the potty chair he gave another roar.

"Enough of that," Kristy Mae lectured. "We're settin' you on the pot and leaving. You signal when you're done."

They wrestled him out of the wheelchair and yanked down his pants. He barked and sat down suddenly. "Turn on the baby-minder, Dellisha. He can't holler for us, leastwise not in English."

They left, closing the door behind them, and found refuge in the dining room bay, sinking into the two facing platform rockers. The bay had been the setting of constant care drama, turmoil, and staff turnover, including the firing of the old care manager and hiring of Momma Cass. Kristy Mae regretted her earlier goading of Dellisha. Such an unsettling morning called for solidarity. "He don't seem like himself at all," she said. "All this grunting and snarling ain't like him."

"That's just because he can't talk. He's always had his moods. He can be downright hateful," Dellisha said.

"That's mean. He can't help himself."

They heard thumping through the baby-minder and realized Major had left the potty chair. "Oh sweet Jesus!" Kristy Mae exclaimed. "Let's go."

They intercepted him at the door of the front room, forced him into the wheelchair and transported him to the provisional shower that had been set up in the back hall after Miss Beatrice died. She would never permit the construction of a downstairs bathroom while she lived. "Now you take your sit-down shower, Major. You can wash yourself if you want, but Dellisha and I are going to stand by to make sure you do it right."

Dellisha kneeled down to slip off his socks and gasped. "Look at these feet, would you?" They were callused and gnarled with bunions. "They look like a farmer's feet!"

"Now you know Major's never done a day of hard labor in his life. Major's feet are smooth and straight as a young boy's. How'd they get this way after one night in the hospital?"

"His hands too," Dellisha said, grabbing one of them and turning it over. As gnarled and callused as the feet. "Can this really be Major?"

Kristy Mae had been too upset by his behavior to notice his hands. "Who else can it be?" she asked, perplexed.

"I'll give him a manicure after his bath."

"You do that," Kristy Mae said, as if that would solve the mystery. "I'll go clean out the potty."

By the time Cass got back from her supply run to the Walmart in Buckfield, in the neighboring county, the women had the cleaned-up Major sitting in the La-Z-Boy in the corner of the front room, watching television. The two caregivers were worn out from their bathing and grooming battles with him, and from trying to decipher what he wanted from his weird noises that sometimes approximated speech but had no meaning. So Dellisha had brought in the small TV from the parlor across the hall from the front room, rarely visited these past three months by Major, the Oriental rugs and antique furniture forming obstacles to the navigation of his wheelchair. "Let's see if we can find something he'll watch."

"You know he don't much like TV," Kristy Mae said.

The only thing on was *Days of Our Lives*. Amazingly, the old man was instantly riveted.

"Well I be!" Kristy Mae said. "This can't be Major."

"Who else can it be?" Dellisha said.

They heard the door slam and went to meet Cass in the kitchen. "Everything OK?" Cass greeted them.

"Everything is strange," Kristy Mae said. "He's like a different person."

"Don't be silly," Cass said breezily. "Help me unload the groceries." She turned her back on them and started taking things out of bags. The girls went out to her car to bring in more bags and stock the refrigerator with quart jars of mayonnaise and mustard, gallons of milk and half & half, family-sized packages of baloney and turkey slices. When Ruth visited her father she always criticized the over-filled refrigerator for one old man who rarely got out of bed, but these women had survived for generations by buying in bulk on discount and stuffing their large families as full as they could when they had the opportunity. Of the girls, only Kristy Mae and Loretta were skinny, and that was on account of their metabolisms, not because they didn't eat buttered popcorn and pizza with the rest. The others ranged from full-figured to very full. More than once Major had fired a girl for being overweight. And Miss Beatrice, in her time, had prohibited the staff from sitting on her spindly-legged loveseats, telling them they were too fat.

"Angeline will be coming at two to check Major," Cass told them when the unpacking was done. Angeline was the hospice nurse who came once a week. "She'll be pleased to see him up and looking frisky."

The house phone rang. Dellisha looked at the caller ID. "It's Hume."

"I'll take it," Cass said, picked up the telephone, and wandered with it into the dining room, away from the girls' prying ears. Still they could hear her telling Hume, "Your dad can't talk to you right now. He had a spell last night and it affected his speech … no, he's fine … you'll be down on Friday?"

Hume came every Friday to have lunch with Major and write checks for the staff.

Later, when the girls were eating lunch and waiting for Angeline to arrive, Cass said, "I was talking to Jeanie at the pharmacy this morning. She tells me Trisha is still spreading lies about me." Trisha was the former care manager. "Trisha says I won't let her visit Major. She thinks I'm poisoning him."

"Trisha is always lying on people. Don't pay her no mind," Dellisha said. Dellisha and Cass went way back.

"That's why Ruth fired her," Kristy Mae said. She had been around for the drama in the Box Room. "Ruth don't want her visiting Major. She'd only rile him up, Ruth says." Trisha had been with the Major the longest, since his first stroke five years earlier, when he just needed help getting up and down the stairs.

Before Cass left to teach her class in medical ethics at Sweetwater Community College—a job she qualified for as a Certified Medical Assistant—she checked in on the front room. "He's napping," she told the girls. "I turned off the TV."

"I can't believe he sat through *The Dukes of Hazzard*," Kristy Mae said. "Something is seriously wrong."

"What can be wrong?" Cass said. "He ate a good lunch. When he wakes up you can put on that Bartok CD he likes."

"We tried that this morning and he yelled at us," Kristy Mae said. "I'm telling you, he's not himself."

"Nonsense," Cass snapped. "I have to run or I'll be late to class." She hurried at a clip from the room.

"Is she hiding something?" Kristy Mae asked. "You've known her a long time."

"She seems normal to me," Dellisha answered.

When Angeline arrived Major was still sleeping. She looked at the notes the caregivers kept of his input, output, meds, and vitals. Kristy Mae explained there'd been an event in the night, she wasn't sure what. "OK," Angeline said. "Let me take a look." They all went into the front room together.

"Major Thorndike. How're you doing?" Angeline asked. The Major's eyelids fluttered open and he sat up with a start.

"Grrr arum argle."

"Hmm …" Angeline took his hand. "Major, can you squeeze my hand?"

Kristy Mae and Dellisha watched anxiously, waiting for him to leap up and attack. But he just fixed his glare on Angeline and squeezed. "Good!" she said, and took his other hand. "Now this one."

He squeezed again. Kristy Mae gave a sigh of relief. Angeline spread his eyelids open and peered into his eyes. "You get another attack like you had last night, you should let the girls take you to the hospital."

The Major shook his head violently and made more sounds.

"He *did* go to the hospital," Kristy Mae explained. "I just don't know what happened there."

Loretta and Tammy came in at three, going right on in to see the Major. "Don't you look good!" Loretta told him and winked. "The girls got you cleaned up handsome."

He beamed up at her. "How is he doing?" Loretta asked Kristy Mae. She didn't like the suspicious look on Kristy Mae's face.

"Why didn't the hospital keep him for tests? Why is he acting so strange? If this is our Major, why don't he look like Major?" Kristy Mae fired off questions like bullets.

"He looks like Major to me!" Loretta felt her heart contracting.

"Where'd he get them bunions?"

"What bunions? What are you talking about?"

Kristy Mae yanked off his slipper that was resting on the La-Z-Boy footrest. "What did you do to him last night?"

Panic seized Loretta. "Nothing! I done nothing! He died all of his own accord and the Lord sent us this new Major. It was Major's plan all along."

"What?!" Dellisha and Kristy Mae chorused.

"He told me not to tell anyone, just to bury him in the High Place and bring in his double."

"His *what*?!" Dellisha exclaimed.

"This dear old man I been taking care of for close on to a year and needs us. I told you Major had a double."

"You mean ... this ain't Major?" Kristy Mae asked, incredulity in her voice.

"He is now. He's our new Major. We'll take care of him and he'll take care of us. No one will know the difference."

"You went along with this?" Kristy Mae asked Tammy, who had retreated across the room.

"She told us we were doing a good deed for Major and all his family. And we keep our jobs. It ain't easy being a single mom, daughter about to go to college."

"I've got four kids. You think you have problems! Who else knows about this?" Kristy Mae demanded.

"Just Cass," Loretta said.

"I knew she was acting fishy!" Kristy Mae said.

"Now you two," Loretta added.

Dellisha spoke up. "If I didn't have a wedding to pay for, I wouldn't have no part in this. It can't be legal."

"You're one to talk." Loretta stiffened. "Ain't you marrying an ex-con?"

"You've got a nasty mouth! At least I know my Jeremy's not a cheater."

The old man at the center of this debate had been looking from one woman to the next as if he were watching a match on TV. He broke in. "Goryar!"

"Don't worry, Major" Loretta comforted him. "They aren't mad at you. They're going to take good care of you, aren't you, girls?" she wheedled. She was behind on the car payments. Even though she had let Beaver go back to work at Hard Rock Construction when he couldn't find another source of income besides work around the Thorndike place, and even with her extra hours at the Family Dollar, things were tight at her house with three plump children to feed, all still living at home even though the older two had already finished high school. Her oldest, Jewel, had worked for a time at Thorndikes' before Major fired her for falling asleep on the night shift and leaving him to stew in his wet diaper. Loretta had tried to argue for leniency, but Major wasn't having it. "We've all got mouths to feed," she added when they didn't immediately give in.

"I reckon," Dellisha said grudgingly.

"I'm just hoping you can keep this from the other girls. Some of them have mighty loose lips." With this parting shot, Kristy Mae left, Dellisha by her side, newly allied.

3

Miss Beatrice Shuffles Off the Mortal Coil

A MONDAY MORNING IN 2012

"Ruth, this is your father." As if she couldn't recognize that querulous voice anywhere, even when the phone rang in the dark and roused her out of deep slumber.

"Dad, what time is it?" She didn't disguise her exasperation.

"Six. I waited until morning, a decent hour. Your mother has been up all night vomiting and, if you'll pardon the expression, shitting blood. She's on her way to the emergency room. You need to come."

"A hurricane landed here last night. Did you hear?"

"Yes, Hume told me."

"Manhattan is shut down. The bridges are closed. The tunnels are full of water. My power is out. I'm talking to you on the last corded phone in America." It was so like her father to think she could just drop everything and run when he called. "What's wrong with Mother?"

Beatrice was 89 and had never been sick. She was indomitable. She didn't believe in sickness, and had never permitted it in her offspring. Ruth had inherited her mother's lack of sympathy, to the point of disgust, for bodily weakness.

"I don't know. She's gone to the hospital, didn't I tell you? In an ambulance. A half hour ago. It's not like her. What am I supposed to do?" His tone said *I am weak.* His tone played on her heartstrings, against her will, creeping past her defenses, reminding her of when he'd been her precious daddy, so long ago.

"Just wait, Dad. I'm sure she'll be fine. Keep me posted." She slammed down the receiver. That was the satisfying thing about an old-fashioned phone. You could slam it. Lower the gates! Shore up thick skin! Now thoroughly awake, Ruth heard the bitterness in her voice. She had recently left her gallery job on bad terms with her boss. At 62 her art career, which had started out so promisingly, was a bust. She continued to make large kaleidoscopic montages of painted and photographed material that she manipulated digitally, her best work ever. But she no longer showed her work to dealers and curators. She was tired of rejection. The gallery job had been her last remaining link to the art world. She had thought about filing an age-discrimination suit against her ex-boss but gave it up when she considered all the forms of discrimination (against the fat, the ugly, the fashion-challenged, the uncouth) that were tolerated in cutting-edge galleries.

Adding to the pressure of her suppressed fury, her lover Walker was threatening to divorce his wife and become available. What was he thinking? Who would support him? The last thing Ruth wanted was a full-time lover, certainly not a neurotic out-of-work actor. She had her hands full with two children making their way through their angst-ridden twenties; though no longer under her roof, they were always under her worried inner eye.

Let her brother Hume take care of their high-maintenance father. He was the patient one; she didn't have emotional room.

Two days and many phone calls later the bridges and tunnels reopened, and her mother's diagnosis came back: terminal cancer. Ruth was flabbergasted. Undone. It had never occurred to her that her mother might actually be capable of dying. Beatrice defied mortality. On their walks around the farm in recent years, her mother would shake her fist at the vultures circling overhead and yell, "Not yet!"

Hume had called with the diagnosis. "In addition to the cancer, she has a massive infection in the colon and her heart rate has spiked. The doctors asked me what our instructions are and I told them: Do Not Resuscitate. I hope you're OK with that."

"Hold on!" Ruth shouted into the phone. She well knew the DNR directives from both her parents, but they'd always been hypothetical. "She can't die before I get there!" She reeled with uncharacteristic panic, packed in a rush, and left New York late that afternoon to drive all night. In the widespread blackout left by the hurricane, isolated gas stations glowed like oases in an apocalyptic landscape, presaging the end of everything she knew. The world without her mother appeared an unfathomable vastness. She pressed down on the accelerator to outrun the specter. Lo and behold, to her great relief Beatrice was still extant when she walked into the ICU in the morning.

"I've been told I have three days to get my affairs in order," Beatrice told her daughter. Her mother was not one to beat around the bush. Ruth had never seen her like this, laid out on a bed, wired to machines, helpless. She had never seen her mother so vulnerable. She looked accusingly at her brother and at the ICU nurse, who raised her eyebrows and said to Beatrice, "I don't know who told you that! It wasn't me."

She winked reassurance at Ruth and Hume. They were in good hands. The ICU nurse knew how to take care of them.

Beatrice was adamant even through her morphine fog. "The horses go to Make-A-Wish Riding Center. The dog goes to Trisha."

No mention, Ruth noticed, of the husband of sixty-three years. Perhaps Beatrice had already washed her hands of him. Later, Ruth and Hume were in the middle of a meeting with the doctor and a social worker to discuss end-of-life options when their father called on Ruth's cellphone. "You know, I'm anxiously awaiting your presence."

As if he were jealous of the attention Beatrice was getting from her bewildered and grieving children. Well, Ruth thought more charitably, he would be heartbroken too. He'd never spent a night apart from his wife. Pressed by the urgency of her father's impending loss and need, she left the hospital in Buckfield and sped down to Amity in the early afternoon, leaving Hume with their mother. She anticipated histrionics and tears from her father. She prepared herself to let bygones be bygones, forget the years of hurts he'd inflicted on her since she left home at seventeen, and coddle the darling daddy he'd once been. Trisha met her at the door. "Your dad's been waiting for you all day. He's in a mood."

She found Roger ensconced in his throne-like La-Z-Boy in the parlor. "Your mother and I are completely estranged. This proves it. I intend to die first. Neither of us will miss the other," he declared.

The heartless bastard! His self-centeredness still had the ability to astonish her. The marital battles since her father's stroke and subsequent decline had been reported to her by the caregivers—Beatrice throwing plates, Roger hurling curses and threatening her with divorce. Roger's cruelty to her mother had made Ruth furious. But when she'd tried to pry, Beatrice had defended him, saying, "He can't help himself. He's suffering."

If Ruth had expected a change of heart now, given the circumstances, was she a fool? She tried to contain her rage and fan the dying embers of pity in its place. She made excuses; he was in shock. She made him dinner and sat with him until the caregivers put him to bed. "I'll stay as long as you need me," she told him before bidding him goodnight.

She moved her things into her mother's room, where she'd never before slept. Her mother's paintings were on the walls; her meager wardrobe hung in the closet, leaving Ruth plenty of space. She looked out the window at a black sky filled with stars. Her mother's room and its familiar objects gave her resolve. In the morning she rose at dawn, anxious to get back to the hospital. Her car had a flat. In the early light she stared at the driver's manual despondently, trying to figure out where the jack and spare were stowed. Loretta Hardwick pulled into the gravel parking area beside her and said, "You need help with that?"

Tough and scrappy, Loretta was Ruth's favorite of the caregivers she'd gotten to know on her increasingly frequent visits. Loretta got out of her car. "Your Yankee book-learning won't change a tire. You need a hillbilly."

"You're my hillbilly," Ruth said. It was their running joke.

Loretta took over and between the two of them they jacked up the car. Loretta jumped on the tire iron to get the lug nuts loose. "This donut spare won't take you far, but it'll get you to Leroy's to get your tire fixed."

Hume one time had pointed out to Ruth that Loretta had no teeth. Ruth had never noticed. Loretta kept her lips pulled over her gums so you never saw them. She had a brilliant smile and the most expressive eyebrows Ruth had ever seen. To Ruth she was beautiful.

"Can you tell me how to get to Leroy's?" she asked. Everyone seemed to assume she knew her way around Amity. They forgot that she'd never lived there. When they gave directions they used landmarks that had gone out of existence years ago.

Before she could leave, Loretta's brother-in-law Nate arrived in his pickup truck. Nate was the thin and scruffy brother with the ponytail down his back. "Nate," she said. "Perfect timing. My mother gave me some instructions for the horses."

Nate answered her with a sentence in a drawl so thick she couldn't pick out a single recognizable word. "Let me show you," she said. Sign language might work better. She led him through the orchard and they went into the pasture through the gate beside the stable. Each horse had its separate paddock. The Tennessee walker galloped over to them as they crossed his space. Nate reached out a hand to greet and calm the horse, to Ruth's approval. Horses made her nervous. Nate had a natural ease with them, like her mother.

"Beatrice wants you to move the fences back a few feet, to give them more grass." Ruth pointed to the lush green grass in the pasture beyond the low electric fences. November, and the grass was still growing like crazy. Beatrice had said she'd never seen anything like it. She had to ration out the pasture as if it were high summer.

"Global warming, Mum," Ruth had said.

In the ensuing days Ruth shuttled between her father and the hospital. Every morning she set her alarm at 5:30 for a cup of coffee before the half-hour drive across the frosted fields to Buckfield. She treasured her time in the hospital away from her father. She read her mother *New Yorker* and *Smithsonian Magazine* articles. When they ran out of articles she looked around the house for books and found the *Just So Stories*. She read the news off the Internet. They talked about everything except death. At four in the afternoon Hume arrived and Ruth drove back to Amity to give her father his gin and tonic and cook his dinner. His hard-heartedness had turned to tears the second day, and he'd focused the full force of his neediness on her. She felt herself taking over her mother's life, managing the difficult man, the household, and the care staff.

The chief of staff was Trisha. Ruth couldn't stand Trisha—large, obsequious, rocking back and forth from foot to foot while wringing her hands and complaining about the other caregivers. She complained the most about Faith, who had been with Beatrice the night her illness struck, had held Beatrice in her arms and called the ambulance. Trisha would close the door to the front room so the other caregivers wouldn't hear her pour out her heart to the Major, as the staff called Ruth's father. (He liked respect, Ruth knew from hard experience, and probably wouldn't mind a salute.)

"I don't know what's happened to Faith," Trisha said in a teary voice. "We used to be friends but she's turned on me. Do you know what she said when I got home from Roanoke? She called me ... I don't use this word ... I can barely say it ... a *bitch*! Out of the blue. What did I ever do to her?"

Trisha's husband had almost died in Roanoke, from advanced pulmonary disorder. Meanwhile Trisha's adult son was at home on a feeding tube. Trisha loved sickness, and Ruth suspected her of Munchausen's syndrome by proxy, faking illnesses to gain sympathy, a term she'd found in a newspaper article on elder abuse, raising her concerns about Trisha. She'd never seen the husband or the son; were they part of some ploy? But when she suggested this to her father, he scoffed. He had a soft heart for Trisha.

And why, thought Ruth, nursing her gin and tonic at her father's side, did he have to listen to this litany while his wife lay dying?

"She's trying to take you away from me, Major. And you're all I've got." Trisha dissolved into sobs.

"For God's sake, Ruth, get her a tissue. Pull yourself together. I'm surrounded by hysterical women!"

The most hysterical among them, thought Ruth, was Trisha. But she had become indispensable, trusted by both parents. Trisha had worked alongside Miss Beatrice in the maintenance of the house, the garden and orchard and swimming pool, and had become the guardian of her mother's secrets as Beatrice's memory began to fail. The last time Ruth had visited, just the previous month, her mother was making it through the day by ticking off a dozen Post-it note reminders stuck to the kitchen counter. "We're going down the tubes," she'd told Ruth. The caregivers would find her stopped between the house and the stable, having forgotten what she went outside to do. Meanwhile, she was still driving her car to Buckfield once a week to meet with her art group, and riding her tractor around the farm with the bush hog, mowing the pastures on a regular basis; still riding horseback alone into the mountains. It had been terrifying. But if you suggested to her that she give up any of these activities, she would look at you without comprehension. "This is what I do. This is who I am."

Her sudden hospitalization and death sentence felt like deliverance from something far worse. At least she could die still being Beatrice, strong and brave.

After two weeks that felt much longer—as if time had lost all meaning to those perched on the brink of oblivion—Ruth brought Beatrice home. Beatrice, debilitated by the weeks in bed, was unable to walk. She had to be helped into the front passenger seat of Ruth's car by hospital staff. Beatrice had never expected to see the world outside the hospital again. Ruth drove her over the country two-lane that had become so familiar from her daily commute. Beatrice watched the sunset over her beloved West Virginia and exclaimed, "Oh, the purple mountains. Oh! The fruited plain."

The entire Hardwick family and care staff welcomed Beatrice home and rallied around her. Roger entered into a sentimental phase. He wheeled in to sit beside her and reminisce about their early days of romance. The days resonated with sacramental depth. Ruth had never worked so hard, the emotional work of giving comfort to her parents when they most needed it.

"I don't know what's the matter with that priest from Amity Episcopal," Beatrice complained not long after her return. "When my mother got sick their minister used to come to the house to give Communion."

"What priest?" Ruth asked, startled.

"Father Dave. After your father had his stroke, Father Dave called to ask if he should come around. Your father said no. They'd had a falling out over the school board and your father was never one to let go of an argument. But Father Dave should never have given up so easily."

Beatrice spoke with formality, as if discussing rules of etiquette. But Ruth read between the lines and saw secret places she'd never known existed inside her mother's austere exterior. Beatrice really *wanted* the priest to come. This surprised Ruth. Never religious, Beatrice had raised her children as rainy-Sunday Episcopalians, preferring to worship under the blue dome of the sky when the sun shone. Now, with her death looming—the subject she refused to discuss, although her husband had liked until recently to joke about it—Beatrice apparently longed for the comfort of tradition and the poetry of King James. Ruth could hardly blame her. She acquired Father Dave's number and called him.

When he arrived, a stocky middle-aged man in khaki pants and a clerical collar carrying a leather briefcase, Ruth warned Roger, "Dad, Father Dave is here to see Mother. You don't have to talk to him if you don't want to." Full disclosure.

"Have him come in for a chat with me when he's done with her," the Major said from his private domain in the front room.

Ruth led Father Dave upstairs. "It's good to see you Beatrice," he said at her bedside. "It's been too long, and it's my fault."

"Roger hasn't been getting out, you know. It's not you."

"No, I should never have gotten involved in the school board. It came between me and several of the parishioners. I realized my mistake when Roger quit the vestry."

Every day she spent in Amity, Ruth learned more about her parents' lives than she'd known since she was a child. She discovered that Dave Hancock was a pleasant, easy-going man who'd gone to seminary after his military career and returned to his native town to serve its parish as a volunteer. This he explained to Ruth as he opened the briefcase, took out a clerical stole, and draped it over his sport jacket. He spread out a small white cloth that he called his traveling altar, and set up the portable chalice and hosts in a Tupperware container. "I keep my traveling Communion Service short and sweet," he said in his country twang. Ruth had been a believer for a few brief years in her childhood, until her passion for Christ faded in comparison to the more powerful passions of adolescence. The familiar words of the consecration carried her back to that time. The reverend's voice would deepen as he spoke. "For in the night in which he was betrayed, he took Bread; and when he had given thanks, he brake it," and a small bell would ting at the moment of transubstantiation. The child Ruth would feel it in her spine. The deep voice would continue, "and gave it to his disciples, saying, Take, eat; this is my Body which is given for you; Do this in remembrance of me. ..."

Sitting at her mother's bedside, no longer a child, Ruth remembered her mother caring for her through sickness, dispelling her nightmares—the escaped circus lion climbing through her bedroom window, little men marching over green hills on the eve of nuclear destruction—with the glow of lamplight and midnight ice cream. She'd never imagined their roles reversed, that it would be her job to ease her strong mother toward death. Tears came to Ruth's eyes.

The work was exhilarating. And exhausting. She carried the cordless house phone out into the yard for long conversations with people in the real world, out of earshot from her father and caregivers. She stood under the large oak tree still covered in bronze-colored leaves, dropping one by one. "My mother won't let her 92-year-old brother visit her one last time," she told her son Zeke in New York. "I don't think she's seen him in thirty years."

"Is she mad at him?"

"No. She talks to him on the phone. 'You sound just like yourself, Bucky,' she says, all sweet and tender. Then he buys a plane ticket and she tells me, 'Don't let him come. I won't have it!'"

"What's wrong with these people!" Zeke exclaimed, laughing. Her son's humor buoyed her. She spoke to him often, and to her daughter, to remind herself of normal life.

After she'd been in Amity for a month, and the pharmacist and grocer and gas station attendant all knew her by name, she called Zeke again. The rich dialect of West Virginia fascinated her. She'd been collecting vocabulary and practicing silently in her mind. "Guess what," she told Zeke, "I just had a conversation with Nate Hardwick, and I understood every word."

"You've been in West Virginia too long, Mom."

She didn't feel that way. She wanted this time to last forever.

Two weeks later Beatrice drew her last breath, literally, with Ruth sitting on her bed and holding her hand. The hospice nurse had told Ruth that dying was a process. Knowing every step made it less fearsome, if still deeply mysterious. The hospice nurse had said that hearing was the last sense to go. Beatrice's eyes were closed, her breathing labored, her pulse slowing. How do you tell your mother goodbye? "Sweet dreams, Mummy," Ruth said. A tear escaped from the corner of her mother's right eye.

4

How to Shoot Yourself in the Foot

Cass Furrow met the daughter at the Kalico Kitchen on Main Street. Ruth Blitzer, who was visiting from New York City, had told Cass to pick a place for the job interview, someplace discreet. Ha! In Amity, population 564 in the most recent census, there was no such thing, but at least they got a booth. At least the waitress who came to take their lunch order was no one Cass knew. That was surprising, since all of Amity, she had thought, made it at one time or another to Dr. Nightingale's office.

"I'll have a BLT on whole wheat toast, no mayo," Ruth said.

"That sounds good," Cass said, wanting to seem agreeable. "Make my BLT on white toast with *plenty* of mayo. And a side of fries." No wonder Ruth was scarecrow thin, Cass thought. Then she added defensively, "I missed breakfast. I'm starved."

"Don't let me stop you," Ruth said, giving her menu to the waitress. "Do you have unsweetened ice tea?" Cass shuddered and ordered a Coke.

Ruth's short-cropped hair was dark gray, like iron filings. A good color job would make her look ten years younger. Cass had dressed well for this meeting, in a conservative skirt and blazer, but she wasn't surprised that Ruth wore jeans. It wasn't an office job.

"Trisha spoke highly of you," Ruth said, sipping her bitter tea. "She said you might be leaving Dr. Nightingale's office. Can you tell me a little bit more about your ... background?"

What did she want to know? Probably that Cass had attended some kind of high-toned college. She forged ahead. "I was a homemaker while my four kids were little and my husband was on the road most of the time. He's a long-haul trucker. Once my kids were grown I wanted a profession I could rely on, so I enrolled in an accredited medical assistant training program—academic and clinical training in human anatomy, physiology, and pathology; medical terminology; record keeping and accounting; computer applications, coding and insurance processing; laboratory techniques like collecting and preparing specimens; clinical and diagnostic procedures like venipuncture, blood work, patient positioning, electrocardiograms ...." Was she overdoing it? Cass wondered. Would Ruth be impressed or bored? She decided to wrap up. "First aid practices, office practices, patient relations, medical law and ethics. I completed my practicum and got certified in Bluefield and stayed on to work at the medical center there, but the commute was getting me down. So I took the job with Dr. Nightingale."

"May I ask why you want to leave?"

"Dr. Nightingale loves me, and she's a dear. But I have problems with the way she runs her office. Her son works for her." Cass picked her words carefully. "He doesn't want to be there, and it shows. He's immature. He tells dead baby jokes in front of the patients. He accused an old man of pulling out his colostomy bag on purpose to stink up the waiting room and jump the line. He says to the poor old guy, who's as embarrassed as all get-out, 'I'm not cleaning up your shit again!' It's terrible, but I can't do anything. Dr. Nightingale spoils him. There's no professionalism." Their sandwiches arrived. Cass momentarily regretted the graphic reference to feces.

"That's what I want in our care manager," Ruth said. "Professionalism." They let the word hang between them while they bit into their sandwiches. "Trisha has been with my father since his first stroke four years ago," Ruth said. "She has a big heart, but ...." She didn't continue.

"She told me she's staying on," Cass said. She only knew Trisha from their hushed conversation in the doctor's office, while Trisha's husband was inside with the doctor. It had been hard for Cass to get a read on Trisha, who had quizzed Cass on her work as office manager for Dr. Nightingale and told Cass about this great job she, Trisha, was giving up on account of a string of misfortunes—a sick husband, a dying son, a general conspiracy by fate to overwhelm her with responsibilities. Trisha spoke fast, hardly pausing for breath, and Cass had lost track of a bewildering cast of characters in her tale. Besides Trisha's star-crossed family there was the nefarious family of her employer, a saintly old military man, and countless caregivers some of whom were undyingly loyal to Trisha and others who had it in for her, to the point where she was nearing a nervous breakdown. In the end Trisha had seemed to be handing over her job to Cass on the basis of a half-hour conversation in which Trisha had done most of the talking. Cass had necessarily been circumspect. Was she getting a job or a quagmire?

"Yes, to work as caregiver," Ruth said. "Nothing more," she added sharply. Trisha had warned Cass to be wary of the daughter. "Trisha doesn't want to manage the staff any more. There's been *way* too much drama."

"I'll put an end to that," Cass said. She straightened her shoulders and attacked her french fries. And so the deal was struck, pending the father's approval.

The next day she met her soon-to-be employer, a sharp-eyed man with an aquiline nose and a high domed head. "You can call me Major. All the girls do, although I left the military in '49. The army drummed me out, after the geisha girl affair." Wink, wink.

"He's joking," Ruth said, rolling her eyes. "He served in Japan after the war."

"Repaying my debt to fair Hahvard. That's where I spent my war: reveille at six, daily white-glove room inspections, drilling in Harvard Yard, studying all night with a blanket over your window after taps. No college pranks. Oh no! The least bit of jiggery-pokery and you'd be out on your ear and off to the front lines. We learned discipline."

"ROTC," Ruth elaborated. "After he left the army he worked for the government."

"US Department of Radiological Health, making the world safe from radiation," the Major said. Ruth smiled. Father and daughter were quite an act. But under the banter Cass sensed they shared pride in the old man's life.

"Most of his career was in Washington. That's where he met my mother."

"A shy Georgetown debutante," the Major said. "I was smitten!" Another word Cass had never heard anyone use in conversation. This family spoke in lines out of old books. "As soon as we were married she hauled me out to Virginia horse country."

"Where my brother and I grew up," Ruth added.

"She died last year, the love of my life. I'm a lonely man, desperate for female companionship." Major deepened his voice and let it tremble.

"But Dad, you're surrounded by females all day long." Ruth pulled out a tissue to staunch the flow of tears down his cheeks. "He's prone to weeping fits. We're trying to get his Zoloft prescription right."

"It isn't the same," he said, gazing above his daughter's head to stare piteously at Cass. Her heart quivered. He was a romantic. Her life was bare of romance these days, now that her kids had grown up and moved out and she realized there was nothing left between her and Jimmy. The precarious state of her marriage was all the more incentive to land a steady job, something more reliable than Dr. Nightingale's office, where she worried constantly about malpractice suits.

She gave Dr. Nightingale her notice.

Cass's job, as outlined by Ruth, was to schedule and oversee the care staff, order supplies, and run all the many errands required by the operation of a one-person nursing home, as the Major liked to call it. Trisha told her that when *she* was care manager the job took her eighty hours a week. Cass wondered how. There just wasn't that much work to do. She organized the house, which had been a disaster when she arrived, with medical supplies, wipes and pads and diapers, latex gloves and paper products, cleaning supplies and the girls' personal stuff scattered randomly in every room. She set up her computer on the dining room table and got her son-in-law to install Wi-Fi, so that she could order online. For all this she had Ruth's approval, by phone from New York City.

Hume Thorndike took off every Friday from his veterinary practice in Powhatan County and came to look over the books and receipts she kept and to write checks. At first Cass was nervous about this, even with all her experience as an office manager. She went to great lengths to explain every purchase.

"Your dad insisted on this new electric wheelchair. But I found a great bargain on E-bay." She showed him the website, the retail price, the discount.

"It's fine, Cass. Whatever you say." Hume was a gentle soul, the opposite of his sister. When he arrived the caregivers gathered around like a swarm of angry bees, airing their problems and complaints. He couldn't be riled. "It's fine. Let Cass take care of it," he would tell them, spreading his mellow. They would take him aside to ask for a loan, for a car payment, a kid in trouble, a sick parent, promising to pay it back out of their next paycheck and he would say, "Fine. How much do you need?"

Trisha was always around, checking up on her. Cass felt her presence like a grenade waiting to go off. She would take Hume outside and engage him in private conversation. Cass wondered what was going on.

After the second Friday, she asked Tammy and Andrea, the weekend team. They had settled Major in for the night when Cass found them in the dining room, just as she was preparing to go home. "Can y'all tell me what Trisha's talking to Hume about?" she asked. Contrary to how she'd been brought up, she'd found direct confrontation was the best solution to staffing issues.

"I don't know as I can," Andrea said. She and Trisha were close, Cass knew. Andrea, perennially unlucky in love, was dating Trisha's nephew, a dubious guy much younger than Andrea but willing to overlook her delinquent daughter and half-Black grandbaby.

"Tammy?"

"Trisha thinks you're playing favorites, hiring your relatives and taking hours away from girls who've been here the longest," Tammy said, matter-of-fact.

"Playing favorites! Last week Kristy May called in sick last minute and I happened to know my niece was available to cover for her. I told Hume that."

"Then you hired her on."

"Only to cover in emergencies, not to put on the regular schedule. Laurel's a registered nurse, and I have to worry about Major's care. Some of you girls are working sixty hours a week." She didn't mention the two of them in front of her, who would be working forty-eight without a break. "People get sick. People have emergencies."

"I'm just telling you what Trisha said."

"Trisha should mind her own business." Cass left, feeling unsettled. Driving home, she called Ruth. She didn't want Ruth hearing from Trisha first.

"Don't worry about Trisha," Ruth told her. "Be nice, but firm. Tell her you're care manager now."

"I want to hire my former student at Sweetwater Community, Dellisha." Cass still taught a course in medical ethics at the local college. "She has her certification. She and my niece Laurel won't have regular hours, just fill in as needed."

There was silence on the line. Cass wondered if she'd lost the connection. "Some of these girls never finished school, never worked as caregivers before they came to Major's. I'm worried about their professionalism," Cass prompted.

"OK," Ruth said. "I'm not crazy about the idea of hiring relatives but I'll trust your judgment. I suppose everyone in Sinkhole County is related one way or another."

Then, two weeks later, came the drama of the Box Room.

Saturday morning Ruth's phone rang, the dreaded sound of West Virginia calling. "Ruth, you know I never lie," Trisha's voice.

"What is it?" she asked. How is it that the guilty feel compelled to first proclaim their innocence?

"Cass. I don't know what she's up to. She and her husband have been out in the Box Room all morning. I think they're going through your family's precious heirlooms."

Precious heirlooms? Ruth didn't know what her parents had stashed in the shed out back. She'd been out there and seen the shelves lined with broken lamps, outdated stereo equipment, mildewed camping gear, and dozens of cardboard cartons, dusty, unopened for decades, labeled in her mother's hand—letters from World War I, old photos, great-grandmother's dresses, canceled checks. She didn't think there were any treasures there, unless the antique Buttercup silverware her mother had obsessed over was hidden among the boxes but she didn't think it was. "What do you want me to do about it?"

It was perfectly obvious what Trisha wanted: Cass was Trisha's latest enemy. Hume had told Ruth it was coming. How many caregivers had she been forced to fire on trumped up charges because of Trisha's jealousy?! The last thing she'd done before she left West Virginia after her mother's funeral was to fire Faith, the woman who'd held Beatrice in her arms and nursed her gently to her end. Now Trisha was after Cass, despite having brought her on board herself. It hadn't taken Trisha long to have regrets. Cass had been working at the Thorndikes' barely a month. Long enough for Trisha to feel threatened by her, Ruth supposed. "If you don't believe me," Trisha said, "talk to Loretta and Tammy. They saw her."

"OK, Trisha. I'll get to the bottom of this."

Later that day she called Cass, who said, "What would I be doing in the Box Room?"

She talked to Tammy. "Trisha told me what to tell you, but I ain't lyin' on anyone for Trisha."

She talked to Loretta who said, "If you fire Trisha, don't let her come round and sweet-talk Major and start in on him with her tears. She turned him against you once, she can do it again. Be Ruthless."

"You're a wiseass, Loretta." Only Loretta had the balls to use her nickname to her face. "I love that about you."

Eight months earlier, not long after Beatrice died, rumors had been flying around Amity that the Thorndike property was up for sale. Bo Hardwick had told Ruth about them when she called him to discuss the construction of the downstairs bathroom. "It's only natural. He's alone; he's old. There are going to be rumors," Ruth had said. "Just tell everyone he's not going anywhere."

Next, Trisha told her he was trying to track down old girl-friends from the '40s, to call them up and ask them to visit. He invited a local Amity widow to lunch, someone Ruth had never heard of but had apparently been friends of her parents in their younger, more social days. Trisha described the scene: on a mild winter day the widow's daughter dropped her off at Thorndikes' and the caregivers helped her hobble to the house on her walker. They had set the dining room table and wheeled the Major in, and he and Iris Smithson had barely started in on the chicken salads the caregivers had served on the best china when the Major said, "You see what a great setup I have here. You should move in with me. I have everything you could possibly need."

She had brushed him off politely at first. "Thank you Roger, but I'm quite happy where I am. My daughter and son-in-law are next door and take good care of me."

"But how long has it been since you had sexual intercourse? You don't want to know how long it's been for me! Beatrice lost interest years ago." Trisha told Ruth that when she overheard this she almost dropped the cherry pie she was taking out of the freezer to prepare for their dessert.

"Really, Roger, let's change the subject," the widow had choked.

"Of course, we could just be friends until we get to know each other better. There's plenty of space here. You could have a room of your own." The lunch had gone awkwardly after this, with Iris Smithson struggling to steer the conversation away from domestic arrangements toward reminiscences of earlier, happier times. As soon as they were done eating she'd called her daughter to come pick her up, claiming exhaustion. Trisha told Ruth the story over the phone, saying, "I don't like telling you this, but you need to know."

Ruth was appalled. Even before her mother had died, Roger's libido had been a problem. He'd made inappropriate suggestions to the younger caregivers. Ruth's visits had been a series of crisis interventions. "It sounds like he's lost any sense of socially acceptable behavior."

"When Dinah—lives up the road, used to work for Major before she was fired—heard about the lunch, she came down to show Major pictures of her mother, who lives in a nursing home way up in the northern part of the state. She wants to move her mother closer to home, but she can't afford it."

"How did she hear about the lunch?" Ruth asked.

"Probably one of the girls told her. You can't stop them from talking." The one who talked the most, Ruth thought, was Trisha.

Her days were spent spreading gossip around Amity. Ruth, on her visits, had seen Trisha standing on the sidewalk in front of the bank or the pharmacy or post office, engaged in lengthy conversations with people she ran into. She seemed to know everyone.

"Major turned Dinah's mother down," Trisha said. "But I'm worried sooner or later some woman will come along and take advantage of him. Someone's going to marry him and clean him out."

Ruth was worried as well, not least of all about Trisha. Although Trisha was married, she told everyone her husband might die at any minute. Ruth didn't trust her. Roger had Trisha going through his bank and Morgan Stanley statements, against Ruth's warnings. She knew that her father's savings after a lifetime of pinching pennies and careful investing would seem like vast wealth to any of the locals. She called his lawyer, who suggested she talk to her father about removing himself as a trustee from his own trust. The lawyer had set up the trust containing all Roger's money and property, and explained it to Ruth. "Tell your father it's for his own good, to protect himself from scammers. He knows he can't rely on his thinking faculties any more. He's told me." The lawyer understood the situation; he liked her father, and wanted to help the family through tricky times.

Ruth brought it up in a delicate phone conversation with Roger. She told him it was to prevent people from trying to get at his land. At first he seemed receptive to the idea. "We'll do the paperwork when you come down to visit," he'd told her.

Her relief was short-lived. Next thing she knew, he'd changed his mind. Then Hume called her. Roger wanted to remove her power of attorney. Someone had convinced him that she wanted to put him into a nursing home.

"Who?" Ruth asked Hume over the phone.

"I asked him that. He says he can't remember. He's furious at you. I can't convince him it's nonsense. He's really confused, Ruth. His dementia is getting much worse."

"It has to be Trisha. She has the most influence over him."

The lawyer received an email, purportedly from Roger, instructing him to cut Ruth out of his will. "He's never used a computer. He has no Internet. He couldn't have sent you an email," Ruth said. "Can we get a doctor to declare him incompetent?"

"The bar for competence is set low here in West Virginia," the lawyer told her, with a hint of irony. "If he knows his name and who you are, that's all it takes. Who sent the email?"

"I think I know." She called Hume, always her go-to. "This is crazy. What are we going to do?"

"You'd better come down," Hume said.

She flew into Charleston, rented a car, and drove to Amity, arriving late at night. Next morning she went into her father's room.

"Ruth! How good to see you." He looked at her tenderly, as if he hadn't just tried to disinherit her.

"I phoned. I told you I was coming."

"Oh. I must have forgotten. You know, my memory's awful these days."

"Daddy," she said, drowning in a toxic brew of pity and hurt and rage. "All I want is to keep you safe here in your own home. Do you believe me?"

"Of course. Of course I do. You're my daughter. How could it be otherwise?" As if he really didn't know. As if he had forgotten he'd ever been mad at her, much less why.

Pity rose to the surface. She sighed. "That's good."

Later, she asked Trisha for a word in private. They sat in Trisha's car with the engine running and the heat on. "You sent that email, didn't you?" Ruth said.

Trisha burst into tears. "How could you think that? I love your family. I would never do such a thing. I'm an honest person." She dug a Kleenex out of her pocket and wept loudly into it. Ruth watched her without speaking. "It must have been someone else, trying to get me in trouble. You have to believe me, Ruth. I need this job. I have nothing else."

Ruth didn't believe her. It had to have been Trisha. What Trisha had hoped to accomplish was unclear, but fit with her pattern of bizarre behavior. However, care managers were hard to come by in Amity, West Virginia. Roger was attached to Trisha and would balk at firing her. Given her own fragile reconciliation with her father, Ruth was loath to rock the boat. She felt she had no choice. "OK Trisha. Dry your eyes. Let's go back inside."

Keeping the snake firmly planted in her yard.

Eight months later had come the drama of the Box Room. After spending the entire weekend on the phone investigating Trisha's allegations as promised, Ruth called her back. "I can't confirm your story. No one backs you up." She fired Trisha, and banned her from the Thorndike house. It felt like an act of war. It felt great.

5

What Lies Beneath the Surface

FRIDAY

"Hume!" He heard his name over the muzak assaulting him in the automotive aisle of Walmart, where he was studying the shelves for an oil filter for the Miata. He was looking for K&N, but all they had was Fram. He turned to see who was calling—bellowing—his name and breathed, "Oh no."

Trisha's imposing figure moved swiftly down the wide aisle toward him, skirting other equally portly shoppers in her determination to reach him. How long since she'd been fired? Almost a year, and he hadn't seen her since.

"Have you talked to your father?" She rocked from side to side, first one foot and then the other, blocking his escape route.

"I talk to him every day." Usually. But this week when he'd called on Monday the caregivers had told him Roger wasn't speaking. A TIA or something.

"Something funny is going on in that house. Cass won't let me see him. I never even got a chance to say goodbye." Trisha had a remarkable ability to hold onto a grudge. Had she found other work? Hume couldn't remember if he'd heard.

"He's gone downhill in the last few months. His mind is wandering." Hume wondered if he could fake an emergency phone call to get him out of there. But Trisha knew that Friday was his day to leave the animal clinic in the hands of his technician and go to Amity.

"Four years I worked for your father! I want to explain to him why I had to leave. I want to tell him some jokes and sing 'You Are My Sunshine.' His favorite, you know." She wrung her hands as she rocked. Tears welled in her light eyes.

"I'll see what I can do. We don't want to upset him."

"It's Cass who upsets him! What's she hiding? People are talking all around town—the bank, the pharmacy, the Family Dollar. There are things about Cass you and your sister don't know."

"Thanks, Trisha. I'll look into it. I'm on my way there now." Trisha's endless conspiracy theories. He was used to them. He pulled out his phone and looked at it. "I've got to run." He darted around her, the oil filter forgotten.

He'd driven with the top down today, taking advantage of the good weather and the fact that he was alone. Maryanne was the best thing that had ever happened to him, but like most women she didn't like the wind to muss her hair. Hume let it blow his ponytail. The pasta sauce he'd made for his father's lunch was in the Miata's tiny trunk. All was well with the world, as well as could be expected, given where he was going.

Cass came out to meet him when he parked next to the Thorndike house. "That sure is a pretty car," she said as she did every time he drove it. Sunflower yellow made the car a real attention-grabber. Hume was used to the attention.

"How's my father?" he asked, retrieving the container of sauce from the back.

"That's what I wanted to tell you. His speech still hasn't come back. And he's a little … off."

"Off?"

"He seems like he understands you. But sometimes he reacts strange. Like he doesn't know who you are." She trotted at his side toward the kitchen door. He felt the nervous energy coming off her.

"Has Dr. Nightingale seen him?"

"No, but the nurse said it was probably just a small stroke. Otherwise, he's fine."

"Hmm. It doesn't sound so small to me."

In the kitchen he dumped the crab marinara into a saucepan and put on water to boil. Cass opened the binder of timesheets. "We finally heard from Andrea. She wants her job back."

"I didn't know she'd lost her job." Hume left the caregiving management to Cass and Ruth.

"Ruth fired her last weekend. She didn't show up for work, didn't call, didn't answer her phone. We had to get Loretta to sub for her. It was the second time. She disappeared on us last spring. You remember."

Hume didn't remember.

"She claimed she'd had a nervous breakdown and her sister had her committed to a psych ward, then cleaned out her bank account. But I think that was a lie. She was with that boyfriend in Kentucky."

Hume's head was spinning. "Do you think she's lying now?"

"No. The boyfriend has dumped her. She really needs the job."

"It's up to you, Cass. You and Ruth," Hume said, and started signing the checks Cass put in front of him. He made a show of going over the books, but as long as the expenses stayed below his personal redline, he didn't bother with the details.

Loretta appeared in the doorway. "He's ready for you, Hume."

Odd that Loretta was here. She usually showed up later, as he was leaving. But the caregiver schedules were always changing, and he didn't keep track. Sensitive to the barely perceptible signals given off by mute creatures, Hume felt the nervous energy thrumming as both women followed him into the front room. The Major was sitting up in bed, staring at the blank TV screen. Apparently it had been moved in from the parlor. "Hello, Dad. What are you watching?"

The old man's gaze darted around the room, first at Hume, at the television screen, then at the caregivers waiting with breath seemingly bated, perhaps anticipating that the sight of his son would jar Roger's ability to speak.

Loretta piped up. "We been going through his concert DVDs. This morning it was Pierre Boulez conducting Gustav Mahler." Pronouncing the names as the Major had taught her.

The old man fixed his attention on Loretta and smiled.

"Oh yeah. You liked that one, didn't you Major?"

The old man snorted and looked at Hume again. Hume studied his father's face in the light streaming in through the window. A peculiar sensation prickled the hairs on the back of Hume's neck. Something was missing. Some light of recognition. Either the stroke had robbed Roger of his memory of his son, or something weirder had happened. Never had his father's face looked so unlike itself. The familiar hollow cheeks had an almost ruddy glow, as if they'd been exposed to quantities of outdoor air sometime in the last decade. The brow was high, sweeping as usual to the bare hilltop of his scalp. But the eyes lacked their usual dying spark of a great intelligence. The eyes peered at him suspiciously. This was nothing new. Hume was used to his father's paranoia. The Major hated losing control and feared that his son and daughter were trying to take over his life. Sometimes Roger was frightened and bewildered. But never at a loss for words. He could still recite Latin and discuss Samuel Barber's dark despair in "Dover Beach" for baritone and string quartet, quoting his favorite verse, the last:

> *Ah, love, let us be true*
> *To one another! for the world, which seems*
> *To lie before us like a land of dreams,*
> *So various, so beautiful, so new,*
> *Hath really neither joy, nor love, nor light,*
> *Nor certitude, nor peace, nor help for pain;*
> *And we are here as on a darkling plain*
> *Swept with confused alarms of struggle and flight,*
> *Where ignorant armies clash by night.*

"You're not talking, they tell me." Hume patted the old man's arm. He took his father's hand and almost dropped it. Freshly manicured, scrubbed clean, wrinkled and spotted with age, and callused. Callused! Could this be his father's hand? "Wow! Looks like you've been out digging ditches." Beside him, Hume sensed Loretta stiffen slightly.

The old man shook his head.

When had he last held his father's hand? Normally they were engaged in conversation, arguing over the evils of capitalism and right-wing Republicans, subjects dear to Hume. Was it the silence that made him notice the hands in a new way? What else could it be? Nothing else made sense. Hume was a scientist; evidence needed to add up to something reasonable.

Cass spoke up. "Hume, you want me and Loretta to bring in the lunch?"

"Sure. I'll read him the headlines from the *Wall Street Journal* while you get it ready." His usual Friday routine with his father.

"Just don't get him riled up when he can't answer you back," Loretta said, and the two women left.

Hume picked up the paper from the bedside table where the girls had left it and began reading, not knowing what else to do, feeling the need to fill the silence, to reach into that blank gaze and penetrate the brain he thought he knew. He turned the paper at intervals to show the old man, who looked at it without apparent interest. It was unnerving. If the mind was gone, was this shell still his father? Hume felt a tightening in his chest.

Loretta and Cass returned with the plates of spaghetti and a bottle of beer for Hume. They bustled about, setting places on the Major's tray table, snapping a bib on the old man and fluffing his pillow. "Now Major, you show Hume how good you're eating," Loretta said in a loud and cheery voice. She turned to Hume. "Since his episode he's been feeding himself. It's a wonder!"

Hume ate his lunch without appetite, watching the old man shovel in the food with unusual enthusiasm. "So one part of the brain shuts down and another opens up. Is that what you're saying?"

"I ain't a doctor," Loretta said. "I just know what I see."

Hume didn't know what he saw. So many times his father had had a crisis and the caregivers would think he was about to die, and Hume would be hit with worry and sadness. Bottomless sadness. But Hume was used to crises, in his career as well as with his father. The caregivers were much like pet-owners, going off at the least little thing—a minor infection, a missed bowel movement. Today there was something different in their fretting, a forced and anxious quality. They were watching him observe his apparently healthy, although speechless, father eating with gusto. He sensed them wanting him to be heartened. Instead, he couldn't help the feeling that someone or something else had taken over his father's body. But that was impossible. That was science fiction. What was he thinking?

After lunch Hume carried the plates into the kitchen to wash up while the girls cleaned up the old man. He let the hot water run over his hands, wanting it to soothe him. He dried and put away the dishes, wanting to bring order to his thoughts. He went back in for one more look at his father. Loretta was sitting by the bed while Cass took the old man's blood pressure. Hume looked down at him and tried to believe that this was indeed his father who would, in a few days time, return to normal and call him up to complain about his stereo or his physical therapist or some new affliction. "OK, Dad. I have to go. See you next Friday."

"It's time for his nap. You have a safe trip home, Hume," Loretta said.

Outside he walked to the Miata, stowed the leftovers in the trunk, put his hand on the driver's door, and stopped. He felt rattled. His lunch was sitting in an undigested lump in his stomach. He needed to walk off its acid burn. He went through the orchard to the stables, empty and abandoned now that his mother was gone, and circled around to where he couldn't be seen from the house. He didn't want the caregivers watching him any more. He climbed through the fields toward his favorite spot on the farm, the High Place, now the site of his mother's grave. Scrambling up the steep hill depressed him. The grass was high and full of weeds. The farm had grown raggedy since his mother was no longer around; her ceaseless maintenance had kept the pastures park-like. Now there were thistles and burdock everywhere. He noted a dead limb on the big oak up at the High Place. He should get Beaver Hardwick to take it down he supposed, lest it fall and knock over the stone marker Ruth had insisted on. He came over the brow of the hill and stopped in astonishment.

Inside the fence that kept the cattle out was his mother's grave, mown by Beaver and Nate. Beside it there was freshly turned earth. The prickle on the back of his neck reverberated throughout his body. The strangeness of the day exploded in all his nerve endings. He opened the gate and approached the grave with heart pounding. He peered down the farm road through the woods opposite the grave. He saw no one. The Thorndike house below was hidden by the woods and the neighboring farmhouse was tiny in the distance. He was alone with just woods and fields, hills and mountains.

He examined the scene, perplexed. The grass was trimmed around his mother's headstone. What looked exactly like a fresh grave lay alongside it. What, or who, was buried there—without his knowledge or permission—beside his mother? Could it be a stranger? Who would drive right past his father's house on the farm road easily visible to any of the caregivers to bury a stranger on private property? Why and when? The last question he could answer. The grave hadn't been here when he and Ruth were up here a month ago. It couldn't have been here through the recent rains. It had to be the last couple weeks. Or even the last few days. He circled around the grave looking for clues. There were faint tire tracks in the meadow grass leading to the farm road.

Could the caregivers be behind this? That could explain the tension in the house today. Could it be a neighboring farmer, or one of his parents' friends from town, in this new grave? But they had been here when Beatrice was buried. The Episcopal priest had read the burial service right here. All the world knew that this was supposed to be his father's place. Could it be … No, it was too bizarre, unthinkable. So how could he even think it? He flashed on that strange sensation he'd had in the house watching the old man slurp spaghetti.

Could it be … his father? Was his father in this grave? His grave?

Was the old man in the house not his father?

The evidence that his father might be dead took Hume's breath away. He reeled above the fresh grave, overwhelmed by sudden grief, weighed down by guilt that he hadn't rushed down to Amity earlier in the week when the stroke had been reported. He could have, should have prevented this.

But what was this? What had happened? Was there a stroke? Always in the past whenever there was a crisis he'd been called. Why didn't they call this time? If his father was dead, how did he die? His thoughts swirled, with possibilities that seemed impossible flicking through his mind. An accident. An accidental overdose. His father was on so many medications. A deliberate overdose. There was an abundance of deadly narcotics in his father's house.

Hume felt sick. It was crazy! Who would do such a thing? He knew all the caregivers and trusted them. Who was capable of this? Digging this grave, burying his father, these were not easy tasks. Not something skinny little Loretta or big soft Cass was equipped to do. Conspiracy? But why? What would anyone have to gain by removing Roger Thorndike and replacing him with a double?

Because surely, the old man in the house was not his father. The callused hands, the feeling that Hume had had that his father couldn't be inside that silent shell, were the evidence that was so difficult to believe. The double, who was he? Where had the conspirators found Roger's identical twin? The resemblance was uncanny.

He took out his phone to call the police. There was a text from Maryanne. "Back from Charleston. Greg wants us to come over later. When will you be home?"

He hesitated. What would he tell the police? *My father has died under suspicious circumstances. I think his caregivers are involved.* Which caregivers? He thought about their devotion to his father. They were poor. He knew about their run-ins with the law and social service agencies over the years. Would the police be able to distinguish the innocent from the guilty? Should he confront them first? He could go back down to Loretta and Cass right now and demand an explanation.

His head ached. Suddenly he was exhausted. He tapped in Maryanne's number, desperate to hear her voice. No answer. He didn't leave a message, not knowing what to tell her. He used his phone to take some photos of the fresh grave from different angles and distances, feeling like an actor out of CSI. He took a deep breath, blinked rapidly at a sudden seep of wetness in his eyes, and headed down the farm road toward the house, wracked with ambivalence, walking fast. He didn't care if the caregivers saw him. He didn't go into the house, didn't want to talk to them. He needed to move, needed to talk to Maryanne. He texted her, "Leaving Amity now," got into his little car, and sped away.

6

What Can Blood Tell?

Through the kitchen window Loretta watched Hume come down the farm road from the High Place and go straight to his car without stopping into the house again. *He knows* she thought.

A chill rippled through her from scalp to toes. They'd be busted. The girls would blame it all on her. Loretta's idea, Loretta's old man she brought down the mountain from Mud Lick Hollow to impersonate Major. Is that a crime? Oh dear Jesus, you better believe it is. That hanging judge would lock her up same as he had her father-in-law. He had it in for the Hardwicks, him in his stately old house that had been in the Arbuckle family for five or ten generations. Judge Arbuckle considered the Hardwicks to be redneck trash, she was sure, when he thought about them at all. Loretta felt sick to her stomach. How long would it take Hume to report her to the cops?

Damn the world that made her fight so hard to hold onto this job. Damn Beaver and that twat in his office.

She hadn't believed the rumors flying around about him last year. Beaver wasn't so big a catch that he could afford to be fooling around. Then came the morning he forgot his lunch box, so she picked it up on her way out the door. After she dropped the kids off at school she headed down the highway to Hard Rock Construction. The office was nothing more than a doublewide in the middle of a gravel pit, Beaver's truck and a red Camry the only vehicles in the lot. Loretta parked and strode to the door, which rang a bell as she shoved through it, in a hurry to get to her main project of the day—to turn over the vegetable garden while she had use of the neighbor's rototiller—before she had to go to work.

The office was empty.

"Doris!" Loretta shouted. "My husband here?"

Not waiting for an answer she pushed through to the back room, where she found Beaver and the secretary of Hard Rock Construction in flagrante on an old couch with springs that squeaked in time to Beaver's thrusting through the fleshy thighs.

"Omigod!" Doris shrieked.

"I ain't your God," Loretta snapped, hardly believing her eyes.

Beaver rolled off and struggled to sit, pushing aside the naked legs of the half-dressed secretary. "Loretta. Shit!" His member withered.

"I ain't shit either," Loretta said, enraged, advancing on her husband with murder in her eyes.

Beaver raised his hands to fend her off. Loretta raised the metal lunch box as if to smash it into his face. "Don't do it, baby!" Beaver cried. "It's the first time. Never again, I swear."

Loretta released the latch, raining down a torrent of baloney, bread, ketchup, mayo, relish, and sliced onion onto Beaver's head. She grabbed the quart of Mountain Dew, unscrewed the cap, and emptied it in a shower over both Beaver and Doris. She dropped the bucket on the floor, turned around, and left. "You forgot your lunch," she said on the way out.

She drove home, shut herself in the bathroom, and cried for an hour, loud screaming, wailing cries torn from her belly like she imagined a wild elephant would cry over the death of its mate. She couldn't stop it. Tears and snot poured down her face. She gripped the edge of the sink. The crying subsided into gulping sobs. She looked in the mirror at her bloated red eyes. She washed her face in cold water. Then the crying erupted again, built into anguished keening, juices spouting again from eyes and nose. It went on and on, the cycle repeating, crying and washing and crying and washing, until she was done. Then she went outside and rototilled the garden, finishing just in time for work.

By the time she got home that night a contrite Beaver was anxiously waiting for her. She played the role of wronged woman and she was tough, determined to punish him, no matter the cost. She insisted Beaver quit his job. He'd just have to look for another; meanwhile she'd work more hours, more jobs, whatever it took. So it turned out her own actions had put more pressure on her and made her desperate enough to think this crazy scheme could work.

Cass came into the kitchen. "That went pretty well, I thought," she said.

"Oh yeah." No point in telling Cass that she knew Hume knew. Loretta would bide her time, wait for Hume to make a move, prepare as best she could. A honk came from outside.

"Now what?" Cass asked.

"Looks like we got more visitors," Loretta said. "Dr. Nightingale's car."

"She couldn't call first?"

It was typical of the doctor—who had too many patients spread out all over two counties and still made house calls, as though it was a hundred years ago—to show up unannounced.

"I'll go wake up Major," Loretta said. Deeper and deeper she was sinking into guilt. Wider and wider things were spinning out of control. She felt the approach of the judge. It wasn't fair. All she did was work and fight and lose. When had it started? Before Beaver's affair, when she was doing what she could to raise three troublesome kids? Everybody knows what that's like! There was Jewel running around with her bad boyfriend everybody said was a meth head. Loretta was just praying he'd get arrested and locked up before he got Jewel in trouble, addicted or something. Jewel swore it wasn't true, but Loretta remembered lying to her own mother about beer and pot when she was in high school. Those were simpler times.

Then there was Tiffany, her middle child—sweet Tiffany who hadn't learned to read until fifth grade. Loretta had spent hours in teacher's conferences being told that Tiffany was getting bullied, that Tiffany had special needs, that Loretta had to coach her daughter every day and work miracles the teacher couldn't supply. Not a book person herself, Loretta had thought *Why me*? But finally the miracle was worked and Tiffany learned to read, only to sprout boobs and a full womanly figure before any other girl in elementary school, so that the taunts never stopped, just changed subject. "You are beautiful inside and out," Loretta had told her.

Junior, all boy, hadn't caused her problems. Yet. He would save that for some girl, no doubt. Like the men always did. All the men except her Major. She put her hand gently on his shoulder. His eyes flew open.

"Doctor's here to see you." She knelt down to put her face close to his. "Don't you worry about a thing. Loretta's going to take care of you."

He smiled. Loretta straightened up and stepped away when Dr. Nightingale came in with Cass. With her flowing black hair and kohl-rimmed eyes, the doc looked like an aging hippie or gypsy fortuneteller, but at least she was wearing a pink lab coat. "Major Thorndike!" she greeted him, in a voice as large as her persona. "How are you, sweetie?" She bent over to hug him.

Loretta stiffened with alarm, but kept a reassuring gaze fixed on him, and he submitted to the embrace, still smiling at her.

"Major, can you say *Hello*?" the doctor asked.

The Major looked at her with a puzzled expression and remained silent, not even growling or speaking his usual unintelligible language.

She tried again. "Do you remember me, honey? You just saw me two weeks ago."

"Yum."

"I can't tell if that's a yes or a no." She took his hand in hers. Loretta held her breath, remembering Hume's reaction to the gnarled hand. Dr. Nightingale didn't seem to notice. "Can you squeeze my hand?" she asked, peering into his eyes. He glanced again at Loretta.

"No squeeze," the doctor said. "Global aphasia without hemiparesis. That's pretty unusual."

"He squeezed for Angeline on Monday," Cass said. "He may just be tired. He's had a long day."

"We should really get you in for a CAT scan, Major," Dr. Nightingale said.

He shook his head, as he had when Angeline had suggested the hospital.

"There! He understood that," Cass said. "Last time he came home from Sweetwater Valley," Cass said, "he had such a bad MRSA infection I thought we were going to lose him."

"I remember," Dr. Nightingale said. She sat down next to the old man and opened her bag. "We'll do some blood tests first." She pulled out her tourniquet, needle, and several vials.

Blood test? Loretta thought. They hadn't planned on that. Dr. Nightingale was more likely to apply a laying on of hands than actual science. What made her decide today to act like a doctor?

7

A Moral Dilemma

MORE FRIDAY

Hume pushed the Miata on the two-lane—a bolt of yellow light, a lemon zinger—around blind curves, up and down steep hills, down-shifting, alternating rapidly between brake and accelerator, passing slow pickups, fast muscle cars, a logging truck, a flatbed loaded with giant round hay bales, putting the little car through its paces. Even so he couldn't outrun the emotional tangle he'd left behind in Amity.

The fresh grave. The false Major. His grief mingled alarmingly with relief. His father was so much better off dead. The last four years had been a slow, grim descent into misery. Roger's suffering, anger, delusion, and his loss after loss after loss. One night, before Beatrice died, when Roger was still somewhat able to walk, still sleeping in his own room upstairs, he'd fallen in the bathroom and lain on the floor for hours, weeping, unable to get up, unable to wake his wife with his cries, cold and helpless and humiliated by his weakness. Hume would hear about it over the phone. He could bear the sadness in small weekly doses, by keeping to the routines of his visits, paying the bills, fixing the stereo, reading the mail, and then leaving it behind. But he couldn't escape the constant worry, since his mother had died, that his father would do something crazy, that he'd be taken advantage of, hurt and abandoned. When he left Amity each week he carried the weight of that worry.

Suddenly, the weight had lifted. The suffering was over. Roger was in the ground next to Beatrice, safely planted out of harm's way. Hume almost felt glad. But gladness turned to anger. There was that imposter in his father's house, and a conspiracy. Who was behind it, and why? The caregivers. What did they hope to gain? Roger's bank account and assets were out of their reach. The imposter couldn't make it past Hume's power of attorney. Roger hadn't been able to sign a check in years. Even if the girls managed to wheel the old man into the bank in Amity, they'd get nothing for their efforts but a phone call to Hume from Debby, the bank manager. What if this plot had been long in the planning; what if they had found the replacement and then done away with (Hume couldn't bring himself to use a more brutal word even in his thoughts) his father. That wouldn't have been hard to do. There were lethal drugs aplenty in the house, or a simple pillow over the face, held down by several of the heftier caregivers .... Hume shuddered. Even if, in some corner of his heart, Hume felt his father was better off dead, he didn't want that to have been his fate.

By whatever machinations they'd arrived at this preposterous charade, how had they thought they could pull it off? Did they imagine he wouldn't know his own father? And if the switch had gone undetected, then what? Mystified, Hume arrived at the village of Redbud and turned off the two-lane onto a narrower road, rising across open fields, plunging through deep woods, twisting toward home.

He realized he'd forgotten to stop at Walmart to pick up the oil filter. It could wait. Maryanne saw him coming down the drive and was out of the house before he had a chance to pull the Miata into the garage. "Greg's waiting on us," she said, opening the passenger door and climbing in. "Let's just go. Do you mind, darlin'?"

He didn't mind. One of the things that had attracted him to Maryanne was that she was always ready to get up and go. He turned around and headed back up the drive, winding back toward the village. Maryanne launched into reporting an earlier phone call from her daughter, living in Florida, having problems with her son, Maryanne's grandson. This family of an early unplanned marriage was part of what Hume had willingly inherited when he had joined his life with Maryanne's ten years earlier. They were just getting to Greg's house when she asked how things had gone in Amity.

"Something strange is going on there. I saw my father, but he didn't look right. Then I found ... freshly dug earth, next to my mother's grave. I think my father may be dead."

"What?!"

They were turning into Greg's driveway.

"I think there's someone who looks just like my father in the house. I think somebody switched them." It sounded crazy even as he said it. He parked.

"Why didn't you say something? We have to do something!" Maryanne didn't seem to think he was crazy. She was always ready to believe the incredible.

"I don't know what to do. Maybe I imagined it."

"No. You don't imagine things. What did you see?"

Sitting outside Greg's house, everyone else already inside, he gave her the briefest possible synopsis of what he saw.

"Oh dear God! Who could have done it? Why?"

"That's the problem. I don't know. That's why I didn't call the police."

"You didn't ask Cass, or Loretta?"

The kitchen door opened. Greg himself. "You coming in or spending the night in your car?"

"We're coming in," Maryanne said. Wonderfully decisive.

"Let's not tell them about this." The repercussions of such a revelation could get out of hand in a hurry.

Inside, their Powhatan County friends had already helped themselves to the cauldron of Greg's famous vegetarian curry and were sitting around the capacious kitchen table shooting the shit, as they did regularly on Friday nights in someone's kitchen. Bottles of wine, chipped china plates, and mismatched yard sale silverware were laid out on Greg's ancient red formica countertop. Maryanne grabbed a beer from the fridge and sidled up to the curry. Hume poured himself a generous portion of Jim Beam and sank into a straight wooden chair next to Leigh Kirk. A friend since Hume's early days in the county, Leigh now owned the B&B down by the river. "You coming to the Watershed Association meeting next week, Hume?" she asked the minute he sat down. "It's important. We're organizing the pipeline opposition." Leigh was a native West Virginian involved in every conservation battle raging in the state. There wasn't anyone in Greg's kitchen she hadn't corralled into signing a petition or attending a community meeting. Her latest enemy was fracking.

"I'll try." Hume sighed. He was tired; Leigh's energy wore him out. Greg offered him a plate of curry, but he waved it away. "Thanks, but I had a big lunch. Not hungry right now."

Across the table, Dylan Barnett was eating with enthusiasm and washing his curry down with whiskey. "All your organizing isn't really necessary, you know," he said to Leigh, whom he enjoyed needling. Originally a metal sculptor in New Jersey, Dylan's love of cave exploration had drawn him to West Virginia, where he'd become an expert in demolition, inventing a device he called the Micro-Blaster that could break apart rock with a cartridge of gunpowder half the size of a cigarette. "Economics are killing fracking," he said. "Not enough money in natural gas to build pipelines now."

"Maybe not now! But it won't be long," Leigh retorted. "With the politicians in the pockets of Big Energy, they'll use every kind of sleazy tactic to push pipelines through West Virginia, once the other states outlaw fracking. We're the nation's favorite dumping ground for toxic waste, a sacrifice zone—always have been!"

"Politicians are morally bankrupt," Heather the hippie said. Heather and her husband Aaron—who was out on the front porch smoking a joint (Leigh's rules: no smoking indoors)—lived in a ramshackle place up the road from Hume. They had arrived in the '70s, bought ten acres of clifftop overlooking the Sweetwater River, and clung on since then with few visible means of support. "That's why I haven't voted since 1976."

"Is dropping out of the conversation the moral solution to corruption?" Greg asked. Their host was another East Coast refugee who cobbled together a meager living as a photojournalist.

"Absolutely not! It's immoral not to vote." Maryanne was an activist like Leigh.

Hume felt the tempers around the table rising, the pressure building in his temples, breaking through the whisky-induced haze. He had a mad impulse to change the conversation to the one subject his thoughts couldn't stay away from. Forgetting his earlier resolve he said, "I'll give you a moral dilemma. Suppose you discovered your elderly parent had been switched for a double, what would you do?"

Silence like thunder greeted the proposal. Was it stupefaction or incomprehension? Maryanne looked startled. Hume realized his blunder.

"What do you mean, 'a double'?" Heather asked. "A robot? A life-size inflatable doll?"

Blunder or no, the urge to share his burden in this familiar kitchen pressed him on. "No. A real person, an old guy who looks almost exactly like him. So similar it almost fools you."

"Is this supposed to be a joke?" Leigh asked sharply.

"No, it's not a joke. It's an ethical quandary. What would you do?"

Dylan, the analytical one, asked, "What happened to the elderly parent?" Perhaps treating it as hypothetical situation.

"Suppose you assume, or have reason to believe, that he's dead. You don't know how he died, but he was near death and you expected him to die soon."

"Hume," Leigh said, "Did you go to Amity today? What the fuck?"

Heather looked back and forth from Leigh to Hume. "I'm confused. Are you playing a mind game or did this actually happen?"

Everyone waited. Maryanne said, "Well?"

"I don't want to get ahead of the evidence. Let's say you don't have evidence," Hume said. Maryanne's eyebrows shot up and her mouth opened. *Not yet,* he thought, and sent her a warning glance. "What would you do?"

"Who do you think did the switch?" Dylan asked.

"You don't know. That's the problem. There are a lot of people involved. Any one of them, or more than one, could be suspects."

"Are you kidding?!" Leigh exclaimed. "This really happened and you just left? You didn't get to the bottom of it? That's so like you, Hume! You have to find out who's doing what down there. Geez Louise! You got a whole houseful of crazy women pulling some kind of shit on you."

Heather's husband Aaron had drifted in from the porch. "Get this, Aaron," Dylan greeted him. "Hume's old man in Amity has been switched for an identical twin. Hume has no idea where his dad is, but some geezer is pretending to be him."

"Heavy, man. Did space aliens take him?"

"Don't be ridiculous," Leigh snapped.

"Hey, it's possible," Heather said. "We know a girl who was abducted and has the scars to prove it. The double could be an alien."

"Or maybe that neo-Nazi bunch from over Ragtop Mountain kidnapped him," Dylan suggested, grinning slyly. "You'll be getting a ransom demand soon."

"This is nothing to get funny about," Leigh said. "One of the caregivers has committed a crime, and Hume has to find out who. They all have to be in on it. After all, they bathe him, they brush his teeth, they …" she broke off.

"Wipe his ass," Dylan added.

"Take his vitals, give him meds. They have to know who the imposter is and what happened to Roger. They may have murdered him! And Hume just left them there in his father's house."

"Well, they're not going anywhere tonight," Hume said.

"How long you planning on waiting?"

"Until I find out who's behind it. I don't want to make false accusations."

"I think you need another drink." Dylan shoved the whiskey bottle in Hume's direction. "Have you seen *The Double*? British black comedy, a great doppelganger movie."

The conversation drifted from doppelganger movies to postings on the Internet of people claiming to meet their stranger twins—people who looked just like them but weren't related. Several whiskeys later, Hume said he had to work in the morning and he and Maryanne left.

In the car driving home he said, "I guess I blew it."

"You needed to get it off your chest," Maryanne said.

Or out of the pit of his stomach. "That doesn't resolve the conundrum."

8

More Cats Out of the Bag

L yle woke up enveloped by smooth, sweet-smelling sheets. Confusing. He opened his eyes in a strange room. Early morning light came through a clean window and struck a fancy marble fireplace. Nothing like the dark disorder of his cabin since Annabel died. He blinked several times. At least his eyelids still worked, but his brain formed words with difficulty. Where ... Woman? He felt panic.

He turned his head against the fluffy pillow and took in an array of images he no longer had words to describe. Chairs. Tables. Curtains. Pictures. Where ... pants? Usually left in a pile on the dirty floor, since Annabel died. Where was Woman who reminded him of Annabel?

So difficult waking up these days. Window ... open. Birds ... singing? Starting to remember this room. Yes. Woman came. Brought him to this place. He ran his hands over the top sheet, felt warm ... blanket. He looked at ... hands. Clean. Nails ... trimmed. This place full of women, too many to remember faces, no names. Only one face he remembered, Woman with nice smile. Calm.

Door opening. In comes ... Woman? No, the big one. Woman is little, skinny like Annabel. The big bossy one.

"Good morning, Major. How'd you sleep?"

"Just fine," Lyle said in his thoughts, but he knew the words didn't come out that way. The Boss didn't understand his words.

"Don't you worry. I know you're not used to seeing me this early in the morning. I'm here to introduce you to the weekend staff. Kristy Mae and Dellisha won't be with you today. Here's Laurel, she's my niece, and Andrea. They'll be with you all weekend. Did you know today is Saturday?"

The words came out of the Boss's mouth in perfect order, all strung together like pearls on the Shopping Network Annabel used to watch. Lyle couldn't do that word stringing thing; he'd never been much of a talker, even before .... He marveled at her ability without bothering to process what she was saying. It was too hard, too frustrating. Better just to watch and wait. He watched two more come in. They looked like all the others, young or old, dark or blonde, he couldn't keep track. The Boss put the thing around his arm and started pumping.

"See now, girls, since his stroke last weekend he can't talk. And he's real confused. We don't know how much he remembers. That's why I came in, just to get you started. Don't agitate him. Just give him what he wants and he'll be fine, won't you Major?"

He gave a short reply, which apparently didn't sound like yes from the startled expressions on their faces.

"One-thirty over eighty. Perfect! You mark that down in the book, Laurel; give him his meds and keep records of his output as normal. Let me know if his speech comes back." The Boss took the thing off his arm. "You want to use the potty,

Major?" She cranked up the bed to help him sit up. He didn't need the help but didn't bother to argue since arguing was so difficult and so pointless. He'd argued at first and had them all scurrying around clucking like hens and pushing him this way and that. Now he just tried to do what they wanted. The other two came round the bed and wheeled the chair thing into position and all three made a great to-do about getting him into the chair and wheeling him to the potty, which he remembered now stood next to the marble fireplace and was a big improvement over the outhouse back at his cabin. No, wait … that old outhouse had fallen down years ago and the cabin had … indoor bathroom. Now they were pulling down his pants … not pants, but whatever he'd been sleeping in … and unwrapping him and the Boss was talking again.

"Nice and dry! He doesn't seem to need the urinal at night, but we've been putting on the Depends just in case."

"I guess you'll do whatever you want with me," he said, but they ignored him. One of them startled and tsk-tsked.

"Don't worry about those sounds he makes. He's been eating real good this week, and doing more for himself."

"Imma get started on your chicken salad, Major," the tsker said and turned to leave the room. He followed her with his eyes. She had the largest, most unusually shaped … ass he had ever seen. The sight filled him with strange wonder.

"You love Andrea's chicken salad," the Boss said, settling him on the potty. "We'll leave you to do your business and the girls will get your breakfast ready."

The Boss and the other followed the Ass, leaving him to enjoy the warm stream that had learned to flow from a seated position, although always before in his life he'd pissed standing.

Cass didn't ordinarily go to the Thorndike house on Saturday mornings, but this was no ordinary Saturday. Laurel and Andrea hadn't batted an eye at the sight of the new Major, hadn't suspected a thing. Thank goodness! Cass had been nervous about this morning. They had to keep the circle of those in the know about the switch tight and close. The night crew was still in the dark, since Major had been pretty much sleeping the whole time they were there. It was unfortunate that Dellisha and Kristy Mae had found out. Cass trusted Dellisha, but that Kristy Mae was a presumptuous little thing, just because she'd been with Major so long. She needed to be kept in line. As for the rest of the girls, if word were to get out there was no telling whose heads would roll. Just thinking about it made Cass shiver.

Things had gone well this week—remarkably well!—considering. It was as if the ghastly events of Sunday night had never happened. If she could keep her mind a blank slate beginning with Monday morning's return to normal, she could proceed with a clean conscience, caring for this old man. He clearly needed care, abandoned by his relatives if Loretta was to be believed, as she had to be. Loretta would have to bear any necessary guilt for what she'd done. Cass felt herself straight as a rector as she instructed Laurel and Andrea to continue doing their jobs in the professional manner that Cass had imposed on the once chaotic household. Now that Andrea was back, the weekend crew would work around the clock until Sunday evening, spelling each other in the respite room as needed. Andrea's other job was cooking at the Amity Café; she would make enough of her famous chicken salad to last the Major through the week. Life would go on.

Life was looking up for Cass since she'd finally convinced Jimmy to move out of her house and their marriage. She felt like a new woman with the divorce finalized. She'd lost weight—not a lot, but every pound counts—changed her hairstyle, and actually started dating. And just recently a new man had appeared on the horizon, causing such a rush of optimism that she couldn't let anything bring her down.

Laurel and Andrea discussed the tantalizing morsels they knew of Cass's love life in the kitchen after she'd left, while they waited for Mr. Coffee to create Major's morning brew.

"How'd she meet him?" Andrea asked. She put chicken breasts on to boil, then started the oatmeal.

"On the Internet," Laurel said from her seat at the small kitchen table, where she was studying the Caregivers' Notebook.

"No!" Technology terrified Andrea, Laurel knew.

"No," Laurel conceded. She looked up with a smart little smirk from the notebook. "I'm playing ya. They met in church." Maybe it was mean of her, but Andrea was so gullible.

"That sounds more like Cass."

"I can't believe these entries," Laurel said, flipping through pages and snorting in disgust. "Some of these girls can't write English."

"Not everybody went to college like you, Laurel. Some of us gotta work for a living."

"I work!" It was true, though, that she only worked weekends, while Eric watched the baby. She'd decided to spend a year at home with Anastasia before she looked for a real job. She wasn't worried she'd find one, what with RNs being in such short supply. Eric made enough to keep them going in the meantime, doing IT for Frontier Communications. She didn't put herself in the same category as paycheck-to-pay-check Andrea and the rest of the hand-to-mouth crowd that worked at Thorndikes' and were always in a panic over money.

"So what's the dreamboat do?" Andrea asked, stirring the oatmeal and getting back to the subject of Cass.

"For a living? I don't know. All I know is he sings baritone in the choir and takes her for walks out at Crystal Lake and treats her like a queen."

"She deserves that." Andrea believed all women deserved that, though she hadn't had much luck with men herself, from what she told Laurel.

"I never thought Jimmy was so bad," Laurel said. "He was just never around. That's the life of a long-distance hauler; he couldn't help it."

"I heard he took to drinking after she made him quit driving rigs."

"So Cass said." Laurel never referred to 'Aunt Cass' at work, following her aunt's instructions. "I never saw him drunk."

They heard an articulated roar come over the baby monitor.

"I guess he wants us," Andrea opined. "Is that gibberish he talks normal?"

"For a stroke victim."

"It scares me. He don't seem like our Major any more."

"I'll go get him. You bring his breakfast when it's ready"

Laurel found Major sitting in his wheelchair in the front room with an eager grin on his face. "Reargromp!" he said in what almost sounded like triumph.

"Wow! You got yourself up and dressed," Laurel said. He had changed pretty radically in the week since she'd last seen him, bedridden and helpless. Strange. "Cass wasn't kidding you can do more for yourself. Shall I wheel you to the parlor?"

"Rum!"

Puzzled, Laurel negotiated the wheelchair around the bed, over thresholds and carpets, into the parlor across the hall. "Andrea!" she shouted. "You want to come and help me with a transfer?"

This time, as they hauled Major from the wheelchair into his armchair, Laurel noticed something else. "Has he lost weight?" she asked Andrea.

"Cass says he's eating better."

"I'd swear he's twenty pounds lighter than the last time we lifted him. And look at his face. It's thinner."

"That don't make sense. I'll get his breakfast."

Laurel watched the old man's eyes follow Andrea into the kitchen. Major's libido was out of control, she knew. Not unusual at his age and level of dementia. But there was an animal quality to his gaze that unnerved her. Andrea came back with his oatmeal and coffee and put it on the table next to the armchair. She fastened the bib around his collar.

"Hargum! Nar!"

"I don't think he wants the bib," Laurel said.

"Honey, you always wear it. No big deal." Andrea lifted a spoonful of oatmeal toward his lips. Major grabbed the spoon, and shoved it into his mouth, then spit out the oatmeal. Some of it landed in Andrea's face. He swept the bowl off the table and it crashed to the floor and broke.

"Major!" Andrea shrieked. "What did you do that for? Was it too hot?"

He ripped off the bib and sent it flying.

"What's wrong with you?" Andrea asked, tears of hurt swimming in her eyes.

"He doesn't mean it," Laurel consoled her. "I'll get the dust pan." She rushed out of the room and returned with a broom. Andrea was picking up shards. "Go clean yourself up," she told Andrea.

Laurel looked up at the old man from her knees as she cleaned up the mess. "What *is* wrong with you? I've seen you get mad, but nothing like this." Never so crude.

He looked crushed. Even sorrowful.

"OK. So I guess you really didn't mean it."

An hour later equilibrium had returned. They had made a fresh bowl of oatmeal, made sure it was cool, and let the Major eat it himself. Andrea returned to the kitchen to make the chicken salad. Laurel watched the old man handle the spoon without a tremor. Her eyes narrowed. She'd never heard of Parkinson's disappearing after a stroke. The house phone rang and she picked it up. Loretta's name was on the ID.

"What's up?" Laurel asked.

"Did I leave a set of keys on the kitchen counter?" Loretta said.

"I'll check." Laurel carried the phone into the kitchen where Andrea mixed her secret concoction of mayo, mustard, a tad of Tabasco and other mystery ingredients into the chicken. Next would go in chopped celery, green pepper, hard-boiled egg, chopped grapes, and sweet pickle relish. It was a work of art. "What kind of key?"

"Ford," Loretta said. "It's the spare set to Beaver's truck, and he's lost his."

"It's here." What a harebrained couple, she thought. Bumpkins. She didn't usually work with Loretta, but had the previous Sunday when Loretta was subbing for the missing Andrea. She'd gotten the impression of too much energy and too little forethought.

"I have a question," she said when Loretta arrived in the kitchen a short while later. "It says in the book that you took Major to the hospital last Sunday after I left."

"Yeah. He had a stroke."

"And now he can dress himself, and walk if he feels like it, and his tremors are gone. Did he get a CT scan or MRI?"

"Yes ... no ... I don't remember."

"And he's acting like some kind of wild man of the mountain." When she said that phrase it jogged something in her memory.

"You got something against mountain folk?" Loretta snapped.

The memory came back. "Wait a minute. Didn't I hear a while back that you were working for some old hermit who looks just like Major?"

Loretta's face went scared rabbit white. "That was months ago."

Laurel zeroed in on her. "What happened to him?"

Andrea stopped mixing the chicken salad and looked on, interested.

"His family came for him," Loretta said quickly. "Maybe he died. I don't know."

Laurel folded her arms. "Who died, Loretta? What happened last Sunday?"

Loretta looked past Laurel toward the parlor where the old man sat in his armchair, nursing his coffee after breakfast. Guilt was plastered all over her face. Tears filled her eyes. "Major died. I brought Lyle down here to take his place. I didn't mean no harm."

"Oh my Lord!" Andrea gasped.

"You didn't mean any harm! You committed a crime. I'm calling the police!"

"No, please don't! Your Aunt Cass knows, Tammy knows, Dellisha and Kristy Mae—they'll all go to prison. You can't do that!" Loretta was full out crying now.

"I can't NOT do it! That would make me an accomplice."

"Just leave now," Loretta begged. "Say you got sick. I'll cover for you. Give Cass your notice on Monday. You don't know anything."

"I'm leaving now. I'm not making any promises."

Loretta turned to Andrea after Laurel stormed out. Disaster on disaster. Loretta was drowning in them. "What are you going to do? You quitting too?"

"You know I can't! I need this job. What are we going to do if Laurel rats us out? She and her RN and her highfalutin ways, she might call Family Services on us!" Andrea's voice rose toward a shriek.

"Get a grip. What's Family Services got to do with this?"

"They've been trying to take my daughter's baby away from her. Plaguing her with drug tests, asking who the daddy is. She lives with me. DHHR has it in for me since my breakdown. I'm scared!"

Loretta was scared too, but not of DHHR, more likely the sheriff. She put on a false bravado. "There's nothing to get your knickers in a twist over. It's all under control. I got a plan. I'm going to call Tammy to come over. She always needs more hours. I gotta go. Is Major OK?"

"Major?" Andrea said. "I thought you said …"

"I mean our new Major," Loretta clarified.

"He threw oatmeal at me this morning."

"No!" Loretta thought he had been mellowing as the week went on.

"I don't think he meant it. He got upset."

"I better go talk to him." Loretta pocketed Beaver's keys and headed toward the parlor, resolved. She would put Laurel out of her mind. She had to go to Powhatan County.

Saturday was busy at the clinic, with a steady stream of dogs and cats, and one pet rabbit, rotating in and out of the examination room. Hume didn't have time for lunch. In the early afternoon, he was surprised to find Loretta Hardwick waiting for him in the exam room.

"I didn't sleep at all last night," she blurted out before he could speak. "I had to talk to you."

"What did you tell the receptionist?" She had no animal with her to justify her presence in the clinic.

"I didn't say nothing. Close the door. I know you know."

Hume pulled the door shut behind him and steeled himself.

"Your daddy died real peaceful last Sunday evening. Cass and Tammy were there with me. He went with a smile on his face, I want you to know."

Hume felt grief wash over him again, tears pressuring to burst forth. "What! But why?" he couldn't go on, choked by outrage.

"Why didn't we call you? We were gonna. We were about to. Even though we was all so broke up at losing your dad, nobody wanted to be the one to break it to you. Cass was cryin' her eyes out. Right at that moment, I got a text from Jewel that cops had picked up this old man I take care of that looks just like your dad, and he's in jail for reckless driving. I knew that would be the end of it for poor old Lyle because he can't talk and he's broke with no relatives, so I had to go get him before they put him in prison for the criminally insane. I told the girls about him, how he could be Major's twin, and they said bring him on over here."

"Just like that? My father wasn't even cold and you're running out to pick up his replacement!"

"No, no, not at all! I wanted to rescue Lyle while the girls got your dad fixed up. By the time I finagled Lyle out of the sheriff's clutches and got back, they still hadn't called you because no one had the heart. Or maybe they was scared you'd blame them."

"That's absurd! Inexcusable! Don't you people know your jobs?" Hume's raised voice lashed at Loretta, and he saw her cringe.

"We've been trying to keep your daddy alive, not lose him! When I brought in Lyle the girls almost fainted from astonishment and joy. It was like I'd brought Major back from the dead."

Hume clenched his fists, trying to control himself. "Which you had NOT."

"I know, Hume. Believe me, I regret that night. I'm so sorry I told the girls about your daddy's idea, to just bury him beside Miss Beatrice without telling anyone." Loretta wrung her hands.

"What do you mean, my father's idea?!"

"A couple months ago. Major was peeved at Ruth and I told him about the poor old man I take care of that doesn't have a friend in the world, that could be his double. So he told me to ... switch them out."

"You're kidding. You took him seriously? A temperamental old man with dementia? I can't believe it! You idiot!"

"I know. We wasn't thinking straight that night, upset as we was."

"That's no excuse! I'm appalled, disgusted by you. After all we've done for you and the other caregivers. And your husband, is he in on it too?"

"He and his brothers buried your dad."

"Oh my God!"

Loretta burst into tears. "I know, Hume, believe me. I can't sleep at night, thinking how we took advantage of your kindness. But now, if you turn us in, we'll go to jail. We'll never be able to get work again." She buried her face in her hands.

Hume stared at her, dumbfounded. He didn't like displays of emotion. It was why he worked with animals; they were so much more straightforward. He liked moral clarity. Did he want to send Loretta to prison? Did he want to be responsible for ruining the lives of the women who'd taken care of his father? They had fucked up. Really and truly fucked up! But they had loved his father, difficult though the man was. The last year had been a war between them and Hospice: the caregivers always demanding medical intervention when Hospice—and Hume and Ruth for that matter—wanted to let nature take its course. There was no moral clarity here. "What do you suggest, Loretta? That I continue to support the care of this look-alike with my father's money? Indefinitely? That would make me complicit in the fraud." *Against my own interests*, he thought.

"No! Just a few more days. A week or two at most. I think there's a place he can go. Remember that girlfriend of Trisha's that lives in Kentucky? After Miss Beatrice died and your daddy was trying to get us girls to find him a ... 'companion,' he called it? Trisha was going to introduce him to this divorced lady in Kentucky. But Ruth put a stop to it. Now I could tell Trisha that Major is hankering to leave Amity—too many memories—and wants to meet her girlfriend. We could sneak him away and have him disappear. He's easier to care for now; he'd be fine." Loretta's eyebrows moved beseechingly above her teary eyes.

"And then what?" Nothing in this scheme seemed plausible to Hume, starting with relying on Trisha. Hume suspected Loretta was making it up on the fly. She had to be truly desperate.

"You file a missing persons report. This Major can drive, like I told you. So he went out and got lost, like old people with dementia do."

She was forgetting that all Amity knew his father couldn't drive. "And what do I tell my sister?"

That stopped Loretta. "You're right. Ruth will find out what we done and chop off your head for letting us. We should just turn ourselves in and take our punishment. We never meant to hurt nobody, not you or Ruth, or that old man." She swiped her cheeks with a hand and sobbed.

Hume looked at his watch. He didn't have time for ethical quandaries. "I've got to get back to work. I have patients waiting." He pulled a paper towel out of the dispenser over the sink and patted Loretta awkwardly on the shoulder. "Dry your eyes. Go home. I'll think this over. I won't take any action without calling you first."

Loretta went out, leaving Hume an accomplice in his own defrauding.

9

A Man of the Cloth is Alarmed

Sunday afternoon, Tammy and Andrea were sitting with the Major in the parlor, peacefully watching the game. Tammy, always Loretta's finger-in-the-dike girl, had said no problem to working all weekend. Tammy Oakes was a rock. When the other caregivers were storming around in warring cliques, when the old Major was bellowing and firing girls right and left, when Miss Beatrice was throwing plates (she actually only threw a plate once, in the midst of a heated argument with her husband, and she aimed it carefully at a spot on the kitchen floor where it made a satisfying crash), Tammy stayed calm. Emotional waves could break over her and she remained solid. Saturday afternoon she'd heard all about Loretta's breakdown, Laurel's rage, Andrea's hysteria. She pacified Andrea and they had a pretty good night. Major had slept soundly as the old Major never did. Tammy and Andrea had each had six hours of real sleep in the bed in the respite room.

In the middle of the third inning Tammy saw a familiar car pull up. She grabbed the remote and turned off the TV.

"You've got a visitor, Major," she said. "It's your friend Father Dave." The Major looked blank. "He's the priest who often stops in on you Sundays after church." This Sunday couldn't be different. "Father Dave's just going to sit with you and talk a little about God and Jesus," she told the Major. "You don't have to believe what he says; the old Major didn't (a pity, Tammy thought. She, like all the girls, was a good Christian). Just be grateful there's someone taking an interest in your soul." She went to let the father in.

He came in dressed in the clerical collar that he always wore now when he visited the Major. He'd told the girls the one time he'd shown up without the collar the Major had complained, "Father, I expect you to be appropriately attired for our little discussions." He pulled up a straight chair next to the La-Z-Boy and sat down. "Roger," he said, "how are you? I hear you're not doing so well."

"Mmm," the Major said, peering suspiciously at the priest.

"Oh he's feeling just fine," Andrea chimed in quickly. "He just can't talk since his little old TIA last Sunday. But he's getting around better and perked up a lot."

Father Dave glanced at the TV set and the remote lying on the hassock. "I don't want to interrupt your show."

"The opera was putting him to sleep anyway," Tammy said. The old Major would never have been watching the game. "He'd much rather talk, or at least listen, to you, I'm sure. Can Andrea get you some sweet tea?"

"That would be great. I'm always dry on Sunday afternoons." He chuckled as if this were a joke, and perhaps it had been, between him and the old Major. Andrea got up and the Major's eyes followed her through the dining room to the kitchen. "Well now Roger, would you care to hear the subject of today's sermon?"

The Major looked back at him and uttered a noncommittal "Morble."

The girls usually left Major alone with Father Dave, but Tammy decided she better remain on duty in case of trouble. She didn't like the sharp appraisal the priest was giving the old man or the quizzical look on Father Dave's face. "Go ahead, Father," she said.

"I know we don't usually discuss Bible lessons, but I think you'll find this interesting." Father Dave had told Tammy on previous visits that they talked about history and philosophy and that he enjoyed the older man's intelligence and strong opinions. "The reading for today was from Matthew 15, a rather complex chapter that begins with Jesus reproving the Pharisees. Perhaps you know that the Pharisees were an ancient Jewish sect that enforced strict observance of Jewish law. They accused Jesus of transgressing the traditions of the elders because his disciples didn't wash their hands when they ate bread. Jesus answered the Pharisees back pretty sharply, telling them that they also transgressed God's commandments and pointing out how. I won't go into the details because I don't want to bore you." Father Dave kept his eyes fixed on the Major's as he spoke, as if he were trying to gauge the old man's comprehension. "Jesus called the Pharisees hypocrites, honoring God with their lips but not with their hearts. Then he called out to the multitudes, 'Hear and understand: Not what goes into the mouth (he meant the bread) defiles a man; but what comes out of the mouth, this defiles a man.'

"So it's not breaking the dietary laws that makes a man evil. It's what comes out of his mouth, things that come from his heart—murders, adulteries, fornications, thefts, false witness, blasphemies. Jesus is perceptive in this, I think you and

I would agree." Father Dave paused and looked penetratingly at the old man, who stared back at him with an unreadable expression. Andrea had come back into the room with a glass of iced tea that she gave to the priest and was seated next to Tammy in the loveseat across from the two men.

"I would sure agree," Tammy said for encouragement.

"Well, then," Father Dave said, clearing his throat after sipping his tea. "The chapter gets really interesting after this. Jesus and his disciples left the Pharisees and headed up the coast toward what is now Lebanon and were accosted along the road by a woman of Canaan. That meant she was not an Israelite. In fact, the Canaanites were a Semitic people who inhabited parts of ancient Palestine and were conquered by the Israelites. In the time of Jesus, this woman would have been considered a gentile, not Jewish."

All this historical stuff was making Tammy's head spin. The old Major would have loved it, but this one? At least he appeared to be listening. Tammy hoped the story wouldn't go on too long.

"The gentile woman cried out to Jesus for mercy for her daughter, who was vexed by a devil."

"Vexed?" Tammy asked. "You mean possessed?"

"I believe that's what it means. But Jesus ignored the woman. This upset his disciples. The woman was crying, I imagine pretty hysterical. But Jesus said, 'No, I am not sent to help anybody except the lost sheep of the house of Israel.' In other words, only Jews. What a turnaround! From being wise and generous in rebuking the Pharisees, suddenly Jesus looks as mean and nitpicking as they were. The woman comes at him again and actually worships him, saying, 'Lord, help me.' Again he refuses, saying 'It is not meet to take the children's bread and to cast it to dogs.' Talk about cruel! The woman could have been offended and gone away in a huff. Instead, she says, "Truth, Lord; yet the dogs eat of the crumbs which fall from their masters' table.'

"Finally Jesus relents. 'O woman, great is thy faith; be it unto thee even as thou wilt.' And her daughter was made whole from that very hour."

That was a weird story, Tammy thought. The priest had delivered it as he must have from the pulpit that morning, all the while watching the Major.

"What is going on here?" Father Dave paused for dramatic effect. No one answered him. "Was Jesus testing the woman? Or did he really feel that she didn't deserve his help and then changed his mind? The Bible is ambiguous on this, open to interpretation, as it is in so many places. That's why I thought you'd like it."

The Major grunted politely.

"What I think it means is that God wants us to be persistent," the priest said. "Never give up! When you get your speech back, Roger, we'll discuss it. For now, I'd better be going." He stood up, rather abruptly, Tammy thought.

"You always do him good, Father," she said. "I'll see you out."

Outside, Father Dave turned to her and said, "I'm sorry I couldn't stay longer. That was really upsetting. I've known Roger for years. He didn't seem like himself at all."

"Aphasia has that effect. It's unusual to have such complete loss of speech without paralysis, but it happens sometimes. I read up on global aphasia without hemiparesis cases last night while he was sleeping." Tammy was no RN, but she could do a Google search. She hoped her medical language would be convincing. "The prognosis is good that he'll get his speech back with therapy."

"I certainly hope so." Tammy watched him continue on down the path to his car. She didn't know why she had added that last bit about the prognosis. It was certainly the opposite of her hopes.

Lyle didn't hold much with religion. He'd quit going to church after Annabel died. The priest had interrupted his watching the game and tired him out, so he was glad when he'd left. Lyle made it clear to the two whose names he'd never remember that he wanted to go to his bed, and they obliged him nicely, leaving him alone to rest and recover from all that yakking. Soon enough he heard new voices and his door opened again. His heart, which had been painful of late, gave a hopeful jump. But it wasn't Woman. His face must have shown disappointment because one of them said, "Loretta isn't coming this Sunday, Major. You'll see her tomorrow afternoon."

10

Revelations

From her bed Ruth nursed her cup of coffee and watched Ariel perform his sun salutations. Years earlier Ruth had perfected the art of easing into consciousness by setting up a coffee maker next to the bed the night before, so in the morning all she had to do was press a button and the bitter elixir would be ready by the time she got back from her morning pee and slid back under the covers. She was in the habit of waking early; she could do this ritual, shower, dress, breakfast, and make it to work on time. Now that she no longer worked in the gallery, her schedule remained unchanged.

When Ariel had entered her life he'd tried to get her to try the sun salutation and other stretches. She adamantly refused, saying she was way too old and inflexible for lunges and dog poses. Her preferred form of exercise was rowing on the Hudson River with the bunch of eccentrics from the boathouse. She didn't much care for the spirituality of inner and outer suns, but she did enjoy watching his lithe dancer's body in his boxers. He stretched his arms overhead, palms together, arched his acorn-brown torso, and shook his long black dreads. Ruth knew he was aware of her gaze on him and was performing for her.

Ariel was not exactly her boyfriend. She'd met him at the boozy opening for a hot young art star, while trying not to feel jealous that said star's work was on the walls of the gallery whereas hers was home in her studio since her former boss had made it clear in subtle ways that it would never *never* be on the walls of his or any other reputable Chelsea gallery. She believed that this had less to do with the merits of her work than with all the ways she did not fit the profile—in age, gender, social connections, coolness, etc.—of a hot art star.

"Overrated, don't you think?" the man beside her had said that night in the gallery. She looked around, but no one appeared to be listening to him.

"Are you talking to me?" she asked.

"Who else? You look like a person who knows art." He was a light-skinned Black man of indeterminate age, slim, not much taller than she was, with a luxuriant flood of dreads spilling down his back.

"What makes you think that? I'm not wearing my paint-stained sweats." She was in fact somewhat fashionably dressed in a short black skirt and leopard print blouse.

"A certain je ne sais quoi—perhaps the hint of scorn on your face." He used careful diction, as though English were not his first language, although he spoke it like a native. It was a pickup line! How unexpected at this late date. Ruth had given up Internet dating, had been relieved when Walker renewed his vows with his wife, had given up even wanting a man in her life again, least of all trying to strike up conversations over cheap wine.

"I think you've had too much to drink," she said with a flirty smile.

"I hope you have too. I'm Ariel."

"Ariel! What kind of name is that?"

"Shakespeare. 'The Tempest.' I'm the fairy."

"No you're not." Ruth laughed. What man introduces himself as a fairy? Perhaps one who has no doubts about his masculinity. "Are you a dancer?"

Now it was his turn to ask how did she know.

"By the way you carry yourself."

It turned out he was not currently employed as a dancer, hadn't been for years. He sometimes worked as a stagehand, off-off Broadway. They entered into a getting-to-know-each-other relationship that had been going on for more than six months without Ruth ever being able to give up her trepidations and succumb to his charms. He was appealing, interesting—they argued over his mysticism—a bit of a rogue, but … she felt herself unable to fall in love. She wished she could. Maybe it was his preference for crackpot New Age philosophies over rational thinking. Nevertheless, they had fun. They went to offbeat plays, to jazz clubs, anything cheap; he was always strapped for cash. He usually stayed over on Saturday nights; she let him leave a robe and some toiletries in her loft, but she hadn't introduced him to her children. It disturbed her that she couldn't make up her mind to commit.

"I thought we'd go out to breakfast," she said when he had finished his salutations to the sun.

"Whatever you say." He disappeared nonchalantly into the bathroom to shower. He was easy, didn't pressure her.

They ate breakfast at a little place on MacDougal. "I haven't heard from my father all week," Ruth told Ariel.

"You could call him."

"I could. But it's nice to have a break." In July she'd spent a week in West Virginia, cleaning out the Box Room, capturing the feral cats to have them neutered, sitting beside her father. He'd become less demanding, sleeping a lot, talking little. She'd only been back home a week when the caregivers called, sure that he was about to die. He'd become barely responsive, unable to speak or swallow. Hospice predicted death within seventy-two hours. Ruth began preparations to return, this time planning a funeral. The next day Cass called, "Guess who's shouting 'Yo'!" She canceled the trip.

"I want him to cut me loose. I can't take this roller coaster," she told Ariel. "I think he's doing it on purpose. He's always been a manipulator."

"I think he's suffering," Ariel said.

"I know he's suffering! He hallucinates, thinks he's gone places and done things, and he can't do anything except lie in bed and get fed and bathed like a baby."

"Maybe the hallucinations make his life more bearable," Ariel said.

"He gets anxious and doesn't know where he is. He asks, 'Where is home?' 'Where do the Thorndikes live?' Anybody who thinks dying is easy hasn't watched it. He used to think he would be able to control his death. He loved to talk about suicide, as if he would actually do it. He was fooling himself."

What made Ruth angry was how he'd used his threats of suicide to control her. What had made him so awful?

Roger Thorndike rarely talked about his childhood. There was one story Ruth knew. When he was ten years old he climbed too high in a tree in his backyard. Normally he was a prissy little boy dressed in Little Lord Fauntleroy suits by his mother, a former vaudeville performer, one-time concert mistress of the Fadettes of Boston, an all-woman orchestra whose motto was: "To make good popular music and popular music good." But Roger's tomboy first cousin Clara, older by three years, was visiting from western Massachusetts. Roger's sun rose and set on Clara, and she repaid him with vengeful teasing. Clara dared him to climb the tree.

When a branch he was clinging to broke, Roger had plunged to the ground, shrieking. His mother had been watching from a second-story window and had just raised the window to yell at him to get down. She ran downstairs and outside, crying hysterically. Clara, on the other hand, kept her head and went inside to telephone for an ambulance.

Roger's back was broken. He spent the next year largely in bed, wearing a brace, tended to by his anxious mother, who gave up her violin career for him. She feared he'd never walk again. Her fears were overblown. The doctor was willing to allow him out of bed long before his mother was. She never let Roger forget her sacrifice.

This left Roger with an abiding sense of guilt that translated into a loathing for his mother, an expectation that women were intended to cater to his needs, and, oddly enough, Ruth thought, a passion for music.

After breakfast Ruth and Arial walked through Washington Square Park. It was a lovely August day, not too hot. Ariel wanted to linger by the fountain. Ruth couldn't handle any more of him right now. She wanted to send him on his way and get back to her studio. "Stay busy, sweet lady, don't fret," he said, kissing her lightly on the lips. She watched him glide away on dancer's feet, tossing his dreads.

On her way home she passed the old place on Bleecker where she'd waited on tables forty years earlier. She could never go by it without a moment of time travel. She'd been living with Leo Blitzer in a walkup in Little Italy, working nights while he tried to get gigs. The bar where she worked was in a half basement, downstairs from the club that had cracked open the music world in the '60s. The bar had collected the thirsty overflow during breaks. That scene was over by the time Ruth arrived. All that was left in the empty bar on the late shift, after the underage bridge and tunnel crowd left for New Jersey, was a lone bartender, with whom she sparred, and the cook, with whom she played pong. She filled up the ketchup bottles and saltshakers, wiping off the grease, crunching through the peanut shells and sticky drink spills on the floor, serving free coffee to the local cop on his beat. She collected her meager tips in her apron pocket and walked home through the deserted streets at four a.m. Leo would be asleep on their mattress on the floor. It was a time of struggle and high ambition. They had been so in love.

The city had changed since then, no longer dangerous, dirty, and broke. She picked up her pace to escape nostalgia for lost times and re-entered the present. Stopping at the corner store, she greeted the Korean woman behind the counter. The store had been there as long as Ruth had, since the '70s. Products had changed over the years, to suit the changing tastes in the clientele, but it was marvelous to Ruth how well stocked the small place was, usually with her favorite brands. Thirty years ago the store had sold coffee in the bean, before

Starbucks took over that business. Now it was Greek yogurt, Little Schoolboy cookies, blue corn tortilla chips. "Not jogging today?" Mrs. Kim asked her.

"No," Ruth said. She often stopped in at the end of her run, red-faced and sweaty. "My daughter is coming for dinner. I'm making her favorite pesto." She put fresh basil and dry fusilli on the counter.

"We have to keep our daughters happy. It's not so easy. Mine tells me I should exercise more."

"Tell her you're on your feet all day as it is! My daughter is always trying to improve me. I tell her I'm too old to change."

Claire was coming from Queens, from the apartment in Astoria she shared with two girlfriends from college, all three in that tenuous after-college, waiting-for-life-to-begin phase that Ruth remembered so painfully. Yet the millennials seemed to handle it so much better than she had. They were worldlier and more practical, better prepared for life than she'd been when she arrived in New York City to embark on her art career. So full of impossible dreams! Leo had quickly seen that the pick-up jobs of a striving jazz musician would not satisfy him—the realization struck him on a day he spent his last dollar on a good cigar and a taxicab ride uptown—and had abandoned the saxophone for law school.

And now Claire was preparing to follow in her father's footsteps, not even bothering with the bohemian interlude, unless the year in Astoria while she took the LSATs and interned at a socially responsible nonprofit counted. Ruth knew she shouldn't complain. Leo's ascension on Wall Street had bought them their SoHo loft, back in the early '80s when such spaces were still available to mere mortals—3,000 square feet in a high corner of a cast-iron building. When Leo had abandoned her at the end of the century—astonishing her that he could succumb to the stereotypical midlife crisis that afflicted successful men; she had thought he was different, and never doubted his love—he had left her broken-hearted but mortgage-free. At a meeting over division of property he'd grown wistful (reminiscing over their thirty years together!) and told her, "You earned your half."

She carried her small bag of groceries up the four long, dusty flights of wide wooden stairs; the freight elevator was hand-operated and funky, and she preferred to climb. Inside her loft there was no sign of dust. Light poured through tall windows onto pristine white walls and gleaming hardwood floors. Her studio occupied the space in the back that had been her children's bedrooms. Her latest piece was pinned to the wall. She emptied her mind of thoughts of Ariel and her father, and set to work.

Her method involved cutting, pasting, photoshopping, twisting and manipulating dense layers of imagery that derived from reality—architectural elements, internal organs, exploding rubble, an ear close up, a knee—recognizable details that popped out of the complex abstraction she created. She blew them up, pasted them on great sheets of paper tacked to her studio wall, layered them more, moved them, drew on them, drizzled paint over them, until even the medium couldn't be defined—drawing, painting, or digital?

By the end of the afternoon she was exhausted and turned to dinner making. She was listening to "All Things Considered" and blending the pesto sauce when Claire came in, already looking like a lawyer in her pencil skirt and pumps. Ruth turned off the radio. "Set the table, sweetheart," she said. "I'll open a bottle of wine."

She drained the pasta and stirred the grated Parmesan into the sauce. The beauty of this meal was its simplicity. No need for a salad, with protein, green vegetable, and carbohydrate all included in the main dish. Ruth was old-fashioned in her adherence to food groups. "How was your day?"

She tossed the sauce onto the pasta and served the plated dinner while Claire regaled her with her day in the office of an organization that provided housing for the homeless. Sitting down Ruth said, "Claire, when will you learn? The fork goes on the left."

"I know that, Momma!" Her daughter's tone was aggrieved as she switched the utensils. "I wasn't paying attention."

"Oh well, you have more important things on your mind, no doubt. Ready for your big move?" Ruth had offered to drive her to Boston, but Claire had told her it wasn't necessary. She would be living in a dorm at Harvard, wouldn't need much, and could take the train. It wasn't the same as starting college, when she'd been eighteen and needed her mother's advice on everything from organizing her closet to cleaning supplies. Taking her children to college had terrified Ruth. How could they be expected to survive on their own with the nonexistent supervision in higher education today, much less living in dormitories that were cleaned once a year and would never pass a public health inspection? That they had survived, sometimes thrived, and were on their way to becoming self-sufficient adults was Ruth's greatest source of joy.

They were midway through dinner. Ruth poured herself more wine and passed the bottle to Claire, who put it aside and said, "I have some news."

Ruth noticed that Claire's wineglass was still full. She was drinking instead from her water glass. In that instant Ruth divined what her daughter's next words would be.

"I'm pregnant."

In an effort to prevent a chasm of silence Ruth said, "That's unexpected," hoping the statement was noncommittal.

"It's an accident. I got sloppy. It's no one you know. He's out of the picture."

Claire had always been guarded about her dating life and had never brought home a boyfriend. In high school she'd had a group of friends who did music and theater together, and she'd gone to prom with one of them, a boy she told Ruth was gay. Once or twice she'd asked Ruth about sex but had seemed to know at least as much as Ruth could tell her. In college when Ruth asked her about boys she'd say that there was no one serious, but she would let her mother know when there was. Ruth was eagerly awaiting that announcement. In spite of her own experience with marriage, she wanted it for her children, wanted them to have at least the first twenty-five years before disillusionment set in.

"Don't worry," she said now. "I can refer you to my gynecologist. She'll take care of it."

"I don't want an abortion, Mom. I'm going to have the baby."

Ruth put down her fork.

Claire rushed in with her well-prepared defense. "I've always wanted to have kids. You know that!" As a teen Claire had worked as a camp counselor. She'd been a natural with little children. Ruth did know that.

"But there's plenty of time. You're only twenty-three. You're starting law school in three weeks!"

"I have it all figured out. The baby is due at the end of April. The semester will be almost over. I'll get a clerkship next summer in New York and live with you. You've always said you wanted to be a grandmother."

"What about the baby's father? You want to raise a child with no knowledge of who its father was? Is that fair to the child?"

"My friend Megan doesn't know who her father was. She's fine with it."

So many objections to this logic occurred to Ruth, but she knew how obstinate her daughter could be. She fell back on what she considered to be her ace in the hole. "Have you told your father about this?" Leo had strong opinions and he was paying for Claire's law school education; he didn't want her saddled with debt.

"No. He's doing enough. I was hoping …" Claire broke off, her voice trembling. "I'm hoping you'll be willing to help out with the baby."

"Help out! It sounds like you're hoping I'll raise your baby while you go to law school. How do you expect to get a summer job with your belly sticking out like a blimp? What are you going to do your second and third year? Wear your baby to class in a Snugli? Take it with you to the library and study groups? Crawling and crying and needing your attention?" Ruth heard her own voice screeching out of control.

Claire jumped up from the table, threw down her napkin, and burst into tears. "Never mind! I should have known better than ask you! You hate babies!"

Before Ruth could respond Claire grabbed her purse off the couch and fled the loft, leaving Ruth feeling like a coastal city in the wake of a hundred-year storm. Regret set in immediately, along with the fear that Claire was right. She wanted grandchildren in a theoretical way. But she wasn't a baby person. She didn't hold other people's babies and make googly noises at them. She'd been happy when her children grew into toddlers, and then into little kids, and then into sentient beings with whom she could have conversations; she'd liked each stage better than the one that came before.

She decided to call the one person she could think of who was a worse parent than she was: her father. But it was Tammy who answered the phone in Amity. "Oh Ruth. You haven't talked to Hume? Your dad had a TIA last Sunday and his speech hasn't come back yet."

11

Encounters at the End of the World

STILL SUNDAY

Hume and Maryanne were watching a Netflix DVD, Herzog's meditation on Antarctica's scientists, seals, and subaquatic depths—brilliant and deranged like all of Herzog—when the phone rang. "It's Ruth," Hume said, staring glumly at caller ID. The moment of truth he'd been dreading had arrived.

"Go ahead," Maryanne said, pausing the movie and picking up her book. "You can do it." Hume walked away from the sofa, not to keep Maryanne from overhearing but because he needed to pace.

"What's this about Dad not being able to speak? He had a stroke and you didn't call me!" Ruth accused.

He still hadn't decided what to tell her. "I thought Cass had called you," he said, buying time. He looked back at Maryanne for guidance. She was watching him over her book and shrugged, expressing the quandary they both felt. All that Sunday they'd argued back and forth, since Loretta's revelation at the clinic the day before. Maryanne, whose heart was as tender as her empathy was bottomless, had urged giving Loretta time. A few days, maybe Loretta could figure something out.

"This is going to destroy lives," Maryanne had said. "Not just Loretta's. And it's not going to bring back your daddy."

"You believe Loretta? That Dad died naturally?"

"Absolutely! I've watched them care for him. They may have their faults, but they truly loved your dad."

"The nerve of swapping him out like that! And what did they gain? Nothing but trouble. Disaster. If they confess, do you suppose the police would let him stay buried where he is?" Hume had broken off, feeling his eyes watering.

"We need to figure out what you're going to tell the police."

"But what do I tell my sister? She won't go along with this." Hume had countered. They hadn't come up with any idea of what to do about the imposter or the conspiracy in which they were ensnared.

Hume couldn't remember ever lying to Ruth, discounting the pranks of childhood for which she was a gullible mark. As children in the country, isolated from their own kind, they'd been each other's most constant playmate. They'd squabbled frequently. Hume, two years younger, had to defend himself against Ruth's greater size and sense of importance by frequent teasing and trickery. But their father's rages and threats to improve their conduct by applying his belt had always created instant solidarity.

Hume still remembered occasions of his father coming into his room, the dreaded belt in hand. "Where's your sister?" his father had demanded. He couldn't remember a particular offense, just his response to his father's towering anger.

"I don't know, Daddy. Maybe down at the barn." Ruth would be hiding in his closet, but if the Major went down to the barn where their mother was cleaning stalls she would calm him down.

As adults they were close via long rambling phone calls, even closer after Ruth's divorce, as Ruth had come to rely on Hume's practical advice (Hume avidly followed the stock market, a subject of no interest to his sister) and emotional support. The summer after Ruth and Leo split, an anguished Ruth had asked their father if her son Zeke, then thirteen and at the height of pubescent rebellion, could spend the summer on the farm in West Virginia.

"Absolutely not!" Roger had thundered, according to Ruth. Perhaps she exaggerated. "I cannot be responsible for a troubled adolescent. I'm sorry Ruth, you know I have no patience for children. How you and Hume survived growing up with me is a mystery."

"Did it occur to him," Ruth had told Hume, "that I was going through the worst crisis of my life? That I needed him? All he could think about was number one!"

In the end Hume had solved the problem by inviting Zeke to his own place, to work in his clinic. Zeke's sullen willfulness disappeared in his uncle's presence. He loved animals, and was competent and helpful in the clinic.

With their father's illness and their mother's death, Hume and Ruth's closeness had evolved into a partnership of good cop, bad cop that satisfied them both. They consulted each other on their anxieties and held each other up. They shared everything. Most everything. Hume had never felt as panicked over the prospect of Roger's remarrying as Ruth had. He worried more about the old man's feelings being hurt. It amounted to the same thing; together they tried to protect their father. All this passed through Hume's mind now, with Ruth at the other end of the line. "It was a TIA, they said, not a real stroke." The difference between the two seemed a matter of degree; if the symptoms went away, it was a TIA.

"A week ago and he still can't talk! Did he go to the hospital?"

"You know how much he hates hospitals." He was treading a fine line, not flat out lying. "No."

"Has the doctor seen him?"

"Yes. She says that other than his speech, he's fine." Or so Cass had reported to him. "She's going to do some tests and start him on speech therapy." This part at least was true.

"Should I come down?"

"You were just here, a month ago. I'll let you know if ..." if it turns out the old man has shuffled off the mortal coil. Roger's quip sprang into Hume's mind, distracting him. For all his faults, Roger had had a sharp and sardonic wit. "If he takes a turn."

"Are you sure you don't need me?"

He answered quickly, hating himself for doubling down on the lie, "I'm sure."

"What would I do without you, Hume? Being at the front lines."

She trusted him. He was betraying that trust. He couldn't say anything.

"I've just had the worst fight with Claire. You won't believe this."

The conversation shifted from the dangerous topic of their father to Ruth's shocking news about his niece. Hume sat down at his computer, across the room from Maryanne, and did his brotherly best to reassure Ruth that all was not lost, that Claire would forgive her, that she would manage this new crisis. There was still time to work things out. Finally he hung up and moved back to the sofa, where Maryanne had been listening. "Apparently I'm to be a great uncle," he said.

"I guessed."

"Ruth is pretty flipped out. She suggested an abortion and Claire stormed out in a huff. Claire wants to keep the baby, but not the boyfriend."

"Poor Ruth." Maryanne had tangled with her own daughter over bad boyfriends and bad decisions. "But Claire's got a good head on her shoulders. She's probably thought it through."

"I hope so."

"And single parenthood is a lot easier when there's some money in the picture. I reckon Leo will be good for that." Maryanne had never met Leo, having come into Hume's life after Leo was gone from Ruth's, but she'd heard plenty about him.

"I didn't tell her about the switch."

"It's going to be OK, sweetheart." Maryanne pressed against him and tucked her head under his chin. He put his arm around her.

"It felt weird," he said miserably. "It felt awful."

When Loretta got to work on Monday afternoon she found Major in his big easy chair in the parlor, a place the old Major hadn't been in months. "He was getting bored in his room," Kristy Mae explained. "I moved the TV back in here. Change is good for him." Major looked up at Loretta and nodded, as if in response to Kristy Mae's pronouncement, although Loretta couldn't tell.

"He's smelling like a rose, too," Dellisha said. "Had his bath this morning like a good boy."

"Cass around?" Loretta asked. She dreaded finding out what Laurel had revealed to her aunt.

"In the kitchen, making lists."

"I'll be right back, Major. Y'all can go. I seen Tammy's car coming up the road behind me."

Loretta felt the Major's eyes following her toward the kitchen like a puppy. She felt guilty. Since Saturday she'd been racking her brains about how to get him out of the house. She didn't know how much time Hume would give her. Or Laurel. And there had been Friday's blood test. The switch that had seemed so straightforward a week ago had turned into a ticking time bomb. Anything could blow the whole thing up. Losing her job now looked welcome compared to prison. Suppose Hume didn't believe her about the Major's peaceful passing. Suppose he thought she murdered him. The thought had kept her awake at night.

The idea that had popped into her head at the clinic, to spirit the new Major away to Trisha's friend in Kentucky, that had sounded so preposterous when she proposed it, had been turning round and round in her thoughts. To get him out of the state seemed desirable. She couldn't just take him back up to his cabin and turn the clock back. There was the grave that Hume had seen. Would the sheriff want to dig it up? The thought caused her heart to squelch uncomfortably in her chest. Of course, there were Tammy and Cass to back up her account of the death, the true version, but who would believe any of them? Loretta had destroyed all their credibility. And there was always the chance they would all turn on her and accuse her of ... Lord knows what.

She was stuck worse than a hog on ice with his tail froze in. And she surely couldn't tell Cass what Hume knew. Cass looked up from her lists when Loretta came into the kitchen. "Did you see how good the Major looks? He's having a real good day."

Cass was playing it like nothing was out of the ordinary. What had Laurel told her? Had she forgotten about the blood test and the grave in the High Place? Loretta tried to play along, keep it casual. "With him looking so healthy, you think the doctor may take him out of Hospice?"

"That wouldn't be so bad," Cass said. "Fewer visits from the nurses."

"Was Angeline here today?"

"She was. Happy to see him up and about!"

Not suspicious? If they could fool Angeline, who was pretty sharp, maybe they could fool Dr. Nightingale. Cass's cellphone rang and Loretta listened in on Cass's half of the conversation.

"Yeah, honey ... oh dear ... right away? That will leave us mighty short-handed again ... No, I understand ... You do what you have to do ... OK honey, take care of that little girl of yours." She ended the call and noticed Loretta watching her.

"That was Laurel. She's giving notice. Since Frontier's system crash on Saturday, Eric figures he's going to be getting more weekend emergency calls. He wants her to stay home with the baby."

Loretta pieced together the story Laurel had told her aunt: the husband, IT for the phone company, had to go into work on Saturday, couldn't babysit their daughter. Nothing about the Major, or a ... crime. "That's too bad," she said carefully.

"I don't know. With the Major doing so much better, maybe we don't need two girls on nights any more. That could free people up to work more on the weekend. Y'all are always wanting more hours."

"I'm working at the Family Dollar this weekend," Loretta said. "I can't call in sick again." She put her evening snack in the refrigerator and went back to the parlor, where Tammy had replaced the morning shift. The Major looked up at her and smiled.

"He's in a good mood," Tammy said dryly. "Mellower every day."

"Didn't I tell you you'd like it here?" Loretta said, looking right into the Major's eyes.

He actually seemed to chuckle.

Later, after Cass at last finished fussing about the kitchen and left, Loretta asked Tammy, "Cass don't know what really happened on Saturday?"

"Not yet. I'm surprised Andrea ain't told her. Laurel must have scared her."

"You think Laurel will rat us out?"

"I ain't no prophet."

Loretta couldn't bring herself to reveal to Tammy her dash to Powhatan County and her confession to Hume. She trusted Tammy over any of the other girls, but she had to try to fix things first. She allowed peace to fall over the house. There was precious normalcy in giving Major supper in front of the TV in the parlor. They sat on the Victorian sofa opposite him, eating their own suppers, as they had in the old days before the old Major became bedridden. After dinner he let them help him into the wheelchair and played the invalid as they got him into bed.

"Do you want me to set with you a while?" Loretta asked him. He waved her away and gestured toward the light.

"He's getting more communicative," Tammy observed, turning off the light and switching on the baby monitor. They went out, closing the door behind them.

"I've had such a day," Loretta said, collapsing into the chair in the bay. The desperate plan was starting to form. "I have an awful headache."

"You want to go? It's OK by me. Night crew will be here in another hour. Listen, he's snoring already." The sound of the Major's breathing reverberated through the monitor.

"You sure? I didn't sleep good last night."

"Go on. It'll be fine."

Loretta went outside, lighting a cigarette under the dusk-to-dawn light in the parking area before she got into her car. It was late, but Trisha stayed up late, Loretta knew, if her habits hadn't changed in the last year. So when she pulled out of Forest Bostick Road onto the two-lane, she didn't head toward home. She turned instead toward the south of Amity, where Trisha lived in a trailer with her invalid husband and dying son.

12

An Unexpected Visit Ends Abruptly

MONDAY NIGHT

Trisha had never intended to give her job away. She loved her job! She loved the Major, just as she had loved and comforted Miss Beatrice before she died. Why, Trisha was the only person Miss Beatrice confided in or trusted, although others would take credit.

Trisha had been a caregiver her whole life. First it was her baby sister (the princess), then her sick mother, and her father's needy parishioners. Blood and shit and vomit didn't scare her. Her father, the silent and judgmental pastor, did. When Jason Vance came along—a chef! a catch!—she was eager to get away from the pastor and out of Kentucky. Did she confuse delicious dinners with love? No no! She loved Jason, wiry, energetic, ambitious. She always would, even now when he was such a burden. Back then in Kentucky he was her ticket out. They married, moved to DC, and Trisha got pregnant with Bradley right away. She wanted lots of children! A house full of noise and life and mess, not like the pastor's house. But the birth had gone horribly wrong. Doctors had saved

Bradley, but Trisha could have no more children. So as soon as Bradley was a toddler, they started taking in foster children. Oh how she loved those babies, how they broke her heart. The babies came and went so fast, leaving a trail of suffering. Trisha saw abuse, abandonment; she saw a corrupt system failing babies. She told Jason, I can't do this any more. Jason, whose ambitions were focused on his kitchen at Brasserie, let her run the family. You're the boss, he said, I'm the cook. So they decided to adopt.

Together they picked two little boys out of an album at the adoption agency—little Christopher, just two, and his older brother Benjamin. Trisha fell in love with sweet, clingy Christopher, with his curly black hair and liquid brown eyes, brilliant in his pale face. Benjamin was another matter. He was a four-year-old demon, racing around the house, smashing things, constantly in trouble. And remorseless. When she caught him with a baseball bat and a broken TV he stared back at her with flat, impenetrable eyes. "I didn't do it. He did." Pointing at innocent Christopher.

Damaged by the abuse he'd come from, Benjamin hated Christopher. Trisha couldn't leave them alone together for a second. Once, crossing the parking lot at the supermarket, when Trisha's arms were full of groceries and Benjamin was supposed to be holding Christopher's hand, he pushed the toddler in front of an oncoming car. The driver slammed on the brakes and Christopher was safe. Another time, she caught Benjamin racing toward Christopher with a sharp kitchen knife. Every day, another close call. Counselors didn't help. After three months she told the agency they would have to take Benjamin back. She feared for Christopher's life.

Bradley doted on his adopted brother. With Trisha's care—and Jason's cooking—Christopher grew out of his shyness to be a lively boy. The family had a few years of peace.

The trouble started so gradually that Trisha and the teachers first ascribed it to increasingly complex subject matter. Long division! Fractions! By the end of sixth grade Christopher was falling further and further behind. The school recommended testing. More than a year later after every test under the sun, the diagnosis came back: a rare genetic disorder was destroying his brain. As his body grew older, his brain was growing younger. The doctors predicted a slow-moving disaster: he would regress in intelligence, returning to a childlike state; he would lose the ability to speak and control bodily functions; voluntary movements would shut down; he would waste and die. It was irreversible. Trisha, devastated, prepared to nurse him to the end.

Then, as if the Lord hadn't dished out enough travail on Trisha, more bad luck. Jason's persistent cough and wheezing turned into chronic pulmonary disease. He quit smoking, too late. He had to quit work, the work he loved, that made him who he was, and go on disability. Her heart ached for him, and for his sake she pretended he was still the dynamo she had married. DC's humidity made it hard for him to breathe, so they moved the whole family to West Virginia, where living was cheap and the air clean. "A fresh start will work miracles," she told Jason. "You'll get better. Maybe even Christopher will get better."

Secretly, she liked Christopher the way he was. Now eighteen, he had the large plump body of a man—only his brother Bradley was strong enough to lift him—and the sweetness of a toddler. "More ice cream, please Mommy." He could still talk and he only occasionally wet his pants. Maybe the doctors were wrong.

Meanwhile, money was tight. In the small doctor's office in Amity where everyone seemed to know each other, Trisha heard that a local gentleman had recently had a stroke and was looking for help in his home. She needed a job. She met Major Thorndike in his formal front parlor. He used a walker and had an ugly looking wound in a bald patch on top of his head. "What happened to you there?" she asked him.

"My wife hit me with a frying pan. She has a nasty temper."

Miss Beatrice, the wife, a thin and stiff-backed woman who had helped him into his chair, glanced heavenward. "Skin cancer. He just had surgery. It needs to be cleaned three times a day."

"I can take care of that," Trisha offered.

"Could you? That would be lovely." Miss Beatrice sounded relieved and moved away from the basin that waited beside the Major's chair.

"Do you have any gloves?" Trisha asked.

"Gloves?"

"Never mind. I'll wash my hands." Miss Beatrice led her to the kitchen sink, then escaped through the back door. As Trisha gently washed and dried the wound and applied the Vaseline, he closed his eyes. She thought he was wincing and asked anxiously, "Am I hurting you?"

"No." He sighed with contentment. "You have the touch of an angel."

She loved those words. With them she took on his care. Over the next three years she found herself caring every waking hour—for her son, her husband, and her employer. She bonded with Major and Miss Beatrice, becoming as essential as the air they breathed. Miss Beatrice confided to Trisha,

"I could never do what you do. I couldn't even care for my husband. I can't hold his penis when he pees. Love turns to hate." Miss Beatrice would share many intimate secrets with Trisha. And Trisha told Miss Beatrice the story of her life and troubles, even showing her the album from the adoption agency with the picture of the devil-possessed little boy.

At first there was just one other caregiver at the Thorndikes', a somewhat snotty woman who lorded it over Trisha because, unlike Trisha, she had a nursing degree. Trisha didn't altogether trust Phoebe, not because she was a lesbian. Trisha wasn't biased! People can love who they want. Not because Phoebe and her girlfriend had built a solar-powered house out of straw bales that looked a lot grander than Trisha's doublewide trailer, but she did wonder where the money to build that house had come from. She'd heard some shady rumors about the couple. Then didn't Phoebe quit on the Thorndikes right when Miss Beatrice got sick and they needed all the help they could get? That left Trisha in charge by seniority of what was by then a large staff. At the same time Jason was having medical emergencies and Christopher was getting weaker. The miracles hadn't happened. But Trisha could handle it.

She could handle the aggravation of Faith trying to take her job away from her and Loretta's potty mouth and the gossip and cliques among the caregivers and the stress of their demands for more hours and Ruth's nagging suspicions and threats to put her father in a nursing home (which she'd heard herself because Major always talked to his daughter on speakerphone), because she loved the Major. She would do anything to ease his remaining months or years.

Then Christopher stopped being able to swallow. Trisha insisted on a feeding tube. Some of the doctors thought it was time to let him go, but she would never give up on him. Through all the terrible changes she could still see her little boy. If he couldn't talk, the light of love still shone in his dark eyes. Finally Christopher's care became so arduous, she felt ragged all the time. She suggested to Ruth that they hire Cass. Trisha would stay on as caregiver and let Cass take over the headaches of management, which was never what Trisha had wanted in the first place.

Instead, Trisha returned to her first love—children. She decided to take in a seven-year-old girl she'd come upon weeping in the aisles of the Family Dollar, a skinny little pigtailed thing. Melanie was on the spectrum; the parents couldn't handle her; the county was looking for foster parents. Oh yes, Trisha knew the dangers of foster care, but this was different. This was rural West Virginia, a place of caring people, not the cold-hearted city. A child in the house was just what Jason and Christopher needed to lift their spirits and bring them hope. And the stipend the county paid foster parents would help with their care.

The same week that Cass swept into the Thorndike house like a queen bee, Melanie moved in with the Vances. It was a double storm. Melanie turned out to be the child from hell. She kicked and bit and screamed when Trisha tried to give her a bath. She tore around the doublewide grabbing porcelain knickknacks and smashing them. It was Benjamin all over again. She found the matches Trisha had hidden and set fire to the cat. Trisha saved the cat but realized that the county's Child and Family Services had lied to her about the severity of Melanie's full-blown autism. She had to send Melanie back, never mind the emotional and financial cost. At least she had her work at Thorndikes'.

At work meanwhile Cass was setting the caregivers and Ruth against her. Even her best friend on the staff, Andrea, who was engaged to Trisha's nephew in Kentucky—Trisha had introduced them. It was love at first sight!—started acting funny. There was something malevolent about Cass, something subversive, Trisha was sure. She called Ruth to warn her, "Cass is poking through the house, looking into closets and cupboards like she owns the place. What is she looking for?"

Ruth replied, "I told her to clean up the clutter. She's doing her job."

Then Ruth turned around and fired Trisha. This was her payment for four years of loyalty and service.

Since she was fired, it had been nearly a year of relentless care. A long and lonely time without the respite and sociability she'd found with the other girls at the Major's house. Even Andrea had cut her off. Andrea's fiancé and his mother, Trisha's sister (the princess), weren't speaking to her. Her son Bradley lived up the road with his wife, but they were too busy with their jobs and two kids to be much help. She was shut in with her husband and poor Christopher. Jason had retreated into an almost catatonic dependence on the television.

The TV was on now in the living room of their cramped and crowded doublewide. Trisha could hear it from Christopher's bedroom. Tired from an exhausting day, she sat next to her sleeping boy, watching the steady rise and fall of his chest as if she could keep him breathing by force of will. The sound of the doorbell came like a shriek in the night. Christopher didn't startle, but Trisha jumped up and went into the living room, closing the bedroom door behind her.

The cute wall clock that was shaped like a frog—Miss Beatrice had loved frogs—said almost nine o'clock. Too late for visiting. Her heart raced, thinking Bradley might have been in another car wreck. It might be the police.

"I'll get it," she told Jason, still prone on the couch. He'd been asleep.

She opened the door to see Loretta standing in the black night. "I just come from Major's," she said. "Can I come in?"

"Is he OK?" If the Major had passed, it was highly unlikely that Loretta would come to her door to tell her.

"He's OK," Loretta said quickly. "I just need to talk to you about something."

Trisha's defenses on alert, she backed out of the way to let Loretta in. Jason sat up. "Howdy, Jason. How are ya?" Loretta said and looked around.

Had she ever been there before? Trisha tried to remember. The girls used to stop over when they were all on better terms, to drop off laundry that Trisha did in her machine when Thorndikes' was on the blink or to pick up supplies that Trisha had bought and forgotten to bring over. Yes, Loretta had probably been there before but was taking her sweet time coming in now and looking things over. Trisha sat on the couch next to Jason to wait her out. Jason silenced the sound on the TV. "Not too bad," he answered.

Loretta chose the old upholstered rocking chair Trisha had found at an estate sale and fixed up with ribbons and lace, facing the wall of family photos—Bradley and Christopher as healthy young boys, Jason in the kitchen of Brasserie, Trisha's parents in front of New Lebanon Reformed Church, weddings, grandchildren, and Trisha's favorite photo of Miss Beatrice on horseback, riding through the wild woods the spring before she died, mounted on Ginger, her back ramrod straight as she always carried herself, her shoulders thrust back, her chin high and proud, white hair peeking out below her riding helmet, gazing into the newly green forest where the mountain laurel was blooming in a cloud of white.

"I know you're surprised to see me," Loretta said. "Major is fine." Just today Trisha had run into the hospice nurse Angeline at the Family Dollar and Angeline had told her the Major was looking wonderfully well. Every time Trisha heard gossip about the Major, it felt like a stab to her heart. If he was bedridden and miserable, she wished she could be there for him. If he improved, it was no thanks to her. Loretta continued, "I'm here to tell you things are a mess over at the Major's house. They should never have fired you."

Trisha didn't believe for one minute that Loretta meant that. She was pretty sure Loretta had been behind her firing. She folded her hands in her lap to keep them from trembling with indignation. "What's going on?"

"You know how Major's always changing his mind. First it's Cheerios he wants for breakfast. Then it's gotta be oatmeal or he throws a fit. First he likes one girl, then another and he wants to fire the first one."

Loretta was beating around a bush as big as Kentucky. Where was this going? Trisha remained polite, patient as a crocodile. "Yes?"

"He never wanted to leave his house. Remember when he thought Ruth was going to put him in a nursing home and he nearly busted a gut?"

"I remember."

"Suddenly he can't stand the house no more. He says it's too full of sad memories and yammering women and it's always falling down around his ears and a whole lot of other nonsense. He don't want to be in Amity either, says it's full of busybodies who don't mind their own beeswax. He wants to leave."

"Really?" The other thing Angeline had told her at the Family Dollar was that for the last week the Major hadn't been able to utter a single word, despite his physical robustness.

"I know it's unbelievable. He always said he wanted to die in his own house, in his own bed. Now he thinks a fresh start will give him energy."

"I heard he stays in bed all day."

"That's the crazy thing. He's doing better. Getting stronger. He can actually walk now." Just what Angeline had told Trisha. "He keeps talking about that friend of yours in Kentucky. He wants to pay her a visit."

Trisha folded her arms across her chest and studied little Loretta, rocking nervously in her chair. Jason looked from one of them to the other, then to the silent TV where the picture was still going. He wheezed feebly. He would probably need to sleep with oxygen tonight. "That lady died last winter, Loretta," Trisha said.

"Oh. I'm sorry." She didn't seem to know what to say next. "I can come around and talk to Major. You know I was always good at talking sense to him."

"No. That's OK. You know what Ruth would say if she found out you were there. Cass would skin my hide if she knew I was here tonight."

"I imagine she would. You want a cup of tea or a Coke?" Trisha offered, knowing how eager Loretta was to leave.

"Thanks, Trisha. I gotta go."

After Loretta ran off like a scared cat chased by wolves, Trisha helped Jason to his oxygen tank then sat down at her computer. Now she knew for sure something was going on at Thorndikes'. Loretta was up to no good. Trisha had been waiting for this. She wasn't one to let go of a grievance.

"Dear Sheriff Boggs," she typed. "I'm being held prisoner in my own home by my son and daughter, who are guarding me with the care staff they hired. Since my recent stroke I'm unable to speak or to call anyone for help. The situation is quite desperate. My daughter fired my reliable care manager Trisha Vance when she discovered my intention to leave a generous bequest to Trisha. I have reason to believe that my current care manager is stealing from me, and may be slowly poisoning me. I beg you to investigate at once. An elder crime is being committed in Sinkhole County. Yours truly, Major Roger Thorndike."

She read it over, corrected typos, and clicked print.

13

Insomnia

BACK TO SUNDAY NIGHT

The night after her dinner and fight with Claire, Ruth couldn't sleep. The blast of klieg lights from the retail behemoth across the street poured unobstructed through the ceiling-height windows in her bedroom. Yes, she could install shades. But she hated shades.

One of the things she had loved about her parents' house was how pitch dark it got at night. Not another house to be seen from the farm in West Virginia. One night shortly after her mother died, Ruth woke up in her mother's bed and went to the window. Outside, over the oak tree and outbuildings, the night sky was full of stars, more stars than she'd ever seen, stars upon stars reaching deep into the universe. Ruth was not religious, but she couldn't help but feel that her mother, only gone a few days, lingered close by and spoke to her through the stars. "Sweet dreams, little lamb."

Later, after Cass took over the care management, she'd had the local power company install a dusk-to-dawn light in the parking area near the house. For the safety of the caregivers, who arrived and left at all hours and might break a leg stumbling up the steep path to the house in the dark. Ruth reluctantly gave permission for the light. It was up and running when she came for the one-year anniversary of her mother's death. She stayed in her mother's room; she thought of it as her room now. The closet and dresser had been cleaned out but the room was otherwise unchanged. The same moss-green walls hung with her mother's watercolors—a tree full of cackling blackbirds, storm clouds over Ragtop Mountain—the same small Victorian rocking chair with its faded yellow upholstery, the high four-poster bed that sank like a U-shaped valley when she got into it. She turned out the bedside lamp and cursed. The backyard—oak tree, outbuildings and all—was lit up like a stadium. She felt robbed of a dark night of dreamless sleep and waking up like it was the first morning of the world. She buried her face in the pillow and fumed: the planet was polluted with light. Dusk-to-dawn lights seen from outer space. No place dark enough to see the stars. And did all this light deter crime (the power company's argument)? Or did it just light up the entrances and egresses to make theft easier? And add to Mountain Power's profit.

It made no sense to be angry at nighttime illumination in New York, famed for its sleeplessness. Back in the days when artists had carved out a meager livelihood in these SoHo lofts, Ruth had loved the warm glow of people at home, people who turned out their lights at night, or burned the midnight oil working at human tasks. Not flagship corporate fucking chain stores that lit up an entire loft building 24/7 for no good reason. There were no shoppers of designer sneakers and athletic wear at 1:00 a.m., not even night watchmen. She didn't need shades; she needed a bazooka to shoot the lights out. She needed peace.

Claire's baby invaded her unquiet thoughts. Not a baby, she corrected herself, a pregnancy. It wouldn't be a baby for forty weeks. That's how pregnancy was measured now, like forty days and nights in the wilderness before your crucifixion. And resurrection? Had she been reborn by Zeke's birth? By overwhelming, life-altering love so powerful it blotted out everything—her husband, her ambition, her art career. "Children and art," Marie sang in "Sunday in the Park with George" the year Zeke was born, "What do I do?" Ruth added her own words and sang to her newborn Sondheim's unsingable tune. "What do I do about ambition? What do I do about my life?"

Truth was, Ruth was ambivalent about babies. Yes, she had adored Zeke, and Claire had doubled her joy. With a caveat. Leo had said that those years when Zeke and Claire were little were the happiest of his life. He could say that; he was working seventy hours a week at his law firm, making partner before he was forty. Meanwhile Ruth was home with babies and toddlers, watching her career sink under the tide of motherhood.

Did motherhood come between her and Leo, a dozen years of it turning her brain to mush so that she couldn't hold a candle to the brilliant young associate in his firm he left her for? The edge went out of her art, and the dealers saw it. Twenty years later all the women Ruth knew who had made it in the art world were single and childless. Claire was naïve to think she could have this baby and carry on with her life as though nothing had changed. Ruth knew: once a baby comes, everything changes.

Nevertheless, Claire was her baby. She was not to blame for whatever mistakes Ruth had made. She should never have given Claire such a hard time about this pregnancy. Granted, it was a shock. A baby! What would that make Ruth? Was that what so alarmed her—becoming a grandmother? She wasn't ready to advance to the head of the line. Nothing good lay ahead.

Still and all, she shouldn't have blown up at Claire. That was what had her tossing through the undark night. The pain she had inflicted on her own sweet child. Terrible mother.

In October of 2009 Ruth and Clair had flown to West Virginia for a quick visit, their first since Roger's stroke the previous July. No, Ruth had not rushed to her father's bedside when hearing about his stroke. She and Hume and Maryanne had been in Italy, on an art- and wine-filled vacation.

"No need to come," Beatrice had assured them over the phone. "He's out of danger and doing fine. Enjoy yourselves!"

Canceling the trip and flying to West Virginia would have been a huge expense, and for what? To argue with their parents over their needs? Their parents had always been so independent, resistant to all advice.

It turned out Roger and Beatrice had figured out their needs on their own. They hired Bo Hardwick to install an electric stair lift, to carry Roger up to his bedroom, and handrails in the shower. They hired their first two caregivers, Phoebe and Trisha, to take turns working seven days a week from nine to four, freeing Beatrice to live her normal life.

All was running smoothly by the time Ruth and Claire arrived in Amity, hours late because of a delayed flight. Roger had gone to bed, but Beatrice waited up for them and gave them a cold supper. She seemed ecstatic to see them.

"How's Dad?" Ruth asked.

"He's doing the best he can, given the circumstances. Rage, rage! I tell him." *Against the dying of the light*, Ruth knew.

She'd sent Beatrice a copy of the poem, at her request. Ruth wasn't so keen on old-age burning and raving. She and Claire slept late the next morning and came down to breakfast as Beatrice was coming in from feeding the horses. "I'll make fresh coffee," Beatrice said.

They heard Roger's voice yelling, "Ruth! Come here immediately!"

"He's in the front room," Beatrice said. "You'd better go." Claire stayed in the kitchen with her grandmother.

Ruth found her father in an ugly mood. "Have you no consideration?" he thundered. "What did you mean by keeping your mother up so late, forcing her to make a second supper? She couldn't sleep. She's exhausted. These visits of yours are too hard on her."

"Would you rather I didn't come?" He'd always made her feel unwelcome in his home, and her children were even more unwelcome.

After breakfast the three women walked around the farm. The mountains blazed with full autumn colors. Beatrice's little terrier raced ahead, barking at the cattle, sending them lumbering away in fright. Claire laughed at the sight and recited, "Way down south where bananas grow, a grasshopper stepped on an elephant's toe. The elephant cried with tears in his eyes, 'Why don't you pick on someone your own size?'"

Beatrice chortled. "Claire, you must write down the words for me." Later Beatrice would paint a picture of the elephant and the grasshopper inscribed with the words to the ditty, make copies, and send them to her children and grandchildren. "My memory's so lousy now," she added.

"You remember plenty of things," Claire said. "Just not the nonsense."

Beatrice asked Claire about college—she'd just begun—what courses she was taking, what she aspired to. Claire confessed she didn't know: should she pursue musical theater, her passion in high school, or study something more practical?

"Don't be practical!" Beatrice advised. "College is a time for testing your wings. I wish I'd done more of that in college. It was hard then, with the war on. I was mostly pursuing boys."

"I don't believe that, Grandmother."

"They'd all gone off to war. When I finally found a boyfriend—I was a very late bloomer—my mother put the kibosh on it. She thought he wasn't good enough for me."

Ruth had known her grandmother, a domineering matriarch and unrepentant snob. She loved that Beatrice was telling Claire this story, loved her mother talking girl talk.

"When your grandfather came along," Beatrice said, "I grabbed him quick. Before my mother could do anything about it, we were married."

"Grandfather got a good deal. You were beautiful," Claire said. "You still are."

"We're both going down the tubes now, your grandfather and I."

Ruth felt sad. She wished her children could have spent more time with Beatrice when they were growing up.

Roger's mood had improved by the time they got back. But Ruth noticed he was greatly weakened. He walked hunched over, shuffling, exhausted. He told them he was falling often and having frequent TIAs. He also refused to see a neurologist. "There are no secret cures for this known only to a select elite," he said. "My internal medicine man can do as good a job as anyone."

He introduced them to Phoebe, the new caregiver. "My granddaughter is a talented musician," he said. "Are you still playing violin, Claire?"

She'd given up violin for voice, but cheerily engaged him with talk about music and listened with him to his Anne-Sophie Mutter CD.

That night, tucked into their respective twin beds in the guest room, Ruth said to Claire, "I'm glad you came. You were sweet to them. Grandmother needs sweetness right now."

"She seems more afraid of what's coming than he does," Claire observed.

So perceptive, Ruth thought, surprised at the idea. She'd always thought Beatrice was the strong one.

That had been five years ago. Ruth's admiration of her sensitive and brilliant daughter had increased with the years. Full of remorse in the morning after the fight, she called Claire. There was no answer. Of course Claire kept her phone off; she dashed straight from her shower to her office with her hair still wet and had no time for distraction. Ruth left a message. Of course Claire didn't listen to messages. She was a millennial. Millennials don't talk on phones or read email or use Facebook. How do they communicate, Ruth wondered. Telepathy? Or maybe some technology implanted in their brains that Ruth didn't want to know about.

Ruth didn't text. Landlines can't text, she explained patiently to her friends who refused to learn her contact preferences. She sent Claire an email with the subject line, "Call Mom." No body.

Claire didn't call. She's mad, Ruth thought. She spent the day in her studio cataloguing old image files for future use.

The piece she'd been working for the past month, a swirling vortex of grey and fleshy pink and citrus green, couldn't draw her in. Not if she'd lost her baby girl.

In the late afternoon she tried Claire's number again. About to despair on the third ring, she finally heard Claire's voice, "Hi Mom."

"Oh sweetheart! I'm so sorry. I didn't mean what I said last night."

"Silly Mommy," Claire said. "I knew that."

Ruth spilled tears of relief.

14

What the Heart Knows

2012

When Loretta first went to work at the Thorndikes' she hadn't had a job since she married Beaver, when she was just out of high school and expecting Jewel. She'd never had a care job, never even babysat for money. She admitted this on her first day. "I've pumped gas and chucked hay bales. I don't know as that qualifies me for this job." She was standing on one side of Major's La-Z-Boy, Trisha on the other, and they were preparing to haul him from the armchair to the waiting wheelchair.

"You're qualified," Major quipped. "Just think of me as a bale of hay." Loretta liked him at once.

"You raised three children," Trisha said. "You can give care."

She found out she could. It surprised her. She could give Major sponge baths in the hospital bed that had been set up in the front room now that the caregivers couldn't get him upstairs—the downstairs bathroom hadn't been built yet. She could adjust his penis in the urinal when she tucked him in at night. He didn't scare her with his fearsome shouts that got the other girls running to see what he wanted. The person who scared her was Miss Beatrice, his imperious and angry wife, who seemed to be at war with the caregivers and the Major.

"The most aggravating woman in the world!" he would thunder when Miss Beatrice was out of the house, which she was from eight in the morning until five in the afternoon, when she brought Major his cocktail in the parlor. During the day she was always on a horse, on a tractor, planting, weeding, painting, mending fences, the list went on. "She's ADHD," Major griped. "Always has to be doing, doing. Won't sit still for five minutes for a conversation with her husband of sixty-three years. If I could get up out of this chair I'd divorce her!"

"Now Major, you wouldn't do that," Loretta would say. "Where would you go?"

"Anywhere would be better than here!"

"What! You'd leave us girls?"

"Not you, Loretta. Would you marry me?" And she would joke with him and say, of course, knowing that he'd proposed to all the girls and made unwanted sexual advances to some of them but not to her, thank the Lord. She'd heard about these in titillating detail. It was an exciting place to work, what with the constant drama, the gossip and cliques among the caregivers, the screaming battles between the Major and Miss Beatrice, and the gun in the Major's nightstand.

"Phoebe's making a stink about Major's gun again," Trisha told her after she'd been working there about a month. They were sitting in the dining room and Loretta was trying to write notes in the caregivers' journal, trying not to get distracted by Trisha's chatter. "She's going to try to get Ruth to take it away from him." Big plans were being made for the daughter's upcoming visit over Memorial Day weekend. Everyone seemed to have some grievance or other to present, as if the Yankee daughter was a kind of justice of the peace. Loretta didn't think she was going to like Ruth. All Loretta knew about New York City was from watching TV, and that was more than enough to prejudice her against it as a place of superficial glamor and loose morals.

"What's wrong with his having a gun?" Loretta asked. "I got a Colt 45 Peacemaker my daddy gave me when I was twelve." It was one of her most prized possessions and reminded her of target shooting and hunting with her daddy as a teenager, before he died. "Everybody in Sinkhole County's got a gun."

"Don't I know it. Dinah, who used to work here, lives up the dead end of Holiness Church Road in a A-frame with a yard full of mean dogs and No Trespassing signs, used to walk down here to work carrying a pistol. Major fired her for walking into the parlor waving it around, startling him so bad he almost fell out of his chair. She claimed she just wanted to protect him from the meth-head crowd."

"Can't blame her for that," Loretta said. Her daughter was running around with that crowd and it worried Loretta to death, but she didn't tell Trisha that.

"Major did," Trisha said. "He and Miss Beatrice were having their cocktails, and Miss Beatrice had a conniption. But the reason Phoebe is down on Major's gun is because he's always threatening to use it on himself."

"What?!"

"Sometimes it's just when he's mad, when he and Miss Beatrice have a fight and he tells her he's going to blow his brains out. Then it's just talk. But sometimes he means it. He tells us caregivers that he won't go die in the hospital, that before that happens he plans to commit suicide."

"You think he'd do it?!"

"The elderly do, sometimes. A man down in McDowell did just last year. His brains were splattered all over the bathroom walls." Loretta had already learned that there wasn't a single piece of grisly news from southern West Virginia that Trisha didn't know. "If Major did it, one of us could get blamed. That's what Phoebe's worried about."

"Really?" Not about the horror of finding the Major with his head blown apart and blood spilling out on his pillows, maybe not even all the way dead if the caregivers came running as soon as they heard the shot? Loretta shuddered at the picture in her mind.

"I'm more worried about what happens if Miss Beatrice gets her hands on the gun when she's having one of her temper tantrums." They heard the kitchen door slam and Miss Beatrice come in. "Must be four o'clock," Trisha said. Every day at four, Miss Beatrice came in for the beer that she took out to drink by the pool before returning to cook dinner and make the Major's evening cocktail. "You can set your clock by her."

Trisha got up from her chair in the dining room bay where they'd been chatting and went into the kitchen. "Need me to help you skim the pool, Miss B?"

Loretta had noticed that Trisha fawned on Miss Beatrice, following her around and offering her constant attention, almost adoration, like some kind of pushy little sister. Loretta didn't know what the fierce old woman thought of Trisha.

On the day of the daughter's arrival, Loretta pulled into the parking area and saw an unfamiliar Subaru Forester with New York plates. She headed toward the kitchen door and stopped at an unexpected sight. The clotheslines in the back yard were hung with Oriental rugs. A woman who had to be

Ruth Blitzer was whacking away at them with a broom, while Miss Beatrice looked on smiling. "Oh hello, Loretta," Miss Beatrice said. "Come meet my daughter. Ruth, Loretta is part of the Hardwick clan. We couldn't do without them. They keep this farm going." Loretta was surprised at such praise. She didn't think that Miss Beatrice had noticed her in the bustle of caregivers coming and going, as many as eight or ten in a week, what with overlapping shifts and girls calling in sick and sending subs—daughters or sisters or cousins.

Ruth turned around, wiping sweat from her face with a dirty hand. Short dark hair streaked with gray, face bare of makeup, she was no Carrie Bradshaw. "My mother complained that her vacuum cleaner spews more dust than it sucks, so we decided on an old-fashioned rug-beating."

"Isn't my daughter the bee's knees?" Miss Beatrice said. Loretta thought, *Miss Beatrice is crazy about her daughter. She has a heart after all.*

"That's a lot of work, Miss Ruth," Loretta said. "You want help?"

"Just Ruth. No *Miss*. This isn't the antibellum South. But thanks, I need the exercise. I spent all day yesterday sitting behind the wheel of my car." She seemed friendly, a regular person. Loretta went inside, still putting together her understanding of her employer's family.

Later, Loretta helped Ruth bring in the rugs and spread them in their places while the Major looked on. Miss Beatrice had gone out to feed the horses. Major told Loretta, "My daughter's here in her capacity as marriage counselor."

"I don't know how to do that!" Ruth said, her face reddening.

"What does your mother say on the subject? I trust you've raised it with her." He seemed to have forgotten Loretta was in the room.

"She says there's nothing wrong with the marriage. Come on, Loretta, we have one more rug." Outside, Ruth confided in Loretta. "My parents used to be very private people. This is new to me, all this spilling of their emotions in front of you all."

"It ain't easy, when people get old."

"You got that right. My brother's coming for lunch tomorrow. My father wants to have a big meeting. To discuss their marriage. When I was growing up they always seemed like such a loving couple. Every evening when my father got home from work he would sweep my mother into his arms for a romantic kiss, the kind you'd see on TV in the '60s. She won't talk about what's going on in their relationship now. When I ask, she says it's the same as it's always been." Ruth grabbed one end of the rug while Loretta got the other, and they hoisted it off the line. "Maybe it is. I don't know what's going to happen at this meeting."

Loretta knew more about the meeting than Ruth realized. Major always kept his phone on speaker because he was half deaf, and Loretta could hear both sides of every conversation he had with Ruth and Hume. The week before, she'd heard Ruth tell Major, "We have concerns, Hume and I, about your finances. Do you even know how many loans you've given out to the caregivers?" Ruth had no way of knowing that Loretta could hear her. "Do you record the loans? Do you know you're being accused of sexual harassment?"

"I merely explained that I find it stimulating when they wash my genitals. It's a natural thing, nothing to be alarmed at. I like the sensation!"

"Two of the caregivers report that you've asked them to 'stimulate' you." Loretta had heard about this. It was all the talk of the staff. Trisha was sure the Major would be sued sooner or later.

"Perhaps I did. I don't remember. Is that so terrible?"

"It's sexual harassment. People take it seriously these days." Ruth's voice was stern, like a junior high school teacher.

"It's so unfair! No one ever accuses women of sexual harassment." Loretta could barely keep from cracking up.

"Life isn't fair. That's what you've always told me. There's more. We're worried about Mother's memory and ... mood swings. You need a downstairs bathroom."

"Your mother won't permit it," Major said. He sounded like a little boy denied dessert.

"We'll talk it over with her when I come down. And the caregivers are worried about your gun."

"Put it all on the agenda! I'm tired, can't talk any more. We'll have a formal meeting when you and Hume are here." He had leaned back in his armchair, closed his eyes, and held the phone out with a touch of drama for Loretta to take.

She had thought then that she'd like to be a fly on the wall at that meeting.

That evening, after the rug beating and subsequent cocktails, Loretta and Trisha wheeled Major to the dining table, then sat out on the front porch while the three Thorndikes ate their dinner. The caregivers brought their own snacks to work, and remained close by in case they were needed. It was a warm night. Loretta smoked. "You ought to give that up," Trisha said. "It's what's killing my husband."

"I reckon you're right." Loretta wasn't going to argue with Trisha, although Trisha wasn't her boss. Phoebe, as the senior caregiver (and the one with a nursing degree), put together the schedule, a difficult task with the competing demands of eight or more caregivers. "Ruth isn't as stuck up as I expected."

"Stuck up?"

"Being from New York and all."

"You sound like someone who's never been out of West Virginia."

"Yep. A hillbilly. And proud of it." That shut Trisha up.

When Loretta got to work the following day Hume and Miss Beatrice were washing dishes and Ruth was in the front room with the Major. Loretta took his three-o'clock medication into him. "How was lunch?" she asked. "Y'all have fun?" She didn't ask about the meeting, although that was what she most wanted to know.

"He slept through it!" Ruth said. Loretta thought she heard disgust, like Ruth was suppressing anger at her father.

"I was not asleep!" he said, returning her anger with his own. "I simply closed my eyes to do a little experiment. I wanted to see how long I would be ignored. The world pays no attention to a man with no legs."

"You were snoring," Ruth said. "Mother didn't want to wake you up." She turned to Loretta. "There was no meeting." She sighed.

Later on, after Hume had left and Miss Beatrice had gone out to feed the horses, Loretta was in the kitchen with Ruth. "When are you going back to New York?" Loretta asked. "Not that I'm trying to hurry you," she added.

Ruth gave a short laugh. "Don't worry. I'm leaving tomorrow, and tomorrow can't come soon enough! My father is driving me crazy. If I stay any longer I may have to strangle him."

Loretta thought she had an insight. "He can't help himself. He's lost his manly pride. That's why he's so mad."

Toward the end of that summer, Trisha's husband had gone into the hospital in Roanoke and almost died, and Trisha was away for a month. During that time Loretta got to know Faith, the tough old caregiver who took over Trisha's role in bossing everyone around. Loretta liked Faith; she was funny and shrewd and did great imitations of the other caregivers, the Thorndikes, and anyone else who became a target for her wit.

When Trisha got back from Roanoke, war broke out between her and Faith. Phoebe was leaving to take a job with Hospice, and Trisha felt that the care manager position should naturally go to her. She saw Faith as a threat. Life in the Thorndike household got even more exciting, with cliques of caregivers whispering behind each other's backs. They divided into camps, and Loretta found herself in Faith's camp. In the middle of all this drama, Ruth came to visit for a week, summoned by the Major.

"Staying longer this time?" Loretta asked her on a brilliant October afternoon, the first day of Ruth's visit.

"God help me," Ruth answered.

"I didn't think you believed in God." Another bit of information that Loretta had picked up from the speaker phone. It had shocked her, but she wasn't about to preach at her employer.

"There are no atheists in foxholes, Loretta."

Loretta had no idea what she was talking about. "That vacuum cleaner you ordered for your folks came. It works real good. How do you say its name? Nobody here knows, not even your mother." In fact, when it had arrived by UPS Miss Beatrice had expressed disdain. She'd watched Loretta pull the sleek black oblong out of the box and unwrap its tubes and attachments one by one, shaking her head and muttering, "Ruth is throwing away her money again."

"I think it's pronounced *mee-ly*," Ruth said.

"I put the old one in the Box Room."

"Not in the garbage?" Ruth's tone was incredulous.

"Nope. Your mother wanted it out there with the other old vacuum cleaners." Loretta grinned. "She says we might need them for parts."

Loretta got to know Ruth a little better in that week. She approved of the way Ruth followed Miss Beatrice around, letting her mother be herself but watching closely for signs of danger, as Loretta herself had watched her children when they were little. The Post-it notes on the kitchen counter had clearly alarmed Ruth, but she'd let Miss Beatrice drive her across the fields in four-wheel drive, braving hidden ruts and rocks. When they got back, Ruth said to Loretta, "Despite rumors, she still knows how to drive."

Loretta found herself liking Ruth. In spite of her fancy education she didn't act superior. Of course, there were topics they had to avoid, like religion and politics. Miss Beatrice had planted an Obama placard in her yard, in defiance of the citizens of Sinkhole County, and she and Ruth were filled with fervor about the upcoming election. The placard had disgusted Beaver, who knew for a fact that Obama was born in Kenya and should never have been president, but Loretta kept strong emotions focused on things closer at hand: her family and loved ones.

A few weeks after the October visit, Miss Beatrice went into the hospital and Ruth was back, this time to begin the vigil.

Of that strange intense time, when they had two patients in the house, one of whom they'd never dreamed they'd take care of, several memories stood out to Loretta. Ruth had brought Miss Beatrice home from the hospital, frail and unable to stand on her own, in stark contrast to what she'd always been. On the evening of her arrival, the caregivers gathered at the kitchen door. The Hardwick brothers had come to help. Directed by Bo Hardwick, Ruth drove out into the pasture behind the house, through the gate into the backyard and up to the kitchen door. It was just past sunset, and the sky was streaked with purple and red. The Hardwicks lifted Miss Beatrice out of the car into the waiting wheelchair and pushed her into the kitchen with everyone watching.

"Goodness!" Miss Beatrice had said. "It feels like the arrival of the queen."

They'd rented a second hospital bed and had set it up in the master bedroom upstairs, the room the Major didn't use anymore. That worked for three days; they helped Miss Beatrice up and down the stair lift and wheeled her around the house along with the Major. Then, on Friday, she took a sudden plunge into dire pain and couldn't get out of bed. The pain terrified Miss Beatrice. "I can't bear this," she said to Loretta. "I just want out." There was anguish in her voice.

Loretta sat with her, trying to comfort her, feeling panicked herself, until Ruth got home from shopping at Walmart.

"Did the hospital know this was going to happen?" Miss Beatrice asked Ruth.

"Yes." Loretta admired the calm certainty of Ruth's reply.

"Then why did they send me home?" Miss Beatrice wailed.

"You're better off at home. We're going to get help."

Ruth called in HospiceCare. After a bureaucratic delay of more than a day because it was a weekend, the hospice nurse arrived—Loretta wasn't there but heard about it later—bringing the blessed relief of morphine and some advice: "You have to bring her bed downstairs; that way her husband can wheel in to see her."

Ruth had insisted on the initial placement of the bed upstairs, in accordance with her mother's sensitivity to being on display in her weakened state. On Monday Ruth called the care staff together and summoned the Hardwick brothers back. They carried Miss Beatrice downstairs as gently as they could—every movement caused her pain and made them fear they'd lose her—and placed her on the living room couch, lying down. Then the menfolk disassembled the heavy hospital bed and reassembled it downstairs next to the couch, after which the men retired to let the women transfer Miss Beatrice to the bed. Transfer was a female area of expertise.

But Loretta studied the complicated sections and wires of the bed and, being mechanically inclined, piped up. "Bo set the bed up wrong, with the pillow end at her feet." Her brother-in-law Bo fancied himself a master builder and electrician, and sometimes it irked Loretta how he lorded it over Beaver and Nate. "We got to turn it around before we put her in it."

And so the women did, wheeling it over the cumbersome Oriental rugs with difficulty. They carefully smoothed the sheets and gently transferred Miss Beatrice, who never cried out, only moaned when it was more than the morphine could handle, with Ruth looking on anxious for her mother, Loretta could tell. Ruth called the men back to take away the sofa and reorient the bed lengthwise to the room, so that Miss Beatrice could look out and see the dining room and kitchen and be part of the family again. It was when Bo went to plug in the bed's electronics that he noticed what Loretta had done.

"She's in it backwards. She won't be able to raise her head and feet with the controls. Who switched it? I set it up right."

Shame washed over Loretta.

"Never mind," said Ruth, knowing who the culprit was. "We'll just have to turn her back around."

"Oh no!" Miss Beatrice whimpered.

"I know!" Loretta said. "She ain't heavy. We have enough people to just lift the whole mattress with Miss Beatrice on it, and turn the bed around underneath her."

And that they did. When her mattress was lifted high, Miss Beatrice raised her arms and said in her thin voice, "I'm flying!" To Loretta it seemed like God was with them that night.

2014, TUESDAY

In that sacred time when Miss Beatrice was dying, they had all worked together as a team, despite the rivalries among the caregivers, in partnership with Ruth and Hume. Loretta had broken that partnership when she hatched on the plan to deceive the Thorndike children about their father. She'd had the best of intentions, she was sure. But now, Hume knew what they'd done. If Ruth found out, she would be furious and never trust the caregivers again. And how could she not find out? They were closer to being exposed every day. The night before, Trisha had shot down her desperate plan to spirit the Major away to Kentucky. Loretta was terrified. She was in the front room with the Major watching the *Duck Dynasty* CD she'd brought him, when she saw the sheriff's car pull into the parking area. "Omigod!" she yelled. "Cass, go outside. Quick!" She didn't know what this meant, but she wanted to be ready.

She ran to shut off the Major's TV, the little one that Cass had brought in so they didn't have to keep moving the TV from front room to parlor to follow the Major's whims.

"Let's give this a rest, Major honey. Looks like you have another visitor."

He didn't growl or snarl in response, just looked up at her with his obedient puppy eyes. He was definitely calmer with each passing day, smiling more, even as Loretta got more anxious.

"It's Sheriff J. R. Boggs. Don't think you know him. He ain't been sheriff but for a year." Loretta watched through the window as Cass went out to meet the sheriff. They stood talking for a while by the cars in the orchard. The sheriff showed Cass a piece of paper. Then she led him toward the kitchen door. Minutes later they were in the front room. Loretta tensed.

"Major Thorndike," Cass said. "Sheriff Boggs has a letter here, purported to come from you."

"Dropped off at my office early this morning, not sent through the mail," the sheriff said. "The secretary found it when she opened up the Court House this morning." He held out the letter to show the old man, who stared at it blankly. "Did you write this, sir?" the young sheriff asked.

"Major don't know how to type, Sheriff," Loretta said, looking over the Major's shoulder. "And he ain't been out of the house in more'n three weeks, last time he come home from Sweetwater Valley Medical Center."

"These are serious allegations, Major. Did you have someone type this up and deliver it?" He looked from Loretta to Cass and back to the Major.

"You don't think one of the care staff would write this, do you?" Cass said. "The letter accuses us of poisoning him." Loretta's eyes widened. She couldn't see the letter clearly, as the sheriff waved it in front of the Major.

"Can he answer yes or no questions?"

"Not since his stroke last week," Cass answered.

"So where do you think this came from?"

Loretta figured she knew, but she wasn't going to say anything. More than ever she regretted her impulsive visit to Trisha. Now that she'd let the cat out of the bag, no telling what kind of trouble Trisha could brew. Cass also seemed to connect the dots. Maybe she read Loretta's mind, something she seemed capable of. "There's a former care manager," she said, "who left ten months ago, and I don't think she's gotten over it."

"You think she's responsible?"

"I don't know. But if you want to speak to Major Thorndike's son, he comes every Friday. He can confirm that Trisha Vance was fired for lying and left angry."

Dear God! Inviting the sheriff back into the house seemed like the worst idea. Loretta told Cass so later, after the sheriff had gone, promising to return, and *Duck Dynasty* was playing again.

"What were you thinking!" Loretta almost exploded.

"Calm down, Loretta. I've been praying on this, and I've reached a realization. In my heart I know the Major never died. Whatever happened that terrible night, a miracle took place. His soul lives on in this old man who can't speak to tell us he's still our Major. But he is. We have nothing to fear from sheriffs or doctors or blood tests. Once a miracle is set in motion, nothing can stop it—not science or the law."

15

Words Coming Back

STILL TUESDAY

Tammy arrived late on Tuesday, angry at herself. She prided herself on reliability. Tammy Oakes, the rock. But today she had lost it with her daughter Tierra over money. What else? The girl was starting college in a week and was going crazy with online shopping for clothes. Tammy had exploded when Tierra asked to use her credit card yet again.

"I have the money!" Tierra snapped. "I earned it myself! I can pay you back."

"What about the computer I bought you? What about tuition loans? Are you gonna pay me back twelve grand?"

The argument went on and on, until Tammy finally broke down and gave in, as she always did with Tierra. Then kicked herself the whole drive over to the Thorndike house, gripping the steering wheel, barely paying attention to the road. She couldn't believe she was taking her baby girl off to college in a week. Her only child she'd raised herself, a widow mom, guiding her through childhood and adolescence, keeping her out of trouble. Tierra was a little headstrong, but she was a good girl in a time and place where it was so easy to turn out bad. She'd stayed away from the druggies and slackers and set her sights on the School of Pharmacy. She was going to make her mama proud. Only thing was, Tammy didn't know how she could live without her baby girl.

She drove past Cass leaving and pulled into the house to park.

"Didn't think you was coming," Loretta greeted her in the kitchen.

"You know I'd call," Tammy defended herself.

"We just had a visit from the sheriff. You better sit down." They both did, in the platform rockers in the bay, while Loretta unspooled like high-tension wire coming unsprung. Tammy had known Loretta her whole life. They were some kind of distant cousins and had gone to the same high school, Loretta just a couple years behind Tammy. Loretta had been a little wild in high school, but motherhood had settled her down quick. She'd unburdened herself to Tammy when she was going through that thing with Beaver, and Tammy had advised her to stay strong and hang onto her marriage. Tammy had defended Loretta when Cass questioned her. And it had gone both ways. Loretta had been a comfort to Tammy when first her mom and then her dad had died the year before, leaving Tammy and Tierra alone in the world. Tammy liked Loretta and didn't have the heart to tell her what a mess of trouble Loretta had got them all into now. She just listened to her recount the visit from the sheriff.

"The worst of it," Loretta said, "is that after I left here last night, I went to see Trisha."

"What would you do a thing like that for? My God!" Tammy burst out.

When Loretta had finished her tale of the calamitous visit, she admitted, "I don't know what to do, Tammy. Pretty soon the whole county's going to know what we done. Should I go to the sheriff and tell him it was all me? Should I run away and try to hide? I don't know where I'd go."

"Just sit tight. Wait and see. Nothing else we can do now." Although the idea of Loretta taking all the blame was tempting, Tammy didn't think it would work. On top of everything else that was worrying Tammy, now she had to face a new tribulation. How could she have let this happen? She could have found another job. She'd been giving care to elders for years, long before she started with the Major. Right after her husband died, she'd got her first job, leaving the baby in her mother's care. One thing Sinkhole County had in abundance was old people needing help. She regretted not stopping this fiasco the night the Major died, when somehow they'd all got hypnotized by Loretta's energy.

"Hume knows about it," Loretta said. "He figured it out when he came here last week. I went to see him on Saturday." She described her dash to the clinic.

"Cass know any of this?"

"No. I ain't told nobody but you, not even Beaver."

"You've been running around a lot. Time to keep still and take a break. Maybe we'll think of something." Tammy wasn't optimistic.

They heard a car pull up outside, followed by a car door slamming.

"Who's this?" Loretta asked.

"I reckon it's that new therapist, to work on his speech. Remember?"

"I plumb forgot!" Loretta said, jumping up. "Don't look like we're getting a break today." She raced to the front room to turn off the TV and warn the Major yet again.

Tammy followed after her just as a knock came at the front door. Tammy opened it to let in this new challenge in a day that had already been too full of them. But she'd told Loretta there was nothing to do but face them. She just hoped Loretta could keep her cool. The therapist was no one she knew. "Come on in. He's ready for you."

The trim young woman followed Tammy into the front room. Tammy and Loretta hovered nearby, watching and waiting. "Hello, Major Thorndike. I'm Sarah. I'm an occupational therapist. I'm here to help you with your speech." She spoke slowly and clearly, in a normal tone, not loud. "How are you?"

She waited for an answer. Tammy and Loretta waited. All three women were still standing, as if unsure of where to settle themselves. The old man looked up at the therapist, furrowed his brow and frowned. The silence gathered oppressively in the room. Loretta looked as though she were about to break it, so Tammy put a hand on her shoulder and shook her head. The therapist, studying the patient, didn't pay attention to the caregivers. Finally she asked, "Can you say *Hi Sarah*?"

"… Pie Sarah?"

Tammy suppressed a gasp. It was the most coherent response she'd heard from the old man. She glanced at Loretta, feeling uneasy. Loretta was staring at the Major, as if willing him to shut up.

"Very good." Again, the therapist's tone was even, not condescending. "I'd like to do a few simple tests. To understand your speech problems better. May I sit down?"

Before the Major could answer, Loretta pulled a chair up to the tray table at the head of the bed where the Major was lounging. Sarah sat in it, while Loretta and Tammy took chairs by the foot of the bed. Sarah took an iPad out of her bag. "I'm going to make some notes while we talk. Our first test. Can you touch your nose?"

Tammy and Loretta watched in suspense while the Major appeared to ponder this question, then slowly drew out a hand and placed a finger on his nose.

"Good. You used your left hand. Has he always been left-handed?" she turned to ask the caregivers.

"No," Loretta answered quickly. "He's right-handed. He's only been favoring the left since the TIA, but he still has plenty of strength in the right."

What would the therapist make of this, Tammy wondered.

"OK. Now, Major, can you open your mouth and close your eyes?"

Again they watched him take in this command. Tammy felt she could see the wheels turning in his brain. Grudgingly, he complied, opening his mouth, darting his glance left and right, then closing his eyes. He held them shut for three beats, then flew them open.

"Your comprehension seems good. We're not talking about global aphasia here," she said, directing this comment to the caregivers. "If you can understand, you should be able to learn to speak again."

"Oh he can understand just fine," Loretta volunteered. "He don't *want* to talk."

"Really? Was he a reluctant talker before the stroke?"

Oh Lord, Loretta, Tammy thought, *now what are you getting us into?*

"No," Loretta admitted. "He loved to talk your ear off."

"The stroke was when?" The therapist looked down at her iPad. "Over a week ago. He should have gone to the hospital right away." She sounded accusing.

"He refused! We tried to call 911. He grabbed the phone right out of my hand!" Loretta was getting all worked up.

"Really? In the middle of a stroke he did that?"

Tammy knew from her own experience that a stroke victim was more likely to be experiencing paralysis and confusion than grabbing telephones. Loretta burst into tears. "She's remembering a different time," Tammy said, trying to cover. "She's been so upset, blaming herself. I was here that night. We didn't realize the severity of what was happening, he'd had so many TIAs, and he would always recover the next day." Tammy stood up and pulled Loretta to her feet. "Excuse us a moment." She practically dragged Loretta out of the room, closing the door behind her. In the kitchen, she ran water.

"You got to pull yourself together," she said in a low, soothing voice. "I'm going back in there. You stay here for now."

Back in the front room, Tammy didn't know what she'd missed. The therapist was focused on her patient now.

"Major," Sarah said, "Would you like to learn to talk again?"

Major looked down at his hands, resting on top of the blanket, then up at the therapist. He nodded slowly. Then he looked at Tammy, and shook his head.

"Maybe he don't know," Tammy suggested.

"Let's start simple," Sarah said. She picked up the water glass sitting on the tray table. "What is this?"

The old man stared at her stonily. Tammy felt sorry for him. It felt like an interrogation.

After a long wait Sarah asked, "Can you say *glass*?"

He thought about it, opened his mouth experimentally, and said, "Ass."

Tammy kept a straight face. Major smiled. Sarah, keeping her tone easy and pleasant, said, "That's close." She held up her hand and tapped it with her other finger several times, asking, "What is this?"

Major smiled again. "Ass."

Tammy wondered if he was playing with the therapist. Sarah was unperturbed. "Hand," she said.

"... Hand," he finally repeated, clearly enunciated. Tammy felt an unpleasant tingle along her spine.

Sarah clapped her hands together several times. "What am I doing?" she asked.

He said nothing. All eyes were on him. Sarah clapped a few more times. After another long wait she said, "Clap hands."

The Major shook his head.

"I think he's tired," Tammy said.

"Let's try something different." Sarah pulled a deck of large cards out of her bag. "Flash cards," she explained. "I'm going to show you some pictures of animals. Tell me the name of the animal." She held a card out for Major to see.

He studied it a bit and said, "Gorp."

"Close. Can you say *horse*?"

He sighed and said in a low voice, as if struggling, "Horse."

"Very good." She put the card down and held out another. "What is this?"

Tammy looked at her watch. The therapist had been there for nearly twenty minutes, but it felt like an hour. The old man finally got out another word, "Gorp."

Sarah said, "Can you say *cow*?"

"Gow." His voice was sullen.

"He usually has his supper and goes to bed about now," Tammy interjected. "We didn't expect you so late in the day."

"I understand. We'll finish up. Just one more." She held out the card.

This time without hesitation Major replied, "Deer."

"Wonderful! I'm going to leave the flash cards with your caregivers so they can practice with you." She made more notes in her iPad, then stood up. "I'll see you again on Thursday morning. I'll catch you when you're fresh."

After the therapist had gone, and Loretta had recovered to help give Major his supper, clean him up, and get him ready for bed, Tammy and Loretta once again collapsed into the platform rockers in the bay.

"What happens if he actually learns to communicate?" Loretta said. Tammy had filled her in on the progress he'd made with the therapist.

"You know him better than any of us," Tammy said. "What do you think?"

"I think we're fucked."

Lyle got them to leave him alone as soon as he could. Didn't even want Woman around. Too much talking. Wore him out. Headache. And that chest pain that wouldn't quit. He lay back on the pillow and closed his eyes, savoring the darkness. He saw the deer in the picture the Interrogator showed him. Eight-point buck. Words coming back. Best days of his life, spent in his hunting camp.

Long ago, when Lyle was a young man, he'd bought himself a school bus when the county had a fire sale. School buses had to go when they reached 100,000 miles, even in a poorass state like West Virginia. Bus still ran, and Lyle drove it as far up the mountain on an old deer path as he could, then parked it. Fitted it out with a wood stove and old mattress. Thanksgiving week, when his Ma was still alive and he was expected to show up at the dinner table with the brothers and cousins he couldn't abide, he took instead to the woods. With his sleeping bag, a bottle of Early Times, and his rifle, he holed up in the old bus. Oh how peaceful it was to be alone in the woods, the branches stark and bare, the forest floor thick with fallen leaves, sometimes with early snow. He'd be up before dawn to climb to his tree stand above the path, with his rifle and ammo and bottle of whiskey, to sit in quiet meditation and await his prey.

The deer would come sliding by on tiptoe, or leaping in bounds. They'd formed into herds in the early fall, the bucks in theirs, the does and their fawns in their separate ones, each to his own. He'd watch a whole parade of woodland creatures—songbirds, crows, turkeys, eagles, raccoons, possums, foxes, bobcats—while waiting for the right buck to pass below his stand. He favored the mature buck, not just for the rack, though the rack gave satisfaction, but because of the amount of meat to fill his freezer. Some argued that younger bucks were more tender, but if you field dressed the big boy proper, he tasted splendid, chewed easily, and his steaks and roasts were double the size of the young forkhorn.

Lyle was good at killing his buck with a clean shot. He'd dress it and hang it from a tree limb, slice off a bit of tenderloin, and cook it over his gas grill outside the bus. He could stay out in the woods ten days, field dressing and hanging, taking out his kill as needed to get it tagged. He never missed human companionship when he was in the woods.

Even after he met and married Annabel, she understood his need for solitude. She never complained when he left her to go to his hunting camp, or to walk all day through the mountains with a rifle over his shoulder.

16

Up Mud Lick Hollow

OCTOBER, 2013

The first time Loretta had seen Lyle was nearly a year before he became the Major. He was sprawled on the floor of Dixon's IGA, in the canned goods aisle. Wayne Dixon was kneeling by him, trying to rouse him. But the old fellow was out cold. Wayne looked up at her and said, "Loretta, aren't you a nurse? Can you do CPR? Help us out."

Loretta couldn't believe her eyes, the old man on the floor looked so much like the Major. But he couldn't be. She had just come from the Thorndike house, where Major was in a tizzy because they'd run out of chocolate pudding and he couldn't take his pills without it. She'd been sent on a fast run to the store. "What happened?" she said, dropping down beside Wayne. "I'm no nurse." But she took his wrist and felt for a pulse. "His heart's beating. Did he trip and hit his head?"

"I don't know. I heard a thump and found him like this." They looked for signs of his fall. The shelves beside them were undisturbed. The old man's cart was loaded with cans of beans and franks, spaghetti and meatballs, creamed corn, three loaves of Holsum white bread, two dozen eggs.

"Looks like he was stocking up," Loretta said. No blood on the cart. No contusions she could find on his skull.

"I'm calling 911," Wayne said.

Loretta decided to wait with Wayne for the ambulance, out of a mix of curiosity and responsibility. She wasn't a nurse, but the closest thing to it out of the two girls at the registers and the few other shoppers in the store. "Who is he? You know him?"

"A little. He just started coming in six months ago, after his wife died. I knew her better."

"He could be the identical twin of my employer, Major Thorndike."

"Really? I haven't seen the Major in years. These old guys aren't much for doing the marketing. This one is a hard case, from what his wife Annabel told me—no kids, family all dead or in prison or moved to other parts." Wayne nattered on while Loretta stared at the old man, only barely listening. Annabel Dunbar had met Lyle at a Billie Edd Wheeler concert at the state fair sometime in the '60s. She'd come all the way over from Virginia by herself. They must have been the only two unattached young people at the concert—well, Lyle wasn't so young by then. His mother had just died, and he'd run his no-good brothers off and was trying to raise cattle on a little patch of family land. He and Annabel happened to sit next to each other. "It was destined to be, Annabel told me," Wayne said with a chuckle. It was typical of Wayne to hold forth. He was a great talker. Everyone for miles around shopped at his IGA, and he collected their stories the way other men collected hunting trophies. Loretta didn't want to think about what he told people about her.

They saw the ambulance pull up in front of the store. Shoppers gathered around as the medics came in, rolling a stretcher. Loretta decided it was time for her to skedaddle. She bought the chocolate pudding and hurried on back to the Thorndikes'.

Four days later her cellphone rang at 8:30 in the morning. Caller ID said Dixon's IGA. What on earth?

"Loretta, this is Wayne Dixon, wondering if you can do a favor. You remember that old guy who passed out in the store on Monday?"

She did. She hadn't been able to get him out of her head, with his uncanny resemblance to the Major. She'd told Tammy about it Monday evening.

"Sweetwater Valley called. It was a stroke, but they say that Lyle's recovered and they're discharging him. Only thing is, they can't find anyone to come pick him up. His truck is still in my parking lot, so they called me. I'm at the store waiting on a delivery. Can you go up to the hospital and get him and bring him here?"

"Wayne, I got to be at work at three."

"You'll be back in time. That old man doesn't have a soul on earth to care about him. It seems I'm the only one in the county that even knows who he is."

Loretta's tender heart couldn't resist this plea, not to mention she was drawn by something that seemed, later, like fate. An hour after Wayne's call she was at the hospital, where she was confronted at the nurse's station by the discharge planner.

"He's going to need follow-up care. What's your relationship to the patient?"

Loretta, naturally suspicious of hospitals, didn't want to explain she was a total stranger, so she invented. "Niece."

"That's funny. No family listed on his admissions form." She had a stack of papers on the counter between them. Her nametag said *Sue Morgan, MSW.*

"Our families were out of touch until Wayne called to tell us what happened."

"Physically, he's in remarkable shape. It was an ischemic stroke, caught in good time. Medication broke up the clot right away. The CT scan showed infarcts in the left hemisphere of the brain and a blockage of the left carotid artery that was cleared. There's no paralysis, very little weakness. Physical therapists have worked with him. He'll be kept on anticoagulants; you have the prescriptions in your discharge package. Will he be going home with you?"

"I'm taking him to his house."

"Medicare will pay for some home care, but you'll need to look after him. He needs speech therapy. Call us to schedule that." The woman, Sue Morgan, had been flipping through the stack of papers as she spoke. "We need you to sign for him."

A nurse came toward them, guiding the old man by one arm. Loretta felt on display, watched by the discharge planner and everyone else in the nurse's station.

"Hi, Uncle Lyle," she said. "You don't remember me, but Wayne Dixon sent me to pick you up. We're going to take you home."

He stared at her in confusion, without uttering a sound.

"Don't he talk?" she asked.

"His speech should come back in a couple of weeks," Sue Morgan said. "Come with me and we'll go over his discharge summary, med list, and follow-up together. I'm not sure how much he understands."

A half hour later, Loretta took Lyle's arm and two large envelopes Sue Morgan gave her, and he hobbled with her out to her car, limping a little. On the ride back to Amity she put on the radio. "What kind of music do you like?" she asked. He didn't answer. Did he hear her? It was eerie. She needed the radio to fill the silence and turned to the country station. She called Wayne when she got to Amity, and he was standing out in the parking lot when she pulled into the IGA. She rolled the windows down and Wayne said, "You're looking better, Lyle. Glad to be out of the hospital?"

The old man looked up at Wayne and still said nothing.

"He ain't talking, Wayne. Plus, the hospital told me he can't drive."

"That's too bad. Lyle, I need the key to your truck. You got it on you?"

"Gah?" The sound came out strangled, as if forced out with great effort.

"That sounds like an answer of some kind," Wayne said.

Loretta reached into the backseat of her car. "The hospital gave me his personal stuff in this envelope. Think we ought to open it?"

"OK if we open this for you, Lyle?" Wayne asked. He was standing at Lyle's window. Loretta was still in the driver's seat.

"Gah?"

"I guess we got to open it," Wayne said.

Loretta ripped open the fat manila envelope, pulled out a worn leather wallet and the truck key. "There's something else," she said, shaking the envelope. A check fluttered out.

"His Social Security," Wayne said. "Bet you were planning on cashing that when you bought your groceries, huh Lyle?"

"Gah?"

"Why don't I cash it for you. Loretta, can you give me five minutes in the store? Then I'll drive his truck and you follow to bring me back."

Loretta sighed. This was turning into more than she'd bargained for. But she handed Wayne Lyle's wallet and he disappeared inside the store. They waited in the shade of the IGA next to Lyle's battered pickup truck, the windows of Loretta's car rolled down to let in the fresh September morning. Loretta studied the old man. He had more hair on him than the Major, scraggly and silver grey. He had the same furrowed brow, the same high cheekbones, the same beaked nose, but his skin was rougher, ruddier.

"Lyle," she said. The name felt strange to her. "Can you understand me?"

He didn't answer, just pursed his lips as if biting down on words.

"Can you nod your head yes if you understand me?"

He nodded twice.

"Well now! That's a relief. Can you shake your head for no?"

He shook.

"Now we're off to the races in a souped-up Cadillac."

Wayne came out, carrying two shopping bags that he put in Lyle's truck. "I got you a few groceries, Lyle." He walked around to Loretta's window and said, "It's about a half hour up to his place. I was up there a couple times when Annabel's truck broke and I had to give her a ride."

With Lyle beside her, Loretta followed Wayne out of town, windows down, radio on the country station. They drove south past Boiling Spring, turned off the two-lane onto a narrow blacktop road that passed open rolling pasture, then hit the woods and started climbing a ridge, over a fold in the mountains, where a sign said Mud Lick Hollow. A boulder-strewn dirt road led them up the creek to a small clearing, where there were pastures, a pond, a barn. The road ended at a one-story cabin built of unpainted vertical boards, a weathered grey, with an ample porch spanning its width. "Can't go no further," Loretta said, and parked next to the truck.

She helped Lyle out of her car and up the steps of the porch, Wayne following with the groceries. At the door she waited for Lyle to do something, but he hesitated as if in confusion. So she tried the door and it opened. Her first impression was mildew, dirt, and decay. Stained pillows covered the sagging springs of a threadbare couch. A rocking chair was missing an armrest. Cobwebs laced the corners of the moldy ceiling and the legs of the cast-iron wood stove. Dead flies lay piled in the windowsills. Through a doorway to the right, a path of muddy footprints had dried to dust across the peeling linoleum of the kitchen. Lyle limped into the kitchen after Loretta, followed by Wayne, who put the grocery bags on the counter. "You want to put these away for him?"

At least the kitchen counter was wiped clean. A pot in the sink was filled with water soaking some brown sludge, where more dead flies floated. Faded print curtains on the window over the sink must have been the wife's touch, Loretta figured, a pattern from long ago. Red cherries against a white background matched the red formica countertop. She imagined the wife who'd sewed and hung them, who wasn't there to mop and sweep any more. The sight of the cherries nearly broke Loretta's heart. She put the canned goods in the mostly empty cupboard and laid out the loaves of bread on the counter.

"You want to freeze some of this bread, Lyle?"

He didn't reply, so she opened the freezer compartment at the top of the fridge. It was caked with ice and otherwise empty. She stuck in two loaves of bread.

"At least the power's on," Wayne commented. He put some envelopes on the counter. "I found these in his truck.

Bills. He must have been planning to pay them after he cashed his check at the store."

"Lorda mercy Lyle! How are you going to take care of yourself?" She opened the refrigerator. It stank of sour milk and rotten vegetables. She quickly stashed the eggs and closed it. "Is the phone working?"

Wayne picked up the receiver hanging on the kitchen wall. "Yup. It's got dial tone."

"I tell you what," Loretta said, coming to a quick decision. "I got to go to work now. But if it's OK with Lyle, I'll take those bills and pay them with money from his check. I'll fill his prescription and come back tomorrow to clean this place up and see how he's doing. OK?"

Both Loretta and Wayne looked at the old man.

"Gah."

"That don't mean much to me," Loretta said, putting her hands on Lyle's shoulders and leaning in close. "Can you nod or shake your head? Do you want me to come back tomorrow?"

Lyle nodded.

"Men shouldn't outlive their wives," Loretta said, driving Wayne back to Amity. "It's a mistake."

"I'll keep that in mind."

In addition to the bills and Lyle's money, Loretta had a bunch of dirty clothes and towels she'd gathered up in his bedroom and bathroom. She could throw them in her washer and dryer when she got home from work tonight. On the dresser she'd seen a basket of yarn and needles and a half-knit sweater. On the floor a stack of knitting magazines had fallen over.

"I wonder what he's been doing with himself since she died," Loretta said.

"For one thing, he's been chopping wood." In back they'd found a chainsaw and a stack of fresh-split firewood. "He'll need that, come winter."

"If he makes it to winter."

The old man was still in bed when Loretta returned mid-morning of the following day, bringing with her cleaning supplies and his clean and folded laundry. "Wake up and hear the birdies sing!" she called out. He stopped snoring and opened his eyes, looking frightened. "You sleep until ten every day?"

"Gah."

"Now we're having us a conversation."

He'd slept in his clothes. Hygiene would have to come later; she didn't have time today. She cooked him fried eggs with toast for breakfast, then set to work vacuuming, mopping, and scrubbing while he watched her. It was a small house, but the grime was deep. After several hours she'd done what she could. She left the mop and bucket and broom on the small back porch off the kitchen. "Are you able to make yourself supper?" she asked him.

She got a can of spaghetti and meatballs out of the cabinet, gave him the can opener she'd found in a drawer, and said, "I want to see you open the can."

He struggled with the can and had to use both hands to squeeze the jaws of the opener together, but he finally got it to puncture the lid. With effort he held on with one hand and turned the crank with the other, inching the can around most of the way.

"That'll do. Now all you have to do when you get hungry is heat it up. Or eat it straight from the can. I'm coming back tomorrow to make sure you take your pills, and I'll clean out your fridge. OK?"

"Gah."

"Then I guess we can call that number the hospital gave us." Loretta was reluctant for the home-care people to see Lyle's circumstances. She wondered if her name on his discharge form made her somehow legally responsible for him.

He didn't respond but followed her into the living room, where she picked up her vacuum cleaner and looked around at her handiwork. "Looks a lot better. Nice rack of antlers you got." A huge ten-pointer hung on the wall over the wood stove. "You shoot that buck?"

Lyle nodded and smiled.

That evening Loretta told Beaver about Lyle. It was late and she was tired after working twelve straight hours without a break except for driving from one job to the other. Not that Lyle's was a job. It was more a mission of mercy.

"Nobody should have to live that way," she told Beaver. "Even in our hardest times we've had family to help us through."

"You're going back there *tomorrow*?!" Beaver exclaimed. "Don't you have enough to do around the house, Loretta, you have to go work for some stranger for no pay?"

"Tiffany helps me around the house." Since Tiffany's graduation from high school the previous June, one of Loretta's hardest unpaid jobs was over. Now she only had one child left to push, drag, harangue, and bully through school—and Junior was proving to be even more of a challenge than his older sisters. Loretta was proud of Tiffany, who sat with them at the large kitchen table that Beaver had built. He'd done a masterful job of remodeling the kitchen of their modest ranch house. They'd bought the house new in the mid '90s, and they'd almost lost it to foreclosure when they fell behind in their mortgage payments, but the bank renegotiated and they'd squeaked through, as they always did, by sticking together and working their tails off. Beaver had paneled two kitchen walls with rustic boards he'd rescued from old barns. Her family lived in this kitchen, around the kitchen table. Tiffany was with them now, sharing a late-night pizza with her father. Beaver had come home hungry from work. He'd gone back to work for Hard Rock Construction when Loretta had relented and forgiven him his misstep. "Tiffany, you want to come with me tomorrow and help clean out Lyle's fridge?"

"Can't, Mom. I got a babysitting job."

Another good thing about Tiffany. She was always earning.

"You got to draw the line, Loretta," Beaver said. "You can't be working for this old guy for no pay."

"He doesn't have that kind of money. He's living on Social Security."

Next morning when she arrived at the head of Mud Lick Hollow, Lyle was waiting for her, sitting out on his front porch. "Got up early this morning, I see," she greeted him. They went inside so Loretta could turn off the refrigerator and let it start defrosting. She noted that Lyle seemed to be walking more easily, limping less. That was a good sign.

"I'm going to empty this fridge out and clean it good. Meanwhile I want you to take a shower and put on clean clothes." He was still wearing the same clothes he'd been wearing the last two days. "Can you manage the shower?"

"Gah."

Loretta sighed. "When you going to learn to talk, Lyle?"

She went with him into the bathroom. "I'm just going to get you started. Let me see you unbutton your shirt."

He started with the bottom button, fumbled around a while, and got it unbuttoned. He worked his way up from button to button while she watched. When he'd gotten the shirt undone she said, "OK. Take it off. Don't worry, I seen a man's chest before."

He pulled off the shirt and dropped it on the floor.

"Sheesh! You born in a barn, Lyle?" She picked up the shirt. "Imma start you a laundry basket. I'll leave you to take your pants off by yourself. You can set on the toilet lid if it'll make it easier. Can you work the spigots?" She opened the shower curtain and started the hot water. "Yell if you need help." Could he yell?

Cleaning out the fridge, dumping the rotten food in a garbage bag to take home with her, and restocking with stuff that looked nontoxic took a couple hours. Meanwhile, Lyle managed to shower and dress himself and came in to watch her work. He sure had got stuck on her, poor lonely man. When she was done, she sat him down at his little kitchen table and put his money, still in the Social Security envelope, his wallet, and his truck key in front of him. "I paid your bills and spent a little of your money on supplies you need to get you through. Check it out, it's all here."

He shuffled through the money and shoved it away like he wasn't interested. She slid it into his wallet. "I got you a box for your pills. It's got a section for every day of the week. You take them every morning at breakfast. Can you do that?"

He nodded as if he understood. She wondered, and put the box on the counter.

"Now we're going to call the home-care people. They're going to send someone up here to help you." She didn't wait for his permission but took out the discharge papers from the envelope still on the kitchen table. She kept the conversation as short as she could and made his appointment for the next day. "It's the last house up Mud Lick Holler. You can't miss it. He'll be waiting for you."

After she hung up she said to Lyle, "You want me to come back and check on you in a week?"

He nodded eagerly.

She worried about him through the week. When she returned, she had to rouse him from sleep again. Dirty clothes were tumbled on the floor, opened cans were left out on the counter, dirty dishes in the sink. At least he'd been changing his clothes, she thought. It didn't smell like he'd showered again. The pill box was empty, and she hoped he'd taken them in order. He'd been eating, but not as much as she'd like. Two loaves of bread were still in the freezer. She took one out. She cooked him breakfast and sat him down at the table. "What you been doing all week, Lyle?" she asked, sitting across from him.

He puckered up his forehead and looked pained. "Gah," he said.

"That all? You still haven't got your speech back? That ain't good. Did that therapist come?"

He shook his head sorrowfully. That made her mad. She found the number for Home Care Plus and called to complain. When she finally got someone on the line who knew about Lyle Dunbar, that person said, "Miz Hardwick, your uncle refused treatment."

"What do you mean. He can't talk. How could he refuse anything?"

"He stood in his doorway and aimed a shotgun at the therapist. His meaning was clear."

"Oh dear."

"She left."

"Is Lyle in trouble?" Loretta asked, and added to herself, *Am I?*

"The patient has a right to refuse treatment. It's in the Patient Bill of Rights in your discharge package."

"Will his speech come back if he don't get the therapy?"

"I have no way of knowing."

"I'll talk to him, see if I can change his mind."

"Miz Hardwick, your uncle is at risk of having another stroke. This is very serious, especially if he's on his own, as he appears to be. He must take his medications."

"He's been taking them. I seen to that. But I can't be here all the time." The woman was making Loretta feel guilty. She regretted claiming to be his niece.

"He would qualify for a residential treatment program. Did they explain that to you at discharge?"

"We thought he wanted to go home."

"There's still time if he changes his mind."

"Lord, Lyle!" she exclaimed when she got off the phone with Home Care Plus. "What have you got yourself into?"

Sitting across from her at the kitchen table, he just smiled.

"What are you going to do, up here all by yourself? You can't drive in this condition."

Silence. He looked at her patiently.

"Am I the only one you're gonna let through your door?"

He smiled.

She thought for a bit. The envelope from Social Security was still sitting on the table where she'd left it. She found a pencil in a drawer. "Can you write?"

He took the pencil awkwardly, tried it in his right, then his left, then his right hand. Then switched again to the left. She pointed to the envelope. "Can you write your name?"

He drew a scrawl. Another scrawl. Then put the pencil down and shook his head.

"You're going to need help. Someone to remind you to take a bath and clean your place up for you, bring you groceries. I could do it, if you want." He looked at her; his face brightened. "Only thing is, Lyle, I got a family. I got bills to pay. I know you don't have much, I seen your check. If I come up here once a week for a few hours, could you give me thirty-five dollars out of your next check?" Loretta hated to ask, but she couldn't face Beaver if she didn't.

Lyle nodded. Lyle smiled.

"Just until you're back on your feet."

17

Hell Hath No Fury

Waiting was killing Trisha. Two days had gone by since she dropped the letter off at the sheriff's office. In her mind she'd gone over Loretta's strange visit to her house a hundred times, testing and revising various theories. She'd harbored suspicions of foul play for a long time, ever since her firing, which came right after the Major had told her he would be speaking to his lawyer about setting aside a bequest—he'd called it small!—of $100,000 for her in his will. She'd nearly fainted. All he could afford to give her, he said, but enough, he hoped, to make her life a little more comfortable. She'd wept with gratitude, quietly, in private. She wasn't going to tell the other caregivers and suffer their jealousy. She hadn't even told her husband, as if talking about it would make her good fortune vanish. She had guarded her secret until the Major could make it official.

Before he could, just days later, she was fired. By Ruth, over the phone. Unfairly! Had Ruth found out about his intention and decided to block him from carrying it out? Ruth had cut her off from all communication with the Major. She'd tried to call him, only to have Cass answer—screening his calls, no doubt—and threaten her with a restraining order. For what? There was no one she could turn to for justice.

The day she was fired she broke down in tears and told her husband everything. "It must be because of the hundred thousand," she'd said.

"What hundred thousand?" Jason had asked. She'd explained about the bequest for her years of devoted service. But Jason hadn't reacted with the support she needed. Instead he'd said, "You're better off out of that house. We don't need their charity."

Jason and his pride! Jason hated the Major. Sometimes she wondered if there was a little jealousy there, but he said it was because he hated the way the Major treated her. Years earlier, before Miss Beatrice died, Major had blown up and yelled at Trisha for taking time off to care for Christopher, her dying son. Trisha had fled his tirade in tears. Oh, Major could be mean when he was in a temper, but later he'd apologized and she'd forgiven him. Jason never forgave him.

When she told her son Bradley about the hundred thousand the Major had promised her, he said, "That's a lot of money! Are you sure?" Bradley had a way of doubting that irked her.

"He has a lot of money." She'd seen the Major's Morgan Stanley statements.

"Did anybody hear him tell you? Any witnesses?"

"Nobody. I was alone with him, letting him tell me stories and being kind to him the way I always was, and he told me how much he appreciated my paying attention to an old man and how could he ever repay me, and that's when he came up with the bequest idea and promised to call his lawyer the very next day."

"He was pretty moody and on a lot of meds. He probably didn't mean it, Mom."

So she had moved on. Because her caring for the Major had never been about the money. But she monitored what went on in the Thorndike household through the rumor mill. She knew that Beaver Hardwick had gone back to work, that Tammy's mother and father had died within six months of each other, that her former best friend Andrea had gone missing—she had her suspicions about that but these didn't involve the Major—and that Cass had divorced her husband. This last made Trisha more suspicious of Cass than ever. And how could Ruth not be suspicious as well? Unless Ruth was somehow in on the plot.

Then came the supposed stroke, almost two weeks ago. Was it for real or part of the plot? She kept thinking of poison. Maybe Ruth was trying to hurry up her father's death—Trisha read a lot of murder mysteries—before he could marry Cass. Maybe Ruth was in league with Loretta (everyone knew that Ruth had a soft spot for Loretta), manipulating her from afar. And then Loretta had got cold feet and come to Trisha.

Could Loretta be the one who was secretly poisoning the Major? There would be a big cash reward in it from Ruth. He took so many meds; who would notice a daily dose of arsenic in his pudding?

Trisha prowled the streets of Amity, her senses on alert, waiting for the sheriff to take action. She drove past the courthouse several times a day to see the sheriff's car parked in its usual spot in back, as if he had no urgent business. Hadn't he read the letter? "An elder crime is being committed in Sinkhole

County," it said. It was as if she'd dropped a bomb and still hadn't felt its seismic boom. Or maybe a better analogy was she'd lit a fuse that was sizzling its way toward the bomb. In a town the size of Amity, the spark should have made it to the bomb by now but instead seemed to be circling the globe or lost in the forest or ...what?

She tried to slow her thoughts down. She stopped into the pharmacy for a long chat with Jeanie, who liked to fill her in on the town's illnesses. Toward the end of their gossip Trisha asked if there was any news about the Major's condition. Nothing that Jeanie knew. "You know I never stop worrying about him," Trisha said.

"You took care of him a long time," Jeanie offered sympathetically.

"Once you've taken care of someone, you just can't turn it off. Even when people are cruel to you. There are some over in that house who have been very cruel. I had the strangest visit from Loretta Hardwick earlier this week. She told me the Major wants to leave Amity."

"Really?"

"Hard to believe, isn't it. I just hope those girls aren't doing anything to drive him away."

"Now why would they do that?"

"Exactly. Let me know if you hear anything." The street door opened and someone came in. They were no longer alone.

"Did you have something you're picking up?" Jeanie asked Trisha.

"I was just passing by. But that reminds me, I need to go by Dr. Nightingale's and pick up a new prescription for Jason. I better run." She hurried out, feeling the pressure of her racing thoughts. Her next stop was Dixon's IGA. She'd just been there the day before on her weekly shopping run, but somehow had forgotten kitty litter. Plus Wayne Dixon knew more about what went on in Amity than anyone else she knew.

Pushing her cart around the IGA she ran into Wayne in the dairy section holding a clipboard, and asked after his wife and kids. He hadn't been in the store the day before and she hadn't seen him in at least a week, during which any number of calamities could have befallen the Dixons. But they were all fine, and he in turn asked about her family.

"Struggling, you know. Jason and Christopher aren't getting any better, and even if I wanted to work outside the home they couldn't spare me. I do miss getting out, though; I'm practically a shut-in these days."

"You should try and get out more," Wayne agreed. "Why, hello Maggie." He turned to greet another customer coming at them down the aisle.

Worried she would lose her hold on his attention, Trisha plunged ahead. "Do you know anything about what's going on with Major Thorndike? I've heard the most terrible things about his health, and you know I still care about him. Then Loretta Hardwick came by my house in the middle of the night this week to tell me she wished I was still working there because she thinks Cass is mismanaging his meds and making his condition worse."

"Does she?"

"Have you seen Loretta? Has she said anything to you?"

"I see Loretta regularly. Haven't heard anything unusual. You'll have to excuse me. I have to get this order in." He moved away with his clipboard, with a little too much eagerness to be done with the conversation. Trisha's radar detected that he was withholding something, some information about Loretta or the Major. Frustrated that her approach with him had been wrong, she pushed her cart with its lone bag of kitty litter toward the checkout aisle.

She was too impatient to stop at the Family Dollar, although it was another good source of gossip, and went straight to Dr. Nightingale's office. While she waited for the doctor, she chatted up the doctor's loose-lipped son, more and more desperate for some sort of news. "Has your mother been out to see Major Thorndike this week?"

"She went yesterday to get more blood for a test. The first one didn't come out right."

"Blood test for what?" Would arsenic show up in a blood test?

"Figure out why he's not talking."

"He *still* isn't talking! Don't you think he should be in the hospital?" She said this rather loudly, knowing that Dr. Nightingale didn't have hospital privileges. The doctor claimed this gave her more time to treat her patients at home, characterizing herself as a large-hearted old-fashioned doctor who knew all her patients personally. But Trisha suspected that she deliberately steered people away from more expert care in order to keep those Medicare checks coming. Her suspicions were running through her mind as Dr. Nightingale herself came out of her office and handed Trisha the prescription for Jason.

"You know, Mrs. Vance, I can phone this in to the pharmacy. You didn't have to come in person." She said this in a way that made Trisha feel unwelcome. After all the hours she'd spent in this waiting room with her husband and her son, and now she was being shooed out. She felt like she was exploding. She felt rage at her sad lot, indignation at how she'd been cast aside, frustration that no one listened, conviction that there was a conspiracy against her, and anxiety so intense and yet so general she couldn't identify its source. If she kept it all bottled up she'd have a stroke or heart attack herself. She left the doctor's office and took the back way out of town, determined to wait no more. Nothing could stop her now.

In her fury, she could barely see where she was going, but she didn't need to see. She knew every rise and fall on the road to the Thorndike house like her own hand, even after a year. She came to the lot full of farm equipment, and her car made the turnoff almost by itself. On the one-lane she nearly ran smack into a car coming at her. It swerved onto the shoulder and Trisha roared by, glimpsing Cass staring after her. Hah! Let her see. Trisha stomped on the gas and sped on toward the Thorndikes', screaming around blind curves. Fortunately, there were no cows wandering in the road today. Miss Beatrice used to complain about the neighboring farmer who didn't mend his fences. Just thinking about Miss Beatrice, who had trusted her, depended on her, increased Trisha's blood pressure. She pulled into the parking area by the orchard, blood pounding in her ears. She slammed her car door and marched up the path to the front porch. She barged in without knocking—doors were never locked in the Thorndike household—and charged into the front room.

Loretta and the Major stared at her in surprise, like she was a ghost. Tammy said in her flat way, "You might have called to say you was coming."

"What have they done to you, Major?" Trisha said.

"Gorum?" the Major replied. His bright eyes flashed dangerously.

Trisha came closer, peering at Major. She reached out and touched his cheek. He pulled back. "What's the matter?" she asked. "Don't you know your Trisha? Remember our song?"

She sang a bar. "You are my sunshine, my only sunshine …" Her voice fell silent. Something wasn't right. The wound on his head had healed without a scar. His face glowed with ruddy health. The look in his eyes was … wild. Full of alarm, hatred even. He didn't recognize her. He was looking at a complete stranger. Could this be her Major? She couldn't believe what her senses were telling her. She backed away. "You haven't forgotten me. You never knew me."

Was it hypnotism? Drugs? She'd thought they were poisoning him, and now she had evidence. Could this be the man she'd known and cared for? They'd done something worse than a lobotomy to him.

The front door slammed, and Cass came in. She must have turned around and come back. "I thought that was you! What are you doing here?" she demanded. "I'm going to call Hume if you're not out of here in five minutes."

"What have you done to Major? He's not himself!" Trisha countered.

Cass suddenly softened her hostility. "Now, Trisha," she said. "We tried to tell you how sick he's been. Before he lost his speech, his mind was gone. He was hallucinating. It's been hard on all of us." Cass put her arm around Trisha. "And harder on you, seeing him like this after so long." She was almost purring.

Trisha shook her off like she carried a disease. "Don't touch me!" The old man stared at them, his mouth agape. Trisha grabbed his chin and turned his face from side to side, peering at it closely. He shouted and pulled away from her.

"Now you've upset him," Cass said, trying to force herself between Trisha and the Major. Trisha saw Tammy rise up and start coming at her, a scowl on her face. Loretta hunched in the corner mute, looking guilty, looking like she wanted to hide.

"I don't believe a word coming out of any of your lying mouths!" Trisha said. "I'm getting to the bottom of this. You won't get away with it." She grabbed the medication box from the nightstand and stormed out.

"Stop!" She heard Cass yell, along with the lumbering thuds of Cass chasing her. "You're insane!" Fury gave Trisha super powers. She could outrun the bitch. She heard Tammy yelling from the porch, "Let her go! That was just a three-day supply. We got plenty more."

She dove into her car, tossed the pill box onto the passenger seat, and backed out, spitting gravel. Careening toward town she felt herself once again on the edge of explosion. She forced herself to slow down and think. Her first thought in grabbing the meds was that they were drugging him into losing his mind. Maybe it wasn't arsenic after all. She went down the list of drugs that she knew caused memory loss: benzodiazepines, statins, anticonvulsants, tricyclic antidepressants, opioids, dopamine agonists, Z drugs. She used to load the Major's pill box every Monday. She knew he was on a lot of these for his anxiety, his depression, his cholesterol, his Parkinson's, his restless leg. She was careful not to give him any drug cocktails that would exacerbate another drug's amnesic properties.

Maybe the girls were deliberately overdosing him. He shouldn't be on opioids. She'd check the box.

But halfway to town a much larger conviction had taken hold: that she had *not* seen Major Thorndike in that house. She knew every inch of her Major; she'd nursed and cared for his face and scalp, skin and teeth. The person she'd seen was like a wax model of the man she'd known. The lesion on his head was gone, his cheeks were filled out but more weather-beaten than they should be. The lips she had applied moisturizer to so many times were no longer chapped and dry. The teeth were yellower. The Major had spent more time brushing his teeth than any other human being she'd ever known. This man had muscles in his arms the Major never had, and strength when he resisted her. She felt her fury rising as she pulled up and parked in front of the courthouse.

She found Sheriff Boggs in his office and got straight to the point. "I've come from Major Thorndike's home."

"And you are?"

"You know me! Trisha Vance. I took care of Major Thorndike for six years. I know him like my own father. The man they have out there in his bed is not the real Major. They've done something to him."

"Trisha Vance. Your son had that car accident last year. I remember you got pretty hysterical."

"What mother wouldn't?"

"You also called 911 to report that a seven-year-old in your care had set fire to a cat."

Trisha felt her cheeks flaming. "That was not my fault. Child Services lied to me about that child. I'd wanted to adopt her! They told me nothing about her history and diagnosis."

"I was out at the Thorndike house this week. I spoke to his caregivers. Someone sent me a letter." He opened a file drawer and pulled it out. "Did you write this?" He showed her the letter.

Trisha sputtered. "Who told you that?"

"The caregivers. They said Major Thorndike couldn't have written this."

"You have to investigate! They've done something to the real Major Thorndike."

"What do you think they've done?"

"Put an imposter in his place. A paid actor!"

"Why would they do that?"

"I don't know!" Trisha rocked and wrung her hands. "You have to find the real Major. He may be in danger." She snatched the letter from him and ran from the room.

Wimpy little greenhorn sheriff! He didn't believe her. She was sure of that as she drove away, the letter now beside the pill box on the passenger seat. She'd drive to Charleston and give the pills to the state crime lab. It was already four o'clock. She wouldn't get to Charleston until after six. The lab would be closed. Never mind. She'd go straight to headquarters. She'd give them everything. She would tell them it was urgent. It was life and death. Speeding up the two-lane toward the interstate she called her son on her cell. "Bradley, you need to stop over at your dad's, make sure he and Christopher are OK. I'm going to be home late. It's an emergency."

She'd put some real cops on the case. Then she'd call Hume. Or maybe Ruth.

18

Crescendo

FRIDAY

I t was after lunch, and they were going to listen to "Pictures at an Exhibition," one of the more accessible CDs in his father's collection, Hume figured. He closed the door to the front room so that Kristy Mae and Dellisha couldn't spy on them. In their presence he was maintaining the fiction that the old man was his father, but he didn't want to keep pretending, now that they had finished their sandwiches and he had to sit with the silent stranger. He also hadn't bothered to bring a delicious cooked lunch. The old man sat in the easy chair in the far corner of the front room.

"This is Ravel's orchestration of a piano piece written by a Russian composer named Mussorgsky," Hume said by way of introduction, taking out the CD. "It tells the story of Mussorgsky's visit to an exhibition of paintings by an artist friend of his who had died suddenly at a young age, bumming Mussorgsky out." Hume didn't know if the old man was interested in any of this—he doubted it—but he was watching Hume with patience on his face. Hume figured a little music appreciation lesson would be a lot more tolerable than trying to engage the old man in conversation.

"In the music, a suite of ten pieces, Mussorgsky illustrates a wacky assortment of images—a ballet of unhatched chicks, a children's quarrel after games, spooky catacombs, rattling carts, and a hut belonging to Baba Yaga, who was a scary old woman in Russian folklore. Her hut stood on chicken legs. In between each 'painting' Mussorgsky wrote what he called promenades, which showed himself roving through the exhibition, moving fast or slow, depending on his mood, and thinking of his dead friend. The interesting thing" —would the old man find this interesting?— "is that most of the paintings from the original exhibition are lost; only the music survives."

With that preamble, Hume started the CD and sat down across from the old man to listen. Roger would have hated his explanation of "Pictures." He remembered going to a concert with his father in Buckfield's version of Carnegie Hall, his father suffering through the conductor's lengthy attempt to enlighten the audience on how to listen to the piece the orchestra was about to play. Roger's eyes had closed in an attempt to block out the odious conductor. "I don't blame you," the stranger sitting next to him had said after the concert. "Classical music always puts me to sleep."

"Then what, pray tell, are you doing here when you could be at home in your log cabin listening to Merle Haggard?" Roger had retorted, and Hume had choked back a laugh.

What the man sitting next to Roger didn't know was that music moved Roger so violently that he often wept openly at concerts. He believed in a direct emotional connection with the music, without the intervention of tedious blowhards or talking heads. Thinking about his father made Hume sad.

Roger was judgmental and sometimes cruel, especially to Ruth, but Hume missed matching wits with him. He contrasted the double, whose thoughts he couldn't read, with his worldly and intellectual father. How had Loretta ever thought she could fool him with this imposter? What was he going to do about Loretta? He'd promised to give her some time, but waiting was becoming unbearable. On the other hand, no alternative presented itself. Action? What action?

All week, while spending long hours at the clinic trying to keep his mind off the imposter, he'd been weighing alternatives. Get Dr. Nightingale to come out to the house and examine his "father." Maneuver her into making the discovery. He would be shocked, but what happened to the caregivers wouldn't be his fault. Or call Ruth, and ask her to come down after all. Let her share in the decision. But no, both of these scenarios smacked of cowardice. He would have to confront the situation himself, tell the caregivers he knew the truth, call the police.

And what crime exactly had been committed? Impersonating a dead man. Was that even a crime if there were no victims? Roger surely didn't care. Was Hume a victim or a perpetrator? He'd written out the women's paychecks himself, today, in full knowledge of what he was doing. Was that a crime? Ruth would have every right to think so, and yet Ruth, like Roger, had always been generous toward the caregivers, approving loans to them when they were in trouble. They were always in trouble! Mistreated by boyfriends, abandoned by husbands, distressed by drug-addicted children, at the mercy of unsympathetic courts, one payment away from losing everything.

He stopped his thoughts and focused on the music. Like his father, he was an active listener, and he let Mussorgsky/ Ravel absorb him into their world. Somewhere in picture number seven, "Limoges (The Great News)," described in the original program by an influential critic as "French women arguing violently in the market"—squawking horns, racing violins, battling snare drums, triangles chiming—the old man, who had been gazing quietly around the room and looking out the window, suddenly spoke. His voice sounded clear and harsh over the music. "What? …gahnah arble … NO GOOD!"

Real words! The clearest Hume had ever heard the imposter speak, they snapped Hume out of his involvement with the music and brought him back to the present with an electric jolt. What did they mean? The old guy didn't like the music? He focused his attention on the old man, who grabbed his chest, gasping for air, eyes wide with what Hume, practiced at reading the expressions of the inchoate—a look he'd seen on the faces of many a dog he was about to put down as their owners left the room before the injection—saw as terror. "What's wrong?" Hume asked.

The old man leaned forward, the color draining from his face, and repeated "What?" and then slumped back into his chair. His arms and legs started shaking in a violent rhythm. He gasped with a tearing sound.

Seizure? Hume thought. He jumped up and shouted, "Old man! What's wrong?"

No response. The eyes stared at Hume without seeing him. Froth appeared at his quivering lips. The gasps came again and again in disjointed bursts. The arms and legs continued their flailing, like a prisoner's in an electric chair. Hume reached out and placed two fingers on the man's neck to feel for the carotid pulse. There was none. *Cardiac arrest*? Hume thought.

Call 911? He grabbed his cellphone out of his pocket and tapped the screen. No signal. Of course, there was never signal in this house. He looked at the house phone next to him on the bookcase by the easy chair, and saw the orange DNR notice stuck to the shelf. Many times Hume had discussed this very scenario with his father. "Do *not* call 911," Roger always told him. "They're required to try and save your life. I want no CPR. No defibrillator. Once I'm dead, I want to stay that way."

But this old man was not his father.

The twitching and gasping stopped.

"Old man!" Hume shouted again.

No pulse. No respiration.

Now would be the time for Hume to drag him from the chair, lay him out on the floor, and begin chest compressions. How soon could an ambulance get there? Twenty minutes? Half an hour? If the man's heart didn't get restarted within ten minutes, his brain would be dead. Maybe Hume could keep the compressions going long enough for the defibrillator to arrive, to shock him back to life, pulling him out of peacefulness into the excruciating pain of his attack and the bruising and cracked ribs from the paddles. And the questions from hospital intake that Hume would have to answer. This is your father? Bringing Hume back to the dilemma he was in, what to do about the imposter.

"Limoges" had ended with a scurrying coda that led directly into the growling horns of picture number eight, "Catacombs," the artist examining the Paris tombs by the light of a lantern, gloomy and elegiac. Already a minute had passed. Maybe more.

Wouldn't it be easier to let the old man stay where he was? Most victims of sudden cardiac arrest died, in spite of the efforts of onlookers. But how could it be right to let a man die, a man who had never had a chance to give an advance directive? Hume thought of himself as a moral man, but there was no moral solution to his current quandary. He let "Catacombs" lead him down into its mysterious depths. Another two minutes. "The Hut on Hen's Legs" began with the banging of kettledrums. The questions were becoming moot. He moved away from the old man reluctantly; whoever he was, he looked enough like Roger that Hume felt he was experiencing his father's death all over again in real time. He went around the hospital bed, where his father had suffered for so long, past the pictures of his mother on the mantelpiece, and opened the front room door. "Kristy Mae! Dellisha!" he called.

The caregivers came running. It was rare for Hume to raise his voice. All three clustered around the inert figure in the armchair. A whirlwind of violins rose from the speakers. "He had a heart attack," Hume said. "He was gone in a minute. I'm going to call Dr. Nightingale."

Hospice had given the household instructions on what to do in case of death. Call the doctor. If she was unavailable, call HospiceCare. They would send a nurse to issue a death certificate. Call the funeral home. For Hospice this was an ordinary event, to be planned for with step-by-step instructions.

"Oh my Lord," Kristy Mae said.

"Then I'm calling Loretta." He hadn't yet told them that he knew this man was not his father. He didn't yet know what he would tell the doctor, only that it was necessary to make the call.

"You don't have to," Dellisha said. "She's here."

It was three o'clock. Loretta's car pulled in, Tammy's just after. Hume and the caregivers waited, hearing the kitchen door slam. A blast of horns announced "The Great Gate of Kiev."

"In here!" Dellisha yelled.

Loretta came through the doorway, Tammy at her heels. They stopped when they saw the tableau around the easy chair. "He's passed," Hume said in a voice loud enough to hear over the music, which no one had thought to turn off.

"Oh no!" Loretta came around the bed and dropped to her knees beside the old man, shaking with sobs.

Hume picked up the cordless house phone. He hesitated, then put the phone back in its cradle. He waited for Loretta's crying to quiet, then said, "Loretta, I have to know. Who is he?" He saw Kristy Mae and Dellisha startle.

Loretta sat back on her heels. "Lyle Dunbar. I told you that last Saturday. Only me and Wayne Dixon know him. Knew him. Nobody else in or out of the county." Tammy handed her a Kleenex.

Hume remembered Loretta's chaotic story, although he hadn't remembered the name. He wondered if he should google it. "Who knows about the switch?"

Tammy folded her arms, projecting an air of calm stability.

"Just the care staff," Loretta said, paused, then added, "And my husband and his brothers."

If he googled the name would he have to call the police? He'd kept this quiet for a week already, not something he wanted to explain. "My father donated his body to science," he said.

"What!" Loretta got back to her feet.

"To the O School." The West Virginia School of Osteopathic Medicine in Buckfield. "We did the paperwork six months ago."

"But we thought ..."

Hume cut her off. "I know what you thought. Dad didn't want you to know. He thought it would disturb you. He didn't figure it would make any difference to my mother. He didn't believe in an afterlife."

The music came crashing to an end.

"Oh my!" Kristy Mae said into the silence.

"But Loretta said …" Dellisha began.

"I really *did* think he wanted to be up there with Miss Beatrice," Loretta broke in. "I'm sure he told me."

"He may have," Hume said. "He said a lot of things when his mind was wandering. The question is, do you know what Lyle wanted?"

That stopped her. "No way I *could* know. He wasn't talking by the time I met him. I suppose we could ask Wayne."

"We could." *Wayne, did the old man happen to mention his burial plans to you while he was loading his shopping cart?* Hume thought. "But it would complicate things. On the other hand, we could let your scheme play out, and send Lyle to the O School."

Loretta looked shocked. Tammy spoke first. "You'd do that, Hume?"

"I'm not sure yet. First thing I have to do is call Dr. Nightingale."

"There's that blood test," Tammy said.

"Blood test?" Hume asked.

"Dr. Nightingale took his blood last week after the uh … stroke," Tammy said.

"We'll have to hope Lyle was O-positive. A lot of people are." He picked up the cordless phone and left the room.

Dr. Nightingale told him she was heading toward a patient in White Sulphur who had stopped breathing. She'd call him back in ten minutes. If she couldn't make it he could call Hospice. And he should call the funeral home right away. It would take them at least an hour to get to Amity, and time was of the essence in retrieving a body for donation.

Hume carried the cordless phone outside into the yard, stood under the oak tree, and called Maryanne. He wanted to hear her voice. He wanted her advice.

"How are you feeling, darling?" she said when he'd given her the news.

"I don't know. Numb."

"You want to protect the caregivers?"

"I think I do. It wasn't their fault the old guy died. Or my father."

"You think you can get away with it?"

"I guess we'll find out. What I'm really worried about is what to tell Ruth. I have to call her now."

"Tell her Roger died. It was quick and painless."

"I'll have to tell her the truth. The whole story."

"When she gets here."

"She may not like it."

"We'll hope for the best."

Hume went back inside. Kristy Mae was in the kitchen making coffee. "Cass is coming," she told Hume. "Dellisha called her."

"The wagons are circling," Hume said. In the dining room he sat down at the computer to google Lyle Dunbar. Aside from a PO box in Amity, he could find no records. It was as Loretta had said: the man had walked the earth without leaving footprints.

19

More Revelations

BACK TO THURSDAY EVENING

"It's just a theory," Ariel said, and flashed his beguiling grin. "Do you have *any* idea what a theory is in science? It's not just a guess!" Ruth felt herself getting hot. She knew he was goading her. "Evolution explains the natural world. It's the framework of everything!" Going to see *Quest for Fire* at the local art house had been her idea of escape from a pressured week. She remembered the movie being funny and oddly engaging, despite having no intelligible dialogue and instead using body language and lots of grunting to imagine life 80,000 years ago. There were obvious fallacies—such as bands of people at wildly different stages in human development living in close proximity—but hey! It was self-styled as fantasy. Somehow, discussing the scientific underpinnings over dinner after the movie had led them to one of Ariel's favorite topics.

"How can you believe?" he said, pouring more wine into Ruth's glass. Their plates were empty, but they were in a quiet neighborhood restaurant where the waiters knew Ruth and weren't about to hustle her out. "How can you possibly believe that *life*"—pronounced in a deep reverent voice, as though he were narrating a made-for-TV documentary—"with all its incredible complexity, was just an accident? Dependent on mutations to arrive at the human species. *Mutations*! Accidents!"

"I find that easier to believe than the myth of an all-powerful, all-knowing being, whose existence for some reason cannot be substantiated by facts, despite centuries of attempts."

"I'm not talking about God, some white dude sitting on a cloud. I'm talking about the Universe. There has to be some intelligence out there beyond our comprehension!" Ruth groaned, but Ariel was unstoppable. "Take your eye; I've studied this. Your eye is made of interacting parts. Remove one part and the whole system fails. It had to have been produced in one fell swoop. No way it could have evolved step-by-step, in a series of accidents. How do you get from a one-celled animal to a human brain, through mutations?"

"This is giving me a headache, Ariel. I'm the daughter of a scientist, of generations of scientists, you know that. I enjoy reading Carlos Castaneda as fiction, but when it comes to treating cancer I'm going to a doctor who knows a little molecular biology, not to a shaman." She had re-read *The Teachings of Don Juan* when she first met Ariel, based on his enthusiasm, and who doesn't love enthusiasm for a book? It had been a manual for him, a transformative experience. It was still a good read, and reminded her of her own hippie days. But even then, she hadn't taken it seriously.

Ruth wanted to be broad-minded. She wasn't sure she could extend her liberality to someone who didn't believe in evolution. Later she would google it and find that the complexity of the eye was a well-known right wing trope, not worthy of Ariel's intelligence.

"If you would meditate with me," he said coyly, "I could help you with that headache."

"Thanks, but I'm going to turn in early. A good night's sleep is what I need."

She paid the check and they parted at the door to her building, without her inviting him up. He kissed her and said, "Don't worry about Claire. She'll be all right."

She watched him bounce away on dancer's feet, his dreads swinging. The sweet thing about Ariel was that he could sometimes tell what was really on her mind. And yet, it wasn't enough. Something in her resisted him, not because he was broke—she didn't need or want a man paying her bills—but because she couldn't engage with him on an intellectual level. *What bullshit!* she told herself. She thought of the brilliant and controlling men of her life: her father, Leo for the thirty years of their marriage—was that what it took to win her love?

It really wasn't fair to Ariel to string him along this way. He claimed he didn't mind. She didn't believe him.

She had just drifted off to sleep when the phone rang. Startled awake, she grabbed the extension by her bed, the one with no caller ID.

"Ruth! Ruth!" The voice sounded breathless. "This is Trisha. Trisha Vance."

"Trisha?" Ruth hadn't spoken to Trisha since she'd fired her, nearly a year earlier. "What time is it?"

"Midnight. Sorry to call you so late. I just got back from Charleston. From the state police. I'm worried about your dad."

"What!"

"I've reported him missing. I was out there today. I don't know what that Cass has done with him."

"You went to my father's house?"

"He wasn't there! They have some, I don't know what ... *imposter* in his place!"

"What are you talking about?"

"They have some old man there who isn't your father. I don't know what they've done to Major." The voice broke into sobs.

Ruth couldn't make any sense of what she was hearing, but it triggered alarm bells. Trisha was an unguided missile, capable of causing destruction wherever she went. "Trisha, where are you now?"

"Home. You know I have a sick son."

"Good. You stay there. Take care of your son. I'll take care of this." Whatever *this* was. Ruth put the phone down gently, fearing to set off the madwoman. She checked her clock. It was indeed after midnight. She considered calling her father's house, but flashed on the scene in the Box Room, when Trisha had hallucinated Cass pilfering the Thorndikes' treasures. Too late, as well, to call Hume. Had Trisha called him? She should have asked. Had she really gone to the police? Unlikely. She'd probably imagined the whole thing, as she had so many other things. She had no limits when she was out to get someone. Still out to get Cass. Unbelievable that she was obsessed by the Thorndikes after all this time. Ruth wondered if Trisha knew when she was lying or if her lies became truth in her unbalanced mind. She tried to put Trisha out of her thoughts, but ended up worrying about Claire again.

By morning the phone call seemed almost like a bad dream, but she knew it was real. She tried calling Hume to warn him that Trisha was meddling again, but all she got was his voicemail. She tried his mobile; also fruitless. She cursed the unreliable phone connections of West Virginia and called her father's house. Kristy Mae informed her that he was fine, but still not talking. "Tell my brother to call when he gets there," she said. It was Friday, Hume's day to go to Amity. "He should call me on my cell; I'll be out."

She'd planned to meet Rita at MoMA at its opening time, hoping to beat the crowds at the Matisse Cut-Out show. She and Rita had been friends since their art school days together, a friendship that had weathered decades, marriages, divorces, career ups and downs. Had even survived Ruth's jealousy over Rita's comparative success, her large calligraphic abstractions commanding positive reviews and prestigious commissions, despite being, in Ruth's secret opinion, rather easy to produce. The museum was already crowded, but the cut-outs were breathtaking. So full of joy. Matisse, at the end of his life, bedridden and in pain but at the height of his powers, had still been breaking new artistic ground.

"There was a guy not afraid of dying," she commented.

"He knew he was immortal," Rita said.

They had lunch in the museum café. Ruth wanted to divulge her worries over Claire, but Rita launched into a monologue on her favorite subject, herself, and her upcoming show. Her dealer was pressuring her to scale up her paintings. "I'm getting too old to be climbing ladders," she complained.

"Look what Matisse did from bed," Ruth pointed out.

"He had studio assistants. I work alone."

"Consider yourself lucky. You don't have family drama to distract you from your work. My brilliant and sensible daughter has managed to get herself knocked up. Can you believe it?"

Rita looked shocked. "I didn't know she had a boyfriend."

"She doesn't. Of course, I suggested an abortion. But no, she wants to keep the baby and raise it as a single mother." Ruth couldn't keep the skepticism out of her voice.

"And give up law school?" Rita leaned closer.

"No! She thinks she can do it all. The young have no sense of their own limitations. And she wants my help. As live-in babysitter." That wasn't exactly what Claire had said, but Ruth could see it going in that direction. As an artist, why couldn't she rent out her SoHo loft for a couple of years and move to Boston temporarily? "I blew up at her. Now I feel terrible."

"Do you want me to talk to her? She seems pretty clueless about how this is going to affect her life. I could tell her about my own abortion. I've never regretted it for a single moment." Somehow Rita managed to bring every conversation back to herself.

"No," Ruth said. "It might just piss her off that I've talked about it with you. I guess she'll manage. But I'm scared for her. Sometimes I love my daughter so much it hurts."

She still hadn't heard from Hume by the time she got home. She hoped that meant that all was quiet on the Amity front. Her phone buzzed and his name showed up.

"You'll never guess who called me last night at midnight," she said before he had a chance to get a word in. "I've been trying to reach you all day. Trisha Vance, with some crazy story about calling the cops on Cass. What's going on down there?"

"The inevitable."

"The what?"

"Our father. Has passed."

"Oh!" Although it was inevitable, Ruth hadn't expected it. Not today. Not after so many false alarms, each one with its emotional impact growing more complicated as time wore on. After so many dress rehearsals for the main event, she wasn't sure how she felt. A little stunned. Mostly relieved. "When?"

"Just now. I'm waiting for the funeral home to come pick him up."

"What happened?"

"Cardiac arrest. He didn't suffer. I'll explain when you get here."

"Yes. Let me get some things sorted out."

"Take your time," Hume said. "There's a lot to get done once you're here."

"No kidding."

Ruth was the only passenger on the twin-engine turboprop that flew into Sweetwater Valley Airport Sunday afternoon, dodging thunderheads. The 34-seat plane bounced like a rowboat on stormy seas, and lightning flashed outside Ruth's window. The flight attendant had directed her toward the rear of the cabin while he sat in the front to balance their weight. Ruth liked small planes; she enjoyed being tossed about by the forces of nature. In this interlude of solitary thought she tried to take in the magnitude of her father's death.

Claire had come over Friday after work and spent the night with her mother. Dear tender-hearted Claire had shed more tears for her grandfather than Ruth had. On Saturday, when Ruth had booked her flight to West Virginia, Claire had asked, "Do you want me to come with you?"

"It's your last week at your job. Didn't you tell me you're involved in an important presentation at City Council on Wednesday?"

"The Criminal Justice Committee. Yes."

"You can come later. I'll call you when I get there, when I know what the plan is."

This morning Claire had hugged her mother before parting, Claire going back to Queens, Ruth to the airport. "I know he wasn't always nice to you, Momma. But he loved you as best he could."

Wasn't always nice to her! As she bobbed in the hard seat of the plane, Ruth catalogued the many hurts her father had delivered. They began early, when she was sixteen and still adored her Daddy. He ruled the family, and he told her that her dog Sacagawea had to go. Ruth had raised the golden lab herself, trained her, bred her, cared for mama and eight puppies and documented them in her eighth-grade science project. Saca had the run of the Thorndike farm in Virginia and was sweet and docile with children and other pets, of which there were always many. However, she liked to go next door (which was across a pasture and through a wood lot) and beat up the beagles the neighbor kept chained outside, in country hunting-dog fashion. Mr. Chaney called Major Thorndike repeatedly to complain. "Keep your damn yellow bitch chained up," was his solution.

They stopped letting Saca go out. Ruth had to walk her on a leash twice a day, long walks around the pastures while she sang Joan Baez songs and dreamed of the future. Even so, Saca continued to escape and fight with the beagles. The only solution, said the head of the family, was to find a new home for Saca. They advertised in a Washington newspaper for a good home, and a young family came and took Ruth's dog away.

Deep sadness set in. Not only Ruth but also her mother Beatrice mourned for their dear dog. Did they express their grief to Roger? Ruth could no longer remember; she imagined private conversations must have taken place between her parents, because after a week her father relented. "I was wrong," he said. "I'll try to get your dog back."

He called the new owners and offered to buy Saca back. But they had bonded, they said, and refused to return her. The sight of a golden lab could still give Ruth vivid dreams about Saca, her first loss.

The plane came down hard on the single long runway at Sweetwater Valley Airport. Ruth descended the flight of steps onto the tarmac and saw Hume standing outside the low building of the airport holding an umbrella. The sky was beginning to spit, and black clouds raced toward them.

"Let's get to your car before it starts to pour," Ruth said after a brief sibling hug.

The Sweetwater Valley baggage handler obligingly yielded her large suitcase to Hume and they darted inside the small building, past empty car rental desks and out through the front doors, where Hume's BMW SUV was parked close to the entrance and Maryanne waited. She grabbed Ruth in a long embrace and murmured, "Aw, honey."

"You sit up front with your brother," she added, getting in back.

The sky opened up as they started down the highway toward Amity.

"You were going to tell me all about the old man's last days when I got here," Ruth prompted.

"It's complicated."

"So you said over the phone."

"Our father actually died two weeks ago." Hume's voice choked.

"What?" Ruth was confused.

"The guy who died Friday was his double."

There was a moment of stunned silence as Ruth tried to understand her brother's bizarre words. Her head felt like it was exploding. She finally managed to screech, "*What?!*"

"The caregivers buried our father and switched in a man Loretta knew, Lyle Dunbar. A man who looked almost exactly like our father."

"Buried him *how, where*?!" Ruth shouted.

"On the farm, next to our mother. I don't know the details. I didn't ask." Hume's voice sounded low and miserable.

"What! Stuck him in a hole in the ground in the middle of a cow pasture, no casket, nothing to keep the dirt off his face! He was an awful man, but he didn't deserve that."

"I said, I don't know the details ... about ... how they buried him. By the time I found out, he was already in the ground." Was this Hume's defense?

"You didn't do anything about it? You've known this for two weeks and kept it from me?"

"A week. I realized a week ago on Friday when I went to visit. They told me he'd had a stroke and couldn't talk, but something about the ... old man didn't seem right. Then I went up to the High Place and saw the fresh grave. Loretta came to the clinic the next day and confessed." Hume kept his eyes on the road. Rain drummed on the roof.

"Loretta? Loretta's behind all this? I don't believe it. After all we've done for that family."

"On the contrary, I think the Hardwick brothers did more for our parents than vice versa."

"Well, maybe you're right. But this ... *switching bodies*? That has got to be a crime. What are you going to do about it?"

"What do you want to do? Throw them in jail? Exhume our father?"

Maryanne, who had been quiet all this time, piped up. "He didn't know what to do. Those poor women, they loved your father, they took care of him. We were trying to figure out how to get out of this without ruining their lives."

"Then, before we could come up with something, Lyle died. And I just ... let the thing play out." Hume accelerated out of a curve.

"Could you slow down?" Ruth said. "You're making me nervous. You could end up in Stony Bottom for going along with this, you know." The prison was down the road from Hume's house about a mile. She could see the prison lights from his deck in winter when the trees were bare. Sometimes on the Sweetbrier River Trail, they would pass inmates going for walks with their guards.

"I hope not," Hume said.

"Think about it!"

"I'm mostly thinking about how I'm glad our father's ordeal is over. His last few years have been pretty terrible, and getting worse all the time."

"Yeah, and he always claimed he would kill himself first. We took his threats too seriously. Remember when he threatened suicide if I went to my best friend's wedding in Philadelphia?" It was the summer after her graduation from college. She and Leo were living on her parents' farm. Her parents were learning how to be cattle farmers. Leo was working for her father. It was haying season. Roger was worried that if Ruth left for Philadelphia to be a bridesmaid, Leo would go with her. The hay would be spoiled. It would be all her fault. Roger told her that he had suffered from anxiety and depression all his life; that he carried a lethal dose of sleeping pills in his pockets, in case he couldn't take it any more. Ruth hadn't gone to the wedding.

"He didn't mean to be so cruel," Hume said.

"It came naturally," Ruth said dryly. They crossed the bridge into Sinkhole County. "Well, I guess that explains the phone call I got from Trisha. Who else knows about this?"

Hume sighed. "I have no idea. Probably half the county."

"Hume exaggerates," Maryanne said. "But word has gotten out that Roger died. Father Dave called to offer sympathy."

"I asked him to stop over this afternoon. To discuss a memorial service," Hume said.

"For our father, or this Lyle person?"

"Let's forget Lyle and think about our father. He died, you know."

Ruth realized that her sarcasm had touched a raw nerve. Hume's relationship with their father had been more straightforward than hers, less fraught. He seemed bereft. She felt angry, but not at Hume. Poor Hume, just trying to do the right thing. At the caregivers, then? At whom?

By the time they reached Amity, the rain had stopped and the sun had come out. Hume carried Ruth's suitcase inside. "No one is here," Hume said.

"Looks like someone has done some vacuuming," Maryanne observed.

"I asked the caregivers to get the house cleaned up for Ruth yesterday, and take today off. Cass will come tomorrow to help with all the stuff." A lifetime of stuff to be sorted, sold, given away.

A giant bouquet of flowers stood on the dining room table. Ruth read the card sticking out the top, a condolence card signed, "Cass and the girls." She felt oddly moved. The house was quiet, its emptiness palpable; she was used to the bustle and chatter of caregivers and her father's shouted orders. The mantel clock struck four sonorous chimes.

"Beer time!" Maryanne announced.

They took their beers out to the front porch and were there when Father Dave's car pulled up. He took a seat on the porch and accepted Maryanne's offer of a beer. "If it's any comfort to you," he said, looking steadily at Ruth and Hume, seated side by side on the glider, "I gave Roger last rites. Just after Ruth was here, in July. You remember he had a crisis?"

Ruth couldn't forget. The neck-snapping roller coaster of life and death now finally over.

"Cass called me. I came, just to be on the safe side. It's not unusual for a person to receive rites more than once. God doesn't mind."

"There wasn't time this Friday," Hume said. "He went so fast. And then, because he had donated his body to science, we had to call the funeral home right away to pick him up. There's a window of a few hours to get the body into cold storage, and the funeral home the O School designated is over an hour away."

"I understand. Where do you want to hold the memorial service? In the church?"

"No," Hume said. "We'd rather have it here at the house, if that's possible. The caregivers aren't Episcopalians. I think they'd be more comfortable here."

Ruth couldn't point out the irony of Hume's concern for the women who had perpetrated fraud, putting them all at risk. Hume and Maryanne were right: she didn't want to send Loretta to prison for being poor and desperate. Or punish the Hardwicks, the family her parents had loved for decades. She felt herself getting sucked in on the scheme, hoping they could pull it off. What would happen though, if they were found out? Ruth had always been pretty law-abiding, except when it came to speed limits on interstates and No Trespassing signs. But everybody flaunted those laws. Not everybody switched dead bodies.

"It's quite possible," Father Dave answered. "Perhaps next Saturday, to give family time to gather?" He looked inquiringly at Ruth.

"Yes," she said. "My son and daughter will want to be here."

"In the backyard, if the weather's nice," Maryanne added.

They all got up and trooped around to the back of the house to discuss the logistics of folding chairs and a lectern the church could provide and who would speak. Then the priest said he needed to go. As they walked him back to his car Dave said, "You know, I saw Roger last Sunday."

Uh oh, thought Ruth, *here it comes.*

"He wasn't himself after the stroke," Hume said evenly.

"He certainly wasn't. He seemed like an altogether different person. Strange and not all there." Dave took Hume's hand in something between a shake and a clasp. "I'm glad he's at peace now."

After he'd gone Hume said, "That went pretty well."

"If you say so," Ruth said. "But what about Trisha?"

"I was hoping you would figure out how to deal with her."

"Great," Ruth said. "Let's go for a walk."

The three of them—Ruth, Hume, and Maryanne—tramped through the wet pastures up the steep hills, not talking until they got to the High Place. "Here we are," Hume said. "The old man's grave."

Ruth stood at the foot of the bare patch of dirt that lay beside her mother's neatly tended headstone. The end of parents. The thought confused her. She felt sad; she should feel glad that it was over. But it wasn't over. Her father had managed to complicate their lives even after death. She supposed that she couldn't blame him for that. Tender grass shoots poked up through the muddy soil.

"Looks like somebody seeded it," Maryanne commented.

"Probably Nate Hardwick," Hume said. "He's been taking care of Beatrice's grave, and he helped dig this one."

"So, is the idea that our father's grave will stay hidden?" Ruth asked.

"Do you have a better idea?" Hume asked. "I don't. But even with Nate's loving care, it'll be a while before we can let anyone come up here. Meanwhile, we can't sell the farm. One more thing we can thank the caregivers for. Maybe we should bill them for upkeep instead of paying them another week's wages."

"For heaven's sake!" Maryanne exclaimed. "They *need* those wages. You know they live payday to payday."

"I was kidding," Hume said. "Anyway, a week of their wages isn't going to keep the farm salable."

"I always loved this place," Ruth said, looking around, her eyes stinging with unshed tears. "Maybe we shouldn't sell it."

"You want to move to West Virginia and become a farmer? I don't think so! Just maintaining it until we can sell it is more work than I want. Speaking of work, I have early clinic hours tomorrow. Maryanne and I need to get home."

So many issues remained unresolved while they inched their way through moral ambiguity.

20

A Woman's Work Is Never Done

JULY, 2014

The last time Ruth had seen her father alive, in early July, he'd been less judgmental than usual, as if the meanness had gone out of him at last. He didn't talk much. He was happy just to have her in the room, reading or doodling on her computer while he watched the kittens playing through the porch window. He would ask her the same questions over and over, about her mother, about Hume. Sometimes he would ask. "Where am I? Where is our home?"

The cats that lived on the front porch were all feral except for Momma Cat, who kept on producing litter after litter. Ruth hated them. She didn't mind that they killed field mice and rabbits (expendable creatures); she hated that they killed birds. Every day she found bird carcasses on the porch or kitchen steps, where Momma Cat liked to leave her offerings. The wild birds that her mother had so loved. Ruth still filled the bird feeder every morning as her mother used to do, and as Ruth had done the month that Beatrice was dying. At the end, Beatrice had turned away from the domestic animals that had absorbed her life's work—her horses, cattle, even her little dog—toward the wild birds. Five days before she died, she'd had a sudden resurgence of strength. With the caregivers' help she'd gotten out of bed, into her wheelchair, to sit and read her mail. Then Ruth had wheeled her out onto the front porch. It was an unseasonably warm December day. Ruth had asked if she should fetch one of the horses from the barn and lead it up into the yard for Beatrice to greet. No, Beatrice wanted no goodbyes. Instead, she'd wanted to be wheeled to the other end of the porch, where she could see the bird feeder, and she'd sat and watched the birds flying back and forth.

Roger had always been a dog person. But not long after Beatrice had died he'd banished her little dog, a miniature schnauzer named Mitzi. Missing Beatrice's companionship, Mitzi had taken to hounding Roger for attention, scratching and barking at his bedroom door when he shut her out. He couldn't stand the dog's neediness. The barking drove him nuts. One day in a fit of rage he shouted at Trisha, "Take her! Get her out of here today." And Trisha had taken Mitzi home, fulfilling Beatrice's last wishes.

So how had Roger fallen in love with Momma Cat? Maybe it was Trisha who'd brought the cat in one day and put her on the Major's bed. She was soft and calm, low-maintenance, washing her paws and purring without placing any demands on him. Mostly she lived outdoors, where the Thorndike cats had always lived, killing mice in the barn and everything else they could get their claws on. The caregivers started feeding her on the front porch so she could be close to Major and he could watch her kittens.

One of Ruth's projects that week in early July had been to capture Momma Cat and her two kittens in have-a-heart traps and take them to the Amity vet to be neutered. She could have asked Hume to do it, but it was good to have projects; anything to get out of the front room, the tedium of sitting next to her father, needing to talk to fill the silence.

Another of her projects was to start giving away the Thorndikes' vast art collection. Beatrice and both her parents had been amateur artists, and not only the house but also the Box Room and Beatrice's studio were packed with generations of paintings and drawings. Ruth's life didn't have space for sentimentality. She planned to offer the caregivers their choice of her mother's delicate watercolor landscapes, but hadn't thought about her own big cow painting that hung in Major's upstairs bedroom, the product of the summer after college that Ruth spent on her parents' farm. When Loretta let slip that she loved the canvas of the red and white cow, Ruth had immediately said, "You can have it!" She considered it rather clumsy. The cow was bold and round, staring out at the viewer against a flat, almost abstract background of Kelly green pasture and white sky. The thick impasto of pure white oil paint had cracked in the decades since she'd painted it, an embarrassing technical failure.

"Yes," Major agreed. "That's my favorite of Ruth's paintings. Take it. You have good taste, Loretta."

"I can bring it over to your house tomorrow. Will you be home?" Ruth asked.

The next day was Saturday, when the weekend crew would be at the Thorndikes'.

"You don't have to do that. I can get Beaver to pick it up in his truck."

"But I'd like to visit you. Do you mind?"

"I don't mind. But I work at the Family Dollar from eight till five."

Ruth was shocked. She hadn't realized Loretta had a second job. "Sunday?"

"I work there Sunday, too."

"How long have you been working seven days a week?"

"Bout six months. But you can come over tomorrow at 5:30."

"I won't stay long," Ruth promised. "I'll have early dinner with my father before I come over." She didn't want to make Loretta serve her dinner. But she was curious to see the house that the Thorndikes' loan guarantee had kept Loretta from losing to foreclosure. She'd always seen the caregivers at her parents' house; she believed that to really know a person, you needed to see them in their own home. She wanted to know Loretta.

"Love of money is the root of all evil! One of the most misunderstood verses in the Bible," the preacher had shouted from Loretta's car radio the winter before. "Does it mean having money is evil? No! It does not!"

It was a cold morning. Loretta had been working for Lyle since the fall—going to his cabin up Mud Lick Hollow one morning a week before heading down to the Thorndikes' house for her afternoon shift. Then Beaver broke his foot on the job and was out of work, and workman's comp only paid sixty-six percent. Her fifteen-year-old Ford had developed transmission problems. Already its brakes were shot and Beaver told her if she didn't get a new car soon she was going to end up dead at the bottom of a gulch. Where was the money going to come from? They could barely afford to pay their mortgage, let alone new car payments. So she was on her way into Amity for a job interview. The snow on the hillsides sparkled in the sun, and she had switched on her radio to a

Christian station hoping for some uplifting rock. Instead she got a sermon. "No, it is the *pursuit* of money! It's the *greed*! That's the sin, my friends. That's what drives you away from the Word of God."

Greed? Is that what you call needing to feed your babies, put food on the table for your man? Loretta wanted to punch the preacher, whom she imagined living in a mansion and driving a Cadillac with the money he made off this radio spot.

"Is it hard for a rich man to enter the Kingdom of Heaven? Is it easier for a camel to pass through the eye of a needle?" Did he really say that? "Jesus tells us that with *man* it is impossible for the rich man to be saved, but with *God* all things are possible." Loretta snorted. He thinks he's going to Heaven. Ha!

"God WANTS you to prosper," the preacher bellowed. "He WANTS you to enjoy the fruits of your labor!"

Make that the crumbs of my labor, Loretta thought.

"Jesus wants YOU to be in the one percent. And with faith in Jesus you CAN be!"

Sure, Loretta thought. She turned off the radio and pulled into the parking lot of the Family Dollar. She parked, patted her hair, and went into the store, ten minutes early. There was an unfamiliar woman behind the register. Since she knew everyone who worked at the Family Dollar, Loretta figured this must be Brandy, the regional manager, who had agreed to interview her on a Saturday morning.

It turned out that Brandy needed someone to work that same day. So Loretta was hired, at seven twenty-five an hour, minimum wage.

On an unusually hot Saturday afternoon, Andrea of the weekend staff helped Ruth carry the cow painting downstairs and load it into her Subaru. She followed the directions Loretta had given her, driving out the Excelsior Road away from Amity to Second Gap. Here she turned into an unprepossessing housing development called Heavenly View Estates, a dozen modest houses in a single line, each with a large open front yard and not many trees. If Ruth had been imagining a ramshackle cabin or doublewide trailer, she was surprised. The houses were nice-looking—built, she would later learn, in the mid '90s, when Loretta and Beaver bought theirs new. She pulled into the long driveway and Loretta called to her from a small deck at the end of the house. "Hey, Yankee!"

Loretta stubbed out a cigarette and came down a steep flight of wooden stairs to help Ruth get the painting out of the back of the Subaru. "Carry it by its edges," Ruth instructed. "Careful not to dent the canvas with your fingers."

Although it might have been easier to carry it by herself, she let Loretta take the top end as they wrestled the large painting up the narrow staircase. A small boy watched silently from the deck. A door at the end of the house opened and Loretta's daughter emerged.

"Hold the door open, Tiffany," Loretta ordered. "Out of the way, Georgie."

They maneuvered the painting around the tight corner past Tiffany and into the kitchen, where they put it down on the floor, leaning it against a wall. "Come inside, Georgie," Loretta said. "This here's my nephew. He's shy. Come on, Georgie, say hello to our guest." Tiffany reached out to tousle the boy's short blond hair and steer him toward Ruth. He was a plump, beautiful child with rosy cheeks and blue eyes. He held out his hand for Ruth to shake and said, "I'm pleased to meet you."

Loretta laughed at him and explained, "He's my brother's kid. Tiffany's been babysitting him today while Roy's at work. Have a seat." Ruth looked around, impressed by the bright, air-conditioned kitchen, its sink and counters overlooking the front yard, in its center an ample farmhouse table surrounded by six mismatched chairs. Tiffany plopped down at the far end of the table.

"This is so nice!" Ruth exclaimed.

"Yep." Loretta grinned. "Beaver built the table and paneling out of old barns he and Bo salvaged."

The two rustic wood walls sported niches, shelves, and hooks where a large assortment of tools, jars, implements, and sundries were stored. The painting rested against one of these shelves. "Is that one of Major's cows?" Tiffany asked.

"From thirty years ago, when my parents first moved to West Virginia," Ruth said. More than thirty, but she didn't want to count the decades.

"It sure is pretty," Tiffany said.

"It's a gift from Ruth," Loretta said.

"From the Major," Ruth corrected. "He gave it to you."

"Major's always been real good to me. All that yellin' he does, that's just on the outside. Inside he's a helpless little boy. Like our sweet Georgie."

Ruth sat down at the table next to Georgie, who had sidled up to Tiffany. There was something about the boy, his quiet formality perhaps, that reminded Ruth of a photo of Roger from the early 1930s, dressed in his Little Lord Fauntleroy suit. Cousin Clara had showed Ruth the pictures on a family visit to

New Hampshire in the '60s, when Clara had told the story of Roger's fall from the tree and his mother's subsequent smothering love. Roger's mother, Althea, was dead by the '60s, and the cousins—Roger and Clara—gleefully maligned her. "She tried to turn you into a pansy. Her own little house plant!" Clara had said, possibly after a couple of martinis.

"I don't remember my childhood," Roger had replied. "I don't think I ever was a child." Or maybe, Ruth reflected now in Loretta's kitchen, his childhood was too painful to remember.

Loretta's focus turned back to the cow painting. "We'll have to wait until Beaver gets home to figure out where to hang it. He's working late tonight. I got you something." Loretta took a bottle out of the freezer compartment of her refrigerator and brought it to the table. "I don't know anything about wine, so I hope you like what I got you. It was the most expensive bottle at Family Dollar." She paused dramatically. "Five ninety-nine. We have one for two ninety-nine." Her eyebrows jumped up and down with mirth. "Can you open it, Ruth? I don't know how to work these things." She took a corkscrew from a niche in the paneling and gave it to Ruth, then sat down at the head of the table.

Ruth suspected she'd bought the corkscrew for the occasion as well. The wine was a chardonnay from a winery Ruth had never heard of, but she was touched that Loretta had gone to the trouble to make the visit celebratory. While she worked the corkscrew the kitchen door opened again and Loretta's hefty son Junior walked in, followed by a man that Ruth didn't know.

"Hey, baby boy," Loretta said.

"Hey, Momma." Junior leaned over and planted a kiss on top of Loretta's head. Georgie jumped up and ran over to the man, who raised him up in his arms for a hug.

"You been good, sonny?"

"He's been a angel, Uncle Roy," Tiffany said.

Ruth handed the wine bottle back to Loretta, and she poured small amounts in juice glasses and handed them around to everyone except Georgie, who sat on his father's lap across from Ruth. Roy raised his glass and said, "This will be my first drink in four years, ever since I got custody of my boy here. Cheers!"

The announcement worried Ruth. Was he falling off the wagon? Was it her fault?

Loretta took a sip and wrinkled her nose. "Ew! Pure vinegar. I don't know how you can drink this stuff."

"It ain't bad, for five ninety-nine," Junior said, wiping his mouth after downing his glass.

"Like you know!" Tiffany quipped.

It wasn't the worst wine that Ruth had ever tasted. At least it was wine, an unexpected and welcome addition to the evening.

"Roy's been raising Georgie ever since his mother failed a drug test," Loretta explained.

"His mother was a mess. I never lived with her, and she depended on poor Georgie," Roy said. "He was like a little adult when I got him. Always helping out. Been wanting to do the dishes since the age of three. Smart as lightning. Gentle as a summer day."

Georgie squirmed out of Roy's lap and sat in the chair next to him, saying nothing.

"Too gentle," Roy continued. "See this scar?" Roy touched the boy's forehead. "Kid at school threw a rock at him. A known trouble-maker. The school don't do nothin' about it cause the kid's mother is a teacher. What are you gonna do next time he bullies you, Georgie?"

"I don't know," Georgie said thoughtfully.

"Tell the teacher?" Loretta suggested.

"He already done that. It didn't help," Roy said. "The principal advised him to punch the bully in the nose. Can you do that, Georgie? Punch him in the nose?"

Georgie pondered a moment and said in a serious voice, "Yes."

Ruth wondered whether Roger had been bullied at school. She'd never thought about it. And he didn't talk about his childhood.

Junior, who had taken the chair next to his sister that Georgie had abandoned, asked the assembled group, "Anybody know where Jewel's at?"

Loretta's face darkened. "She's out with that damn meth addict boyfriend of hers, you better believe. I ain't heard from her in two days."

"She come by here this morning, Momma, after you was at work," Tiffany said. "She told me to tell you, but I forgot."

"That boy's going to get her killed or locked up," Loretta said.

"She wants to break up with him," Tiffany said.

"Then why don't she?" Junior asked. "It's all over Facebook what she's doing. Makes me sick."

"Maybe she's afraid," Tiffany volunteered.

"Huh!" Junior snorted. "I'll bust that skinny punk's ass."

Junior was going into his last year of high school in the fall, Ruth knew. But because of his size he looked years older than seventeen.

"Be careful, baby boy. He's got mean friends," Loretta warned.

"A fellow's got to stick up for his sister," Roy said. "Junior's man enough. You should have seen him today at the garage, working on the Monte Carlo with me. He knows how to handle tools."

The conversation meandered into a technical discussion of the engine they were rebuilding. Ruth liked the way they bantered on, skipping from topic to topic on family matters, largely ignoring her, while Roy kept refilling her glass and his own. His eyes twinkled. He had a close-cropped beard on a strong chin, a lean and weathered face. He wasn't a bad looking man. Finally he winked at her and she suspected the wine was going to his head. "I hear you're from the big bad city," he said. "I'd like to visit Staten Island someday."

"Staten Island?" Ruth was incredulous. "Why?"

"I saw it on some TV show. So many people in the streets and sidewalks, so many interesting shops. I liked the look of it."

Ruth tried to connect this to what she knew of Staten Island. "What show?"

"I don't remember the name. I just remember skinny women and lots of—cover your ears, Georgie—sex."

Ruth laughed. "*Sex and the City*! That was *Manhattan* Island, where I live."

Roy laughed too. His face was flushed. "You're probably pretty bored around here."

"I grew up in the country. I love West Virginia," Ruth said.

"You need someone to show you around? What kinds of things do you like to do in the country?"

He was flirting with her. How interesting! But not unpleasant. Flattering in a way; she was much older than him. And in a class she would have thought made her unapproachable. Yet he was crossing boundaries to approach her. "Mostly, take walks," she told him. She knew that country people didn't walk through nature for its own sake, without a purpose. For thirty years her parents had given hunting rights on their property to the Hardwicks. In return they'd received fresh venison that they packed in their large freezer. "I don't like fishing," she confessed. "And I'm afraid of guns."

"Ho!" Roy exclaimed. "Show her your Colt 45, Loretta."

"It's in a closet."

"Well, get it out. Come on, girl. Daddy didn't give it to you to keep it hidden away." He stood up and everyone followed him in a general movement through the narrow hallway leading from the kitchen to the living room. Ruth was glad; she wanted to see the rest of the house, and didn't want Roy getting any drunker. The living room occupied the other end of the house, equal in size to the kitchen and facing out on the front yard as well. It featured the usual sofa and TV in one corner, and dominating the front corner, a stuffed black bear, mounted in a half-raised position. "Ain't that a beauty?" Roy asked Ruth. "Beaver shot it."

"Yep. And earlier this summer Junior caught a fifty-pound catfish," Loretta said proudly. "We're having a model made of it to put on the wall."

"About that Peacemaker, sis," Roy said.

Loretta disappeared into a bedroom, came back with the gun, and handed it to her brother. Ruth felt a flutter of dread.

"It ain't loaded," Loretta said. "Show her, Roy."

Roy took a stance—feet slightly spread, shoulders back—that Ruth was pretty sure was intended to be manly. He was a slim man, not very tall. He pointed the revolver toward the blank wall and lifted his left hand to take the weight. He flicked open the loading gate with his right thumb. Holding the gun with both hands, he pulled back the hammer halfway. It clicked twice.

He moved closer to Ruth. "Don't be afraid." He stood behind her and put both arms around her. This was a new development. Ruth wasn't sure where it would go. But really, in the family living room, it couldn't go too far. She decided to enjoy it, despite her nervousness around guns, which she knew was irrational. He pointed the gun at the wall so that she could look down the barrel. "Watch the chambers," he said. With his left hand he spun the cylinder.

"See any bullets?" He spun the cylinder again slowly.

"No," Ruth said, relieved.

"Good. That wasn't hard. Now take it in your hand." He put it there and stepped away from her. It was heavy. She was able to appreciate the beauty of the gun. It looked like something out of an old Western, with its silver barrel, frame, and cylinder covered in old-fashioned engravings. Its grip was textured hard black plastic.

"I think my daddy got it in the '60s," Loretta said.

"I was pissed he gave it to her and not me. Now, hold it up and pull the hammer back all the way."

Ruth hesitated.

"Remember, it's not loaded." She aimed it toward the safety of the blank wall and pulled the hammer back until it clicked.

"It's fully cocked. You can pull the trigger and shoot it now. There's no safety on this gun. But if you change your mind, you can ease the hammer back without firing the trigger. Put your thumb firmly back on the hammer."

She looked at him, wanting this lesson to be over.

"Go on. Take the weight in your left hand and squeeze the trigger just a teeny, tiny bit. This releases the hammer, and you can ease it back into its safe position."

Reluctantly she followed his instructions. Without a sound the hammer returned to the mother ship, and the gun became once more an inoffensive object of art.

"Uncle Roy? I think Georgie's tired," Tiffany said.

The child had been sitting by himself on the sofa while the others watched Ruth's indoctrination into firearms. Tears slid down his pink cheeks. Roy immediately shifted his attention to his son. "What's the matter, little fellow?"

"He's hungry," Junior ventured. "It's seven o'clock and he ain't et."

Loretta took the gun from Ruth's hands. "Tiffany, get a pizza out of the freezer and put it in the oven right away."

"I'll get you some crackers and ham spread, Georgie," Junior said.

"I need to go," Ruth said. "I promised my father I'd be home before he goes to sleep."

The party moved back into the kitchen. Loretta followed Ruth out onto the deck, where the heat of the afternoon had abated. "Thanks for coming," Loretta said, then lowered her voice to a whisper. "My brother just broke up with his girl-friend. Sorry if he's hittin' on ya."

"It's OK. Don't worry," Ruth said feeling conspiratorial. "It's the wine." Somehow between the two of them they had finished the bottle. "He seems like a great guy, a good father."

Driving back on Excelsior Road into the sunset, Ruth took the curves carefully to compensate for a slight buzz. The road was empty and welcoming; the pastures green and glowing, lush despite the harshness of the lives they supported. The lives of Loretta's people, country people struggling against poverty, drugs, and changing times, always one bad break away from disaster. To Ruth, they were admirable, for their grit as well as their love of their land and each other. The words to the old Joan Baez song came back to her, the song she'd sung to herself as a young girl walking her dog in green pastures— *Show me the prison, show me the jail,/ Show me the prisoner whose life has gone stale/ And I'll show you a young man, with so many reasons why/ There but for fortune go you and I.* Years later she would volunteer in jails and homeless shelters, she would march, because from the beginning, woven into her DNA, was *There but for fortune go I.*

21

And They All Died Happily Ever After . . .

BACK TO AUGUST, 2014, THE NEXT WEEK

Monday morning Ruth was coming out of the bank when she ran smack into Trisha. She'd been in to speak to Debby, the bank manager, about closing Roger's account and opening an estate account. Debby had told her that her power of attorney had ended at death (like so many things, Ruth thought). The account was frozen. Only a death certificate from the state capital could thaw it out. Until the wheels of bureaucracy had turned in Charleston, Ruth would have to write checks out of her own account to pay for the funeral expenses (which would be modest, in the absence of a body), the caregivers' severance pay, and the general running of the farm.

"Just the person I wanted to see!" she exclaimed. This was far from the truth. She hadn't decided how to tackle the problem of Trisha. So far, no one seemed to believe Trisha's story of an imposter masquerading as Roger Thorndike (including, apparently, the state police), but for how long? *Keep your friends close and your enemies closer.* Whether it was Michael Corleone or Sun Tzu or Ingo at the boathouse who had said it, Ruth thought now of this advice. "Have you heard the sad news?"

News of her father's death would have been spreading faster than the Elk River chemical spill that had poisoned the tap water of Charleston earlier in the year. Not waiting for a reply she said, "My father ... passed." Ruth hated that expression. Passed what? Why were people so allergic to the plain and honest verb *to die*? But she was willing to swallow her aversion to conventional niceties in order to soften the confrontation with her enemy. "On Friday," she added. "Hume was with him. I just got here yesterday."

Trisha burst into melodramatic tears. Ruth felt obliged to put a comforting hand on her shoulder, felt an urge to put her arms around Trisha. An urge she resisted. Wouldn't it be too hypocritical? They stood on the sidewalk while Trisha wept, exposed to all of Amity—Jeanie in her glass-fronted pharmacy; a woman emerging from the Nearly New, where Miss Beatrice had liked to shop; the Kalico Kitchen where Ruth had interviewed Cass; and, across the street, the stately nineteenth-century brick courthouse. Even now Sheriff J. R. Boggs might be gazing out his window at them.

"I'm sorry," Ruth said. "I know how much he meant to you." Shouldn't the condolences be going in the other direction?

"You never even let me say goodbye to him," Trisha wailed.

Ruth felt an ugly scene coming on. She wanted to snap back at Trisha, to charge her with having been the source of a steady stream of allegations over the years—against her father, that he was making sexual demands on the caregivers, against the caregivers, that they were trying to seduce him or poison him, the source of constant fears of violence, guns being brandished, cars run off the road by drug addicted boyfriends—so much hysteria that it was exhausting. Instead, she had to head off the latest accusation. She wanted to escape. "Can I walk you to your car?" she asked Trisha.

In Amity, people still did such things. The bag boy at Dixon's IGA had startled Ruth the first time she shopped there by grabbing her groceries from the counter and asking her where she had parked.

"Jason dropped me off," Trisha said between sobs. "I was about to call him to pick me up."

"Let me give you a lift." Ruth's hand, still resting uneasily on Trisha's shoulder, reached around to encircle her and propel her around the corner of the bank to where Ruth had parked the Thorndike car. She eased Trisha into the passenger seat and gave her a package of tissues. She got in on the driver's side, started the engine, turned on the AC, but didn't pull out of the space. They were in an alley, shaded by the Bank of Sinkhole County. Without alluding to Trisha's recent unannounced visit to the Thorndike house or the alarming midnight phone call, Ruth said, "He wasn't himself at the end, Hume told me. He didn't even know his own son."

Did Trisha believe her? If she could convince Trisha that the man she had seen in Roger's bed the day before he died was really Roger and not Lyle Dunbar (not that Trisha knew that name), would Trisha call off her bloodhounds? Before she could probe further, Trisha's phone pinged. "It's a text from my husband," she said, peering at the screen. "Something's wrong with Christopher." The dying son.

"OK," Ruth said. "Let's go." She pulled out of the parking space as Trisha texted Jason that she was rushing home.

"Which way?" Ruth had never been to Trisha's house, but she knew it wasn't far. Trisha directed her to the south end of town and out onto a country highway that was unfamiliar to Ruth.

"Jason can't wake Christopher up," Trisha said, staring at her phone. "He's been failing in the last few weeks. Even with the feeding tube he's lost so much weight he's like a scarecrow." Ruth could hear the panic in her voice and felt an unwelcome surge of compassion.

Ten minutes down the two-lane through woods and pastures—ten minutes of silence in the car with Trisha's entire universe focused, Ruth was sure, on anxiety for her son and not on the problem of Roger Thorndike—and Trisha said, "It's the next right, around that curve, by the big rock."

Ruth turned onto an even smaller road.

"First house on the right, the doublewide." Her phone pinged again. Trisha shrieked. "What's he doing?!"

Ruth pulled in and stopped the car. She had no idea what was going on in the house. Should she drop Trisha and run? "Do you want me to come in?"

Trisha didn't answer but flung open the car door and raced to the house. Its door was opened before she got to it by a man who had to be Trisha's husband. She pushed past him. The man stared at Ruth as if he was seeing a ghoul. Ruth got out of the car and went up to him reluctantly. Did he even know who she was? Before she could say a word of explanation, a scream came from inside, a prolonged wailing cry unlike anything Ruth had ever heard. She moved past the husband, who was rooted postlike to his spot, crossed a small living room, and followed the scream into a darkened bedroom. Heavy curtains shut out the day.

On the bed lay the emaciated boy/man. What she could see looked like photos of victims of famine, twisted and yellow, cheeks sunken, lips blue. Trisha lay on top of him, almost obscuring him from Ruth's view, smothering him with her folds of flesh, rocking him, clasping him, seeming almost ready to devour him in her voracious love.

"Come back, Christopher!" Trisha screamed. "Don't die! Don't leave me, baby! He's dead! Noooo! Jason, how could you let this happen? My baby is dead!"

Jason finally came into the room, which was far too crowded with medical supplies and human misery.

"Do you want me to call 911?" Ruth asked. Jason nodded mutely. She had to leave the room to make herself heard by the 911 operator. She closed the bedroom door to let the family have its privacy. The screaming went on and on, barely muffled by the hollow-core door. Ruth heard it over the voice of the operator telling her that help was on its way. She stood, waiting, looking around at the memorabilia of Trisha's life, hardly seeing anything, helpless. She was an intruder. She wanted to leave but didn't dare, not until professionals arrived, people who knew how to handle crisis. She felt like a spy. She heard Jason shouting, "Calm down!"

"Calm down! How can you say that, you fool! You let him go! You knew he was going and you didn't do anything to stop him!"

"Shut up!" Jason yelled back. "What could I do? I've nursed this boy for ten years. What more could I do!"

"You could of prayed for a miracle, like I was every minute of every day. You stopped believing in miracles! That's why he's gone!"

Ruth heard a loud knock on the door and jumped. She opened the door to paramedics, ambulance parked out front. Apparently they didn't use sirens in Sinkhole County.

In a whirlwind of relief, she let in the paramedics and made her escape, speeding away as if pursued by Trisha's howls, harrowed by the depth of Trisha's anguish. It was no act. A mother had lost the son she had fought so hard to save. Not rational, no, but who would demand rational thinking at such a moment? Ruth had never before believed Trisha's histrionics. Yet it was clear that this grief was genuine. Even though the end had been inevitable, on some level Trisha had continued to believe in miracles and had not anticipated the dreaded event. That too seemed real. The emotional truth was so undeniable, so convincing that Ruth felt a spasm of anxiety for her own precious children, who were not sick, not dying, who would live long happy lives, would find their way through the fears and confusion of their youth, would find their places in the world. Unlike Christopher, who for the first time was real to Ruth. Guilt stabbed her for doubting Trisha, for hating Trisha. What could she do for Trisha? How could she make amends? She stopped at the Busy Bee on Main Street and ordered an arrangement of white roses and purple stock to be delivered to Trisha's house the next day. A pitiful gesture in the face of the precariousness of life.

Tuesday morning, Hume and Maryanne were to come down from Powhatan County to help Ruth tackle the shed known as the Box Room. After escaping from Trisha's grief, she had hurtled into the project of restoring the Thorndike house as much as possible to what it had been when her parents were alive, before illness and caregivers and death had invaded. Monday afternoon Cass had come to help, and her solid presence had grounded Ruth in the practical tasks at hand: gathering medical supplies—the ones the hospice nurse hadn't flushed down the toilet—that could be used for other patients, and collecting linens, towels, and the Major's clothing to take to Family Services. Cass had asked hesitantly if she could have the power wheelchair for her mother.

"Yes, of course. Take it, as a gift for all you've done for my father." Including deception and fraud, Ruth thought with some bitterness. But the secret remained unspoken, a wall of tension between the two of them as they sorted through the house, Cass advising Ruth on what could be donated where. Ruth only wanted to get rid of as much clutter as quickly as possible. Cass helped her unroll the Oriental rugs and put them back where they belonged. The care staff had preferred wheelchair-friendly rubber matting. Ruth wanted to see the house one last time as it had always been in her memory.

Much more work lay ahead, all of it freighted with emotion and Ruth's longing for the past. The Box Room, at least, was intriguing. It held mysteries. Not to mention that it would be fun to have Hume and Maryanne as working companions. When they arrived in Hume's pickup truck, Maryanne jumped out and hugged Ruth. "Sweetie! Are you OK?"

Ruth had called the night before to tell them about Christopher's death. "Do you think I should do more?" she asked now. "Than just send flowers, I mean?"

"Like what?" Hume asked.

"I don't know."

"At least maybe this will keep her mind off Roger Thorndike conspiracy theories. The Grim Reaper did us a favor this time," Hume said.

"Hume!" Maryanne exclaimed reprovingly.

"I'm not sure we're off the hook," Ruth said. "Trisha's mind is pretty tenacious when it comes to grievances."

"We better get to work," Maryanne said. "The landfill closes at four."

"The goal for today," Ruth said as they approached the Box Room, "is to get out as much as possible to take to the dump." Knowing her mother's hording habits, Ruth figured there would be plenty of that. "And to go through every box."

The job was not impossible. Although her mother had been loath to throw things away, she also hated to acquire things, so there was a manageable amount of stuff in the shed. Plus, Beatrice had been a meticulous organizer. The boxes were neatly stacked and labeled. They began by pulling out the larger items—more rolled-up rugs, threadbare and full of holes, a toilet (where had that come from?), broken lamps and vacuum cleaners, mildewed camping equipment, a cardboard box containing a mouse nest, complete with a litter of baby mice—and spreading them out on the lawn under the oak tree. Hume set the mouse nest at a distance and said the mother mouse would come for it later. The grass was dry, the day was sunny but not hot, perfect as summer days tended to be in West Virginia.

They found a box labeled by Beatrice: "Snow Boots – Top 2 leaked, mended but not tested. Bottom 2 OK but very worn." Inside were two pairs of black rubber high boots. Ruth laughed, took a picture of the find, and said, "Into the landfill!"

They moved through the boxes inside the shed. They found fifty years worth of canceled checks, neatly stacked. "Into the landfill," Ruth repeated her favorite refrain.

"No," Hume said. "Leave them there. I have to shred them before they go to the dump."

"What! Are you afraid someone will steal the identity of a dead man?" Ruth asked.

"Somebody already did," Hume quipped.

"Very funny." Not, Ruth thought.

They'd brought markers into the shed, to check off the boxes as they went through them and decided what to do with them. There were boxes and trunks that hadn't been opened since their grandparents died more than thirty years earlier. Ruth hadn't realized how much Beatrice had saved from her parents' attic. Wool suits and elegant dresses from the early twentieth century. A white quilt stained and yellowed with age, labeled "This quilt was made by my mother in Albany Wisconsin about the year 1860. I slept under it when a very little boy. It now belongs to Beatrice. L.S. Howell, Baltimore, May, 1939."

"That could be valuable," Maryanne said.

"In this condition?" Ruth was skeptical.

"Put it into the estate sale," Maryanne said. "You never know." Hume's friend Leigh had put them in touch with an antique dealer who ran estate sales. Ruth didn't expect they would make very much in the sale; she just wanted to empty the house.

They found boxes and boxes of letters. Their parents had saved every letter Hume and Ruth had ever written them. Ruth took her letters and put them into the collection of things she would keep. They would provide a window into her past, if she dared look. Hume threw his into the landfill pile. There was a box labeled "Mother and Dad's WWI letters." Inside, the letters from Paris were tied in twine. Beside them rested a small envelope containing half a dozen army insignia cut from a uniform and, beside it, a six-inch length of rusted barbed wire.

"Wow," Ruth said. "This has to have been from the front lines. Can I have this box?" She wanted to read the letters.

"Sure," Hume said.

They were able to divide the items they valued without acrimony. Hume wanted an antique clock and old optical instruments. Ruth wanted diaries, her mother's, her grandfather's, ancestors she didn't know, and the journals Beatrice's great grandfather kept the year he sailed around the world as a ship's carpenter in 1865. Later, she would type up the journals; the handwriting was beautiful—a skill lost to the twenty-first century—but the ink was fading. Hume kept the old photographs from Roger's family; Ruth kept the photo albums from Beatrice's.

The only thing that annoyed Ruth was Hume's pace. She sorted through the boxes at warp speed, taking out what she wanted, leaving the rest, initialing the box, DONE. In the time she sorted through six boxes, Hume would be ruminating over one.

"I'm finishing today," she told Hume. "You live nearby. You can take as long as you want."

They were searching as well as sorting, searching for a set of sterling silver Buttercup flatware that had belonged to Roger's mother. They both remembered its battered leatherette case. In the move from Virginia to Amity thirty years earlier, Beatrice claimed that the Buttercup had been lost, stolen by the movers, she was sure. The family had an obsession with silverware theft. Then Beatrice had found it, announcing the occasion to everyone's joy. She had put it away for safekeeping, to give to Claire. But put it away where?

"Remember Trisha's claim that Cass was going through the Box Room? Looking for precious heirlooms?" Ruth asked.

"That was proven a lie," Hume said.

The shadow of Trisha kept crossing their thoughts.

After a break for lunch by the pool, they attacked the stack of oil paintings leaning against the back of the shed. Beatrice's work was all in her studio, a separate outbuilding, so these were paintings the Thorndikes had bought in galleries in the '60s or inherited from Beatrice's parents. Hume and Ruth recognized the portraits of them that their grandmother had painted. "Ugh!" Ruth exclaimed at the sight of her eight-year-old self in coronet braids and prim cotton dress. "She was a wonderful grandmother, but a lousy painter."

"They're so cute!" Maryanne snapped a photo of the portrait of Hume at six. "Don't you want to keep them as mementos?"

"No!" Hume and Ruth cried in unison.

"Here's something strange," Hume said, pulling a loose-leaf binder from behind the painting closest to the wall of the shed. "Fairfax County Foster and Adoptive Services," he read aloud off the cover.

"We're going to find out we were adopted?" Ruth asked. She and Maryanne crowded in to see what Hume had.

"No. It's dated from 1994." He rested it on top of a box that they had gone through and resealed, so that Ruth and Maryanne could look on as he opened it to its title page, "Children Awaiting Adoption – Creating Connections for Life."

"Were Roger and Beatrice thinking of adopting?" Ruth asked, incredulous.

"I don't think so!" Hume said. "They'd long since left Virginia." He started flipping though pages. They stared at pictures of children of all ages, from babies to teens, accompanied by text.

"Then who …?"

Hume stopped at a page with a circle drawn around a picture of two small boys. Ruth read the text aloud:

"Meet Benjamin and Christopher. Always on the go, Benjamin, 4, is a gold belt at Spirit Tiger Martial Arts. When he's not practicing his karate chops and kicks, you'll find him zooming down the sidewalk on his skateboard or climbing walls and trees. He needs a family with the energy to keep up with him and the patience to give him the structure he needs to thrive.

"His little brother Christopher, 2, will melt your heart with his big brown eyes. Sensitive and affectionate, all Christopher wants is a family to love."

Scrawled next to the printed text in ballpoint pen were the words *Jason and Trisha Vance.*

"Christopher had a brother?" Maryanne asked. "Is that the one that's been helping take care of him?"

"No," Ruth said. "His name is Bradley, and he's Trisha's biological son. When they adopted Christopher, they adopted his older brother as well. She told me about it, not yesterday, but back when Beatrice was dying and I was spending a lot of time with Trisha. They couldn't handle the brother. He was determined to kill Christopher—Trisha's words, pretty extreme I thought."

She and Hume and Maryanne studied the photo. Posed outside a house, on its back steps perhaps, little Christopher sat gazing up at his brother. The older child had his back to Christopher. He was dressed in a white martial arts pajama with his fists raised and one leg thrust high above his shoulders. His eyebrows made a dark V and his mouth was wide open in an angry snarl. Dark hair spiked from the top of his head.

"Yep," Hume mused. "Fratricide looks like a possibility."

"They had to split the boys up, Trisha told me. They sent the brother back to the agency."

"How on earth did this book get in here?" Maryanne asked.

"Beats me," Ruth said. "Trisha's haunting us."

The golden dome of West Virginia's state capitol building was visible from the conference room on the seventeenth floor of the tallest building in Charleston, with its panoramic views of the city spread out along the Kanawha River. Ruth had driven from Amity, Hume and Maryanne from Redbud, Wednesday morning to convene in the lawyer's office. Ruth, who liked to be first to enter a room in order to grab the seat with the best feng shui, sat near the head of the table, facing out at the vista. Beside her sat Hume, flanked by Maryanne. Uriah Krook of Krook Castro & Whiplash PLLC followed them in and sat down at the head of the table. Uriah was an old friend, having helped the Thorndike offspring weather the tempests of their father's moods and delusions since their mother's death. It was Uriah who had counseled them when Roger wanted to disinherit Ruth. It was Uriah who had suggested a family meeting and had attended same to soothe Roger with some tweaking of the trusteeships, acting more as psychotherapist than lawyer. He had a reputation around the capital for being sloppy in his billing practices but basically honest.

On the opposite side of the gleaming stretch of tropical hardwood from Ruth, silhouetted against the sky, were two representatives from Morgan Stanley, including Roger's long-time financial advisor Robinson Hood, recently retired but most knowledgeable about Roger's assets. A secretary (or office manager or administrative assistant or whatever you called them these days) distributed cups of coffee and bottles of water and stacks of paper to the participants, a little like an usher distributing prayer books and hymnals.

"I see you've come prepared," Uriah said, noting the yellow pad in front of Ruth where she'd listed her questions.

"You're in charge," she said. "You start."

The will was a simple boilerplate document, he explained, covering the checking account, contents of the house, vehicles, etc., which were to be divided equally between Hume and Ruth, since Beatrice, who had been named first in the will, was no longer alive. The bulk of the inheritance, however—the house, the land, and the investments—were in two trusts. Each was to be divided: sixty percent to Hume, thirty-five percent to Ruth.

"No," Hume interrupted. "That's not right. It's fifty-fifty."

"Look at the trusts," Uriah said. "Pages four and five. Dated twentieth of September, 2011. I thought you knew about the division."

In 2011 Roger had called both Hume and Ruth, proposing that he split his inheritance unequally, at the time saying two-thirds to Hume, one-third to Ruth, because as he said, Ruth was already well provided for. Would that be acceptable to both, he had asked. Ruth had been surprised by a wave of hurt, as if it were only one-third of his love her father wanted to bequeath her. But she steeled herself to be rational, and told him it was fine with her. Hume hadn't liked it either, but neither sibling wanted to tell their father how to dispose of his money. Later it was Beatrice, backed by Robinson Hood and Uriah Krook, who had prevailed upon Roger that the split must be even. He had acquiesced, or so he told them. But apparently he hadn't. Because there was the document, the thick stack of legalese that none of them had ever bothered to read, with Beatrice's signature as well as Roger's. Ruth felt a great horse kick to the gut.

"That bastard!" she cried. "I'd like to bring him back from the dead so I could shoot him!" She saw the suited men cringe.

"At least he didn't cut you out entirely," Hume sighed.

"What made him so mean?" Soft-spoken Maryanne.

"But wait," Hume said. "What about the other five percent?"

In a voice pained by embarrassment Uriah said, "He told me that Ruth had ... er ... resources and didn't need his money. He carved out a little chunk for someone who did. Look on page six. Trisha Vance."

"What?!" Ruth exploded.

"One hundred thousand dollars in liquid assets go to Mrs. Vance," Uriah said.

A note that the bequest had been added in September of 2013, legally witnessed, right about the time, Ruth realized, that they fired Trisha. How had this never come out in the conversations she'd had with the lawyer? Ruth wanted to scream.

"Roger asked me not to mention it to you. I realized you had ... concerns about Mrs. Vance, but he was my client, and very insistent. I was obliged to carry out his instructions."

Hume scribbled something on the corner of the yellow pad in front of Ruth, where only she could see it. "Hush money."

Hume had a point, Ruth thought. Would Trisha raise a ruckus over Roger's death with this golden egg landing in her lap? Perhaps in Roger's mind he was taking Trisha's portion out of Hume's inheritance, which had originally been sixty-five percent. Did that make it any less hurtful?

Uriah continued, "You can dispute the sixty–thirty-five split if Hume is agreeable and wants it even. There's a legal instrument for doing that."

It would cost more legal fees, Ruth thought. "No. Leave it as it is," she said.

"He always loved you better," she said to Hume with grim humor.

Thursday evening Zeke and Claire arrived, driving down together from New York in Zeke's car. Of course they hadn't gotten an early start, and when Zeke called from the road to give her an ETA Ruth quickly calculated they'd be doing the last forty miles on back roads at sunset—the deer strike hour. Ruth suppressed her panic and said, "You know what to do if you see a deer in the road?"

"I know, Mom," Zeke said. "You've told me a hundred times. Aim for it."

Everyone Ruth knew in West Virginia had hit a deer at least once. One young woman in her mother's art group had died when she swerved to avoid hitting the animal. Trisha's old SUV had been trashed when she hit not one but three deer at once. Was it just Trisha's usual bad luck, or did she not know that deer move in herds? Hume claimed that he had once sped up to hit a deer. It swept up over his hood and windshield, doing no damage to his car, and ran off into the woods unscathed.

Deer strikes: a West Virginia thing. Everyone had a story.

For all her fears, Zeke and Claire showed up at eight, just when they'd said they would. With their arrival her world felt whole again. She gave them cold ham and potato salad for supper, then they all went out to sit by the pool and sip wine in the dark. The evening was cool, as mountain nights usually were. Ruth wore a sweater. Under the cover of darkness she said, "I have something to tell you. You're probably not going to believe it. Your grandfather actually died two weeks ago." She told them about the caregivers switching out Roger for an imposter.

She hadn't known whether it was the right thing to do, to tell them. But she needed their support, and keeping secrets built walls. Their reactions (in retrospect) were predictable. Claire was shocked and angry. "I can't believe it! You trusted them."

"Some of them," Ruth said.

Zeke laughed. "I don't know who's the cooler player in this scam, Loretta or Uncle Hume! You have to give them both points for creativity. The Kafka Award for surrealism in real life."

"This isn't fiction!" Claire objected. "There could be serious legal consequences for everybody who knows about this."

"You're not a lawyer yet, Claire. Hey, Mom, have you heard the news? You're going to be a grandma."

"I know," Ruth said dryly.

"You're going to love it. You should move to Boston and help Claire with the baby."

"Zeke!" Claire reprimanded. "Mom has a life. She has her art career." Now Claire realized what she had seemed to forget only last week. Maybe their fight had made an impression.

"I wasn't suggesting she give up her art. She could rent out the loft for a year and set up a temporary studio in Boston. A change of pace could be good for her work."

It touched Ruth, her children arguing over her well being; two novices planning her life. She smiled and felt life's fullness. This was all she needed, all she wanted. The stars overhead were reflected in the pool. A whippoorwill called.

Maybe I will, she thought. For the first time in a long time, she felt peace.

"I am the resurrection and the life, saith the Lord; he that believeth in me, though he were dead, yet shall he live." Father Dave, in light gray pants and a black shirt with clerical collar (the gray pants featured creases, an elegant touch that Ruth noted), stood at the lectern improvised outside the kitchen door. In the backyard, almost fifty people stood in a large semi-circle, leaving empty the half dozen plastic chairs set up on the brick patio. Ruth was amazed at how many people had shown up, milling around and greeting one another before the priest had called them to order—to all outward appearances an ordinary social gathering of civilized folk who harbored no more than the ordinary secrets we would all rather not admit. Many were Hume's friends from Powhatan County, of course (Leigh and Greg and six or eight others whose names Ruth could never remember), and Maryanne's from all over (Ruth was forever meeting new ones from her sister-in-law's inexhaustible supply). Others were friends of the senior Thorndikes: Miss Beatrice's riding buddy Jane Arbuckle, wife of the hanging judge, along with the judge himself (who had perhaps witnessed more than his share of less ordinary secrets, endowing him with a flint-like steadiness of demeanor); a remarkably talented young artist with a brain injury named Amber whom Miss Beatrice had taken under her wing; the Chowders, a couple of the Major's vintage who were still up and about, defying their antiquity. Robinson Hood was there, looking unwell, but fortunately for Ruth's sanity, Uriah Krook was not. She wanted to put the reading of the will out of her mind. There were people from the Episcopal church: among them Father Dave's gracious wife and a Mennonite couple who still wore the outfits but had "fallen from grace" the Major used to joke—that is, they had left their own church for Christianity lite. Some of the guests might have been interlopers, like the man who delivered water to the Thorndikes' cistern, who had told Ruth, "Your dad was a nice guy. Never could stand that wife of his." What was the water man doing here?

Zeke and Claire stood off to the side of the patio, under the cherry tree, Zeke looking faintly amused, as though he were watching a documentary on village life in old Belarus. Claire looked stressed.

The Hardwick brothers and all the caregivers, some with husbands and children, were lined up against the lattice façade of the pump house, on the opposite side of the patio from the kitchen door, standing at attention as if guarding the well at their backs. Loretta had avoided meeting Ruth when she came in. Perhaps just as well. Ruth didn't know what she had to say to Loretta. Now they were all intent upon the words Father Dave spoke.

"Naked came I out of my mother's womb, and naked shall I return. The Lord gave, and the Lord hath taken away; blessed be the name of the Lord."

Only Ruth wore a black dress. The funeral was country casual. Hume and the judge wore sports jackets and ties; the rest favored polo or tee shirts and khakis or jeans. Among the women nice slacks or denim predominated. Ruth's favorite was Kristy Mae, in jeans and a bright-pink tank top sporting, in large fancy script, the word *LOVE*.

Ruth stood near the kitchen door, sipping a beer, the only way she was going to make it through the afternoon. She was tense. Her eyes ranging over the crowd, she wondered how many knew about the dead ringer. The caregivers and the Hardwick brothers of course. Hume's friends from Powhatan

County. How good were they at keeping a secret? How many of their friends and family members had been let in on the switch? More than half of those now paying their respects to the dear departed, Ruth guessed. How many of the others had seen the imposter in the last two weeks? How many had suspected something amiss?

"I will lift up mine eyes unto the hills, from whence cometh my help. My help cometh from the Lord, which made heaven and earth."

Hume had told her to focus on giving Roger a sendoff, and not think about the bodies—the one in its secret grave in the High Place, where no one in this party would venture; the other immersed in embalming fluid at the O School. The day was pleasant, warm but not too hot, with puffy clouds in a blue sky. In the background, behind Father Dave's voice and the rustling of papers and shuffling of the crowd, country quiet reigned, save for occasional birdcalls and the steady, pulsating buzz of dog-day cicadas, punctuated by the percussive chirp of crickets, sounds that Ruth had always loved, the sounds of summer in the country.

"The Lord is thy keeper; the Lord is thy shade upon thy right hand. The sun shall not smite thee by day, nor the moon by night."

In the distance, something unnatural penetrated. Could it be a siren, or was it just a different insect joining the summer symphony? Or a trick of Ruth's nerves, on edge, alert for disturbance.

"The Lord shall preserve thee from all evil: he shall preserve thy soul. The Lord shall preserve thy going out and thy coming in from this time forth, and even for evermore."

Ruth strained to hear past his words. It couldn't be a siren. It was not a sound she had ever heard at her parents' house.

A sound that she heard so often in New York that she almost didn't hear it. But now she was hearing it, a siren. Here in Sinkhole County the sound was as alien as a Martian invasion. And it was getting louder, coming closer. She felt her heartbeat ratchet up a notch.

Father Dave looked up from his text. In the ensuing pause, others heard the siren. A tremor passed through the crowd. Father Dave continued, "And now a reading from the Gospel. Cass?" The interval in which Cass walked forward from the pump house to the lectern gave the audience a chance to look around. Ruth saw puzzled faces. What were they thinking— fire, accident, emergency? A lawbreaker on the loose? Where was it coming from? Where was it going, and for whom? Father Dave ignored the siren, setting an example that the ritual would proceed, that spiritual matters would overcome worldly concerns. He handed Cass a paper. She stepped up to the podium and commenced to read.

"From the Gospel according to John: I am the good shepherd; the good shepherd giveth his life for the sheep. But he that is an hireling, and not the shepherd, whose own the sheep are not, seeth the wolf coming, and leaveth the sheep, and fleeth: and the wolf catcheth them, and scattereth the sheep." Her voice rose to be heard as the siren grew louder, its wavering cry heading toward them, as if it had left the main road, turned onto Forest Bostic, and was approaching the house. Ruth felt perspiration trickle down from her armpits inside her dress. Her mouth went dry and she took another sip of beer. She noticed terror on Loretta's face. Her daughter Tiffany slipped her hand through her mother's arm. Bo Hardwick's brow wrinkled and he glanced at Judge Arbuckle, who looked at his watch. Hume, standing beside Ruth, caught her eye.

Hume was next on the program, with remembrances of the Major, to be followed by Claire with her own remembrances, and Tammy, who had volunteered to speak for the caregivers. Father Dave had planned to keep the service informal, and let as many people who wanted speak their remembrances. Her heart pounding now, Ruth nodded to Hume, put her beer down on a window ledge, and moved behind the crowd, edging around the corner of the house toward the screaming of the siren in the front yard. The siren died in front of the house. In the sudden silence, Ruth heard Cass practically shout, "The hireling fleeth, because he is an hireling, and careth not for the sheep."

Ruth strode toward the parking area. The orchard was full of parked cars as far as the stable and the fences around the pool and pastures. The cop car had pulled into the mouth of the gravel parking area, still half in the road. The word *SHERIFF* was blazoned in gold letters across the side of the dark SUV. Ruth walked up to it. The driver's tinted window slid down.

"Sheriff J.R. Boggs of Sinkhole County. Looking for Robert and Loretta Hardwick. Are they on the premises?" The sheriff looked to be still on the aspirational side of thirty-five. Next to him, in the passenger seat, a plump girl with tousled blond hair and a puffy eye starting to blacken held a clump of bloody tissue over her mouth. Ruth recognized Jewel Blankenship.

"Yes, officer," Ruth answered carefully. "They're attending the memorial service for my father, which is going on now."

"I told you!" Jewel burst out, removing the tissue and revealing a fat and bloody lip gash. "I'm supposed to be there. I'm late! Because of *him*."

Behind the glass and metal mesh that separated the back seat from law enforcement at the wheel, Ruth saw a scrawny and hirsute young man slouched against the far door. Long scratches across his face oozed blood. Otherwise he appeared unharmed. Was this the boyfriend?

"You sure you don't want to go to the emergency room, miss?" the sheriff asked.

"No! Nothin's broken, just a split lip. I've been beat up worse fallin off my bicycle." She said this with derision.

"And you don't want to press charges?"

"I just want to get out of this car and never see that ass-hole again." Jewel certainly wasn't going to win any awards for politeness around officers of the law, Ruth thought.

The sheriff looked up at Ruth as though he felt an explanation was in order. "I broke up their fight at the Family Dollar when someone called 911. I don't want to interrupt a solemn occasion. She's over twenty-one. She's free to leave, if you're OK with that."

"Yes," Ruth said, eager for the sheriff to be gone. "I'll help clean her up. We have nurses here. But ... the young man. Is she in danger?"

"Hah!" Jewel said, opening her door and scrambling to her feet. "My daddy'll whup his ass good if he ever comes around me again." She slammed the car door shut.

"I'm taking him in. Witnesses told me he was the aggressor. I don't like to see young girls getting intimidated. Witnesses said a urine test might be in order for him."

"Will the siren be necessary again?" Ruth asked, wondering why it had been necessary in the first place. Who had he thought he was chasing?

"Oh that." The sheriff's face reddened. "The young lady got excited, hit the dial hard, and jammed it on wail. It was all I could do to shut it off on arrival. She was a little ... out of control."

And he was letting her walk away?

"I feared violence if I put her in back. In retrospect, well, it was a judgment call. We have to make those on a daily basis, ma'am."

"Thank you for bringing her to us, sheriff. Her people are dear friends of the family." Jewel had come around to Ruth's side of the car. Aside from her face, she didn't look too much worse for wear, in her blue denim work shirt, short black skirt, and cowboy boots. "Come inside, Jewel," Ruth said, steering her toward the front of the house by her elbow.

In the kitchen Jewel threw out the bloody tissues, rinsed her mouth with cool water, and washed her face. Apparently the pressure she'd applied had stopped the bleeding. Ruth gave her an ice cube to suck on. "I wish I had a popsicle," Ruth said, remembering the long-ago accidents of her children.

"Thanks, Miss Ruth. It's OK."

They went back outside through the front door, not wanting to walk out the kitchen door and interrupt the ceremony. They rounded the house and Jewel approached her mother conspicuously, as if broadcasting her presence to all assembled. Loretta's eyebrows jumped up and down, and she embraced her prodigal daughter, touching her damaged face with her lips.

When Loretta, with Tiffany by her side, saw Jewel come round the side of the house with Ruth, she thought her heart would bust. Jewel came right up and put her arm around her mother and whispered, "I'm so sorry I'm late, Momma. I broke up with Jack. It's all over."

"Thank you, Jesus," Loretta whispered back. And thanks also to Ruth, she thought. Oh my! Hadn't Loretta dreaded the coming of the Yankee? Loretta had no way of knowing what had transpired between Hume and his sister, but she feared the worst. When she'd slunk into the back yard to join the caregivers for the funeral, she'd tried to be invisible. Ruth of course had seen her, but gave no clue of what was on her mind. Loretta imagined retribution. Wouldn't Ruth see betrayal in what Loretta had thought at the time was an act of mercy? When she'd heard the siren and seen Ruth go to meet it, Loretta'd had a bout of sheer terror, thinking judgment was at hand, summoned by Ruth. Instead, Ruth had brought her Jewel, as if she were setting her bow in the cloud and promising a covenant between the two of them, between Yankee and hillbilly, between Thorndikes and Hardwicks, that they would defend each other's families evermore. Or so Loretta hoped.

Lined up against the pump house, her family was reunited at last. That was what mattered. Together they could face whatever came against them. Even her fear when Judge Arbuckle's knifelike eyes swept over them. What rumors had reached him? Who in this crowd would talk to him when the service was over and they all moved into the dining room to eat and drink and gossip? He wouldn't hesitate to convict her of a crime if some jabbermouth were to twist his ear into a stroll over the Thorndikes' farm up to the High Place. And that wife of his had been Miss Beatrice's riding buddy and used to ride all over the farm. Would she take it into her head to ride back for one last look at Miss Beatrice's resting place?

Anything could happen. She'd made her mistakes and repented of them, the good Lord knew. If she was arrested she would send out a call on Facebook to her prayer warriors who would rock the heavens, rousing angels with flaming swords. She hoped it wouldn't come to that. Just the thought turned her stomach blinky. But on this afternoon of blue skies and grace, Loretta felt strong in her family. Jewel was back. That had to be a sign. The kindness of the Major shone down on them from the hilltops and surely he'd look out for them from wherever he was.

"He was a kind man, a generous man, a man with a big heart, that's how we knew him," Tammy began from the podium. Oh dear God, Ruth thought. She didn't believe in the Deity but liked to address Him nonetheless. "We who took care of him day in and out, we appreciated his jokes and stories. We didn't pay no mind to his silliness when he'd go off. Because that's what old men do. He was a fine man and treated us good, always helping when we needed it." That at least was true. Trisha, the one who had benefitted most from his generosity, was not present. Ruth hoped that Uriah had reached her, to tell her about the will, and that she had managed to keep quiet about her suspicions, although keeping quiet was not her usual practice. Ruth had not heard from either of them. She didn't know if that was a good sign.

"If he had moods, well, who don't?" Tammy asked the crowd. Indeed. Ruth felt one coming on, a complicated brew of anger and gratitude. She thought about the hundreds of hours Tammy and all the caregivers had spent ministering to her father's needs, both physical and emotional. Such arduous work. Work that she herself could not possibly have done. She had much to be grateful for. She zoned out of Tammy's words and felt instead her love, the love of all the caregivers lined up in front of her against the pump house wall. Maybe the love was misguided, deluded, dangerous, but it was sincere. Whatever they had done, crimes committed, they'd done for love. It was right there on Kristy Mae's pink tank top and on all their faces (Loretta's was now hidden in her hands. Laughter? Tears? Ruth couldn't tell). You couldn't do what they had done for money alone; could they be prosecuted for love?

She glanced around at those assembled. All listening politely, perhaps even enraptured, pondering the mystery of death. She saw her children, her hedge against the reaper. The insects sang. Claire's pregnancy didn't seem so ridiculous, considering. She let herself imagine a granddaughter. With a sharp chin and a will of her own, as all children had, Ruth knew from experience. Yes, she would move to Boston. For how long, only time would tell. Long enough to help usher in the new generation, eyes wide, lips seeking succor. Claire, her capable daughter, would need her mother's help. What better task was left to Ruth, now that she was at the front of the line.

The grass would grow over the High Place. Whether or not in time to hide its buried secrets, the citizens of Amity would decide. That determination was out of Ruth's hands. Her work here was over, the job of escorting her parents into the great nothingness. What a job it had been! Out of that nothingness some new entity would emerge, squalling, something so needy and all-consuming that questions of right and wrong, ambition and love, world worth and self-doubt, would be pushed aside by its demands, forgotten in the daily struggle.

ACKNOWLEDGEMENTS

Readers of my Guatemalan fiction may be surprised that I have turned my gaze to an altogether different part of the world—although perhaps not so different as you might imagine. Fifty years ago my family relocated to West Virginia, drawn by its rugged beauty. What my family found was a generous community of proud mountain people who defy stereotypes, welcome in outsiders, and look out for their neighbors. They have long awaited this novel. Writing it has been a journey, and many have helped along the way.

I am grateful for the inspiration, comradeship, and astute perceptions of my writing group of nearly two decades, 100 Monkeys: Charles Austin, Judy Chicurel, Mary McGrail, Susan Miller, Laura Kruus Reissman, Lauren Sanders, and Iromie Weeramantry. Other first readers who have contributed are Robin Schauffler and David Nicholson, and the indefatigable Rebecca Kimmons. Thanks also to my brilliant editor Victoria Scott, who has been with me through every book. To my enthusiastic and resourceful publicists Louise Crawford and Linda Quigley of Brooklyn Social Media, and to the folks at New Meridian Arts for continuing to believe in the life of letters.

And to Douglas Chadwick and Gina Marie Schrader, who have opened their homes and hearts to me and to so many.

DEBORAH CLEARMAN was born in North Carolina and grew up on a farm in Southern Maryland. She is the author of two novels, *Remedios* and *Todos Santos*; a collection of short fiction, *Concepción and the Baby Brokers and Other Stories Out of Guatemala*; and *The Goose's Tale*, a children's book she wrote and illustrated. Her short stories have appeared in numerous literary journals. She lives in New York City. www.deborahclearman.com.